THE RECKLESS
MISS GRAINGER

Recent Titles by Margaret Pemberton from Severn House

A DARK ENCHANTMENT

THE FORGET-ME-NOT BRIDE

FROM CHINA WITH LOVE

THE GIRL WHO KNEW TOO MUCH

THE LAST LETTER

MOONFLOWER MADNESS

TAPESTRY OF FEAR

UNDYING LOVE

VILLA D'ESTE

A YEAR TO ETERNITY

YORKSHIRE ROSE

THE RECKLESS MISS GRAINGER

Margaret Pemberton

This title first published in Great Britain 2002 by
SEVERN HOUSE PUBLISHERS LTD of
9–15 High Street, Sutton, Surrey SM1 1DF.
First published in 1983 in Great Britain
under the title *Devil's Palace.*
This first world edition published in the USA 2002 by
SEVERN HOUSE PUBLISHERS INC of
595 Madison Avenue, New York, N.Y. 10022.

British Library Cataloguing in Publication Data

Pemberton, Margaret
    The reckless Miss Grainger
    1.   Nobility - Fiction
    2.   Love stories
    I.   Title
    823.9'14 [F]

    ISBN 0-7278-5880-7

Printed and bound in Great Britain by
MPG Books Ltd., Bodmin, Cornwall.

For Mike Pemberton, David Payne and
Martin Conradi. Gamblers all.

Introduction

Inspiration for *The Reckless Miss Grainger* came some years ago when, on a trawl of second-hand book stalls, I bought a book detailing Monte Carlo's history and, in particular, the history of its casino. It described how, in its heyday in the late 1800s, the royal and rich flocked to play at the casino's gaming tables.

In those days the casino was known as 'the Devil's Palace' and it was this period of extravagant excess that caught my imagination. It was the years when grand dukes and Russian princes paraded through the opulent gaming rooms with their bejewelled mistresses; when Sarah Bernhardt lost so much at the tables that she tried to commit suicide and Lillie Langtry won so much it took the croupiers ten minutes to pile up her chips. The famous courtesan Diane de Chandel played the tables wearing her entire collection of jewels and was upstaged by her rival, Caroline Otéro, wearing a plain black dress and not an iota of jewellery. La Belle Otéro was, however, accompanied by her maid, and she was resplendent in a five-roped necklace of pearls that had once been the property of the Empress of Austria. She was also wearing a plethora of rubies, emeralds and sapphires and, as a finishing touch, a diamond corselet valued by Cartier at 2, 275,000 gold francs. The players, apparently, stood up to applaud Otéro as she took her favourite place at the tables without more than a glance at de Chandel.

It was this over-the-top, opulent era that I wanted to live in imaginatively for a little while – and *The Reckless Miss Grainger* is the result. It was written at a time when my own knowledge of gambling and first-hand experience of casinos was minimal and when I had no idea that my youngest daughter would become a croupier. Thanks to her, I now know far more about contemporary 'Devil's Palaces' than is, perhaps, good for me.

M.P. © 2002

CHAPTER
ONE

THE AIR was fragrant, laden with the scent of bougainvillaea and jasmine, roses and orange blossom. A bee
buzzed lazily around the heads of the two figures on the
terrace and was waved bad-temperedly away by a black-
gloved hand.

'Is that the Kaiser's yacht?' Princess Natalya Yakovleva asked her young companion, her hand reposing
once more on her amethyst-topped cane.

Charlotte Graingér narrowed her smoke-green eyes
against the glare of the bright sunshine and studied the
vessel making for Monaco's harbour.

'I am afraid I cannot tell, Your Highness. It looks
smaller and sleeker than the *Hohenzollern* and the flag is
strange.'

The wizened figure at her side crouched over her cane
and squinted at the pennant fluttering in the sea breeze.

'Fetch me my opera glasses, child.'

Obediently Charlotte rose to her feet and hurried into
the shaded interior of the villa. The Princess did not like
to be kept waiting. Previous companions had suffered
the indignity of having books and china thrown at their
heads for such an offence and had departed from the
Princess's employ in tears and umbrage. Charlotte was
glad that they had done so. If they had not, she would be
acting as governess to badly behaved children or as
companion to a far less entertaining employer.

The opera glasses were on the photograph-filled secretaire. Charlotte picked them up and adjusted a silver-
framed likeness of the Grand Duchess of Russia, Marie
Fedorovna, with her two-year-old son Nicholas.

Charlotte paused for a moment. The Grand Duchess was beautiful, but not as beautiful as her sister Alexandra, who was now Princess of Wales. The Prince of Wales was fond of gambling. Perhaps he would visit Monte Carlo. The thought of meeting her future sovereign sent a ripple of excitement down her spine. Incredibly she had begun to regard as normal the day-to-day contact with Polish and Russian nobility. The Princess was related to half the crowned heads of Europe and in her six months as companion Charlotte had been presented to the ill and ageing Tsar Alexander II, to King George I of Greece and to King Leopold II of Belgium.

She smiled to herself as she stepped out on to the terrace, imagining her mother's reaction if she had known her daughter would one day be in the company of kings. The smile held sadness as it always did when she thought of her parents. Her childhood had been happy. Her father was a village parson. Their home had been a shabby, cosy rectory, full of her father's books, her mother's sewing and a strange and varied collection of stray dogs. When fever had broken out in their Sussex village, her father had spent long hours tending the sick. Her mother, too, had fallen ill and her father had nursed her devotedly. Within weeks they were both dead and at seventeen Charlotte was without home and without family.

A position was found for her, caring for the children of one of her father's brother clergymen. The clergyman had none of her father's amiability and his home was a cold, unhappy place. For over a year she had suffered it and then bravely decided that if she must make her own way in the world she would do so on her own terms.

She handed the Princess the opera glasses and sat down, surveying the sunlit sea and the graceful yacht gaining the harbour. She had made a life in a way that had exceeded her wildest imaginings. Monte Carlo and the rich and royal friends of Princess Natalya were a far cry from Sussex and the uneventful day-to-day happenings of rectory life.

'Arrogant young cub,' the Princess said admiringly, her glasses fixed on the approaching yacht. 'Only Sandor would fly his family crest instead of the flag of his country. I can't see any females aboard which is strange behaviour for a Karolyi. Perhaps the rumours from Paris are true.'

'What rumours, Your Highness?' Charlotte asked with interest as the Princess handed her the glasses.

'They say that Irina, Vicomtesse de Salbris, drowned herself when Count Karolyi discarded her.'

Charlotte raised the opera glasses and focused on the yacht as it skimmed past the headland and towards the harbour.

The sailors were busy preparing to berth. A white-suited figure leaned elegantly against the gleaming brass of the deck rail.

'Is that the Count, on the deck?' Charlotte asked curiously.

'If he's handsome as Satan, then it's Sandor,' the Princess confirmed, her black eyes gleaming. 'I shall tell Monsieur Blanc this evening that his Devil's Palace is drawing the attention of the Devil's spawn.'

Charlotte laughed. 'You must not tease Monsieur Blanc so. He takes great offence at the nicknames his family's casino has earned.'

'He takes great offence at nothing that attracts more gold across his tables,' the Princess said practically. 'That is why he was so anxious the Nice–Menton road be completed. Now all the patrons of the German casinos will flock to Monaco.'

Charlotte was no longer listening. Her eyes were resting on the handsome figure of Count Sandor Karolyi. Oblivious of being watched, caught unawares, the passionate Slavic lines of his face were brooding and formidable, far younger than she had anticipated.

The sun caught on the lens of the glasses and flashed. Count Karolyi swung his head round, staring up at the pine-covered hillside and the golden stone of the villa, half-hidden among the trees. Her heart began to race. She knew it was impossible that he could see her, yet for one burning moment storm-dark eyes seemed to hold hers, grief and longing nakedly exposed to her gaze.

Slowly she lowered the glasses. 'Is the Count . . . Russian?' she asked hesitantly.

'Hungarian. His cousin is Count Povzervslay, a devil of a very different colour. Sandor's crimes are all of passion. Povzervslay's are crimes of blood.'

Charlotte wondered if having a mistress take her own life was not a crime of blood also. Certainly Count Karolyi's eyes had been those of a man wracked by an inner hell.

The Princess reached out for the small silver bell on the trestle table at her side and rang it imperiously.

'Champagne,' she ordered the little maid who hastened to answer the summons. 'And lemonade.'

The maid bobbed a curtsey and withdrew. The Princess smoothed an imaginary crease from the black silk of her skirt and adjusted the posy of Parma violets at her waist. 'Do you have the residents list of the Hotel de Paris, Charlotte? Kindly read it to me.'

Charlotte withdrew a piece of embossed notepaper from her reticule.

'Lord and Lady Pethelbridge arrived by carriage yesterday morning. Princess Helena is still in residence, as is the Countess of Bexhall, and Mademoiselle Floretta Rozanko has been joined by Mademoiselle Louise de Remy.'

'Cocottes,' the Princess said disparagingly. 'I'm surprised Princess Helena consents to stay under the same roof. Who else is here? I saw several carriages arrive from the direction of Nice late yesterday evening.'

'Mademoiselle Bernhardt, the actress.'

The Princess sighed with satisfaction. 'Then we must send a card to the Hotel de Paris and inform her immediately that we will be making her acquaintance. Have there been any departures? Has that dreadful Carlyon woman taken her tedious conversation elsewhere?'

'She left this morning for Nice, Your Highness,' Charlotte replied, suppressing a smile.

Mrs Carlyon had been most deferential to the Princess, prudently losing whenever they had played bridge together. Her sacrifice had failed to curry favour. She possessed neither wit nor humour and as such was dismissed contemptuously from the royal presence.

The maid stepped out on to the terrace with a silver tray bearing a glass of champagne and a glass of lemonade. The Princess's black-gloved hand reached for the champagne. Despite the day's heat she made no concession to fashion. Black silk was worn, summer and winter, heavily ornamented by sumptuous jewels.

'I wonder,' she said thoughtfully, sipping her champagne, 'if Monsieur Blanc will be able to persuade Mademoiselle Bernhardt to appear at the casino's theatre in the part of Phaedra? Such a performance would attract great attention and divert from the prominence the newspapers are giving to Monte Carlo's suicide rate.'

Charlotte felt the nape of her neck prickle. She had heard stories of the small, secret cemetery where those who had lost all at the tables and had taken their lives were buried unceremoniously under cover of darkness.

'I shall suggest to Monsieur Blanc that Mademoiselle Bernhardt gives a performance for our entertainment.'

Charlotte smiled and drank her lemonade. It was not an impossible request. The great actress had been at the opening of the gilt and gold Casino Theatre and had recited an impassioned prologue before hurrying to the tables and winning handsomely at roulette.

From where she sat Charlotte could see the tiled and pinnacled twin towers of the theatre and casino. The cream-coloured façade gleamed golden in the sun. Beyond the casino, terraces ablaze with exotic flowers shelved down to the sparkling blue sea.

Her father would have disapproved strongly of gambling, but Charlotte could not. Though she had not the finances to gamble herself, she loved to accompany the Princess on her nightly visits to the casino. She loved the flamboyance and splendour of the red plush sofas and the huge rococo mirrors. Whenever she passed the entrance and the gilded statues of Nubian slaves clutching crystal candelabra, she felt a thrill of excitement and expectation.

Once inside the Devil's Palace anything could happen. Fortunes could be won and lost; reputations made and broken. In her six months with the Princess she had seen ladies of royal blood hiss at each other like alley cats over a dispute at cards. Had seen Prince Roland Bonaparte challenge a member of Britain's aristocracy to a duel; had seen breathtakingly beautiful young women of lowly background accompany kings; had watched love *affaires* flourish, wane and die; had become part of the peculiar society of Monte Carlo. A mixture of international royalty and the twilight world of the *demi-monde*.

'I shall now take my afternoon rest,' the Princess announced, rising to her feet.

'Do you wish me to read to you, Your Highness?'

It was part of Charlotte's duties to read to the Princess the daily French and English newspapers that arrived in Monte Carlo long after their date of publication.

'No. The sun has given me a headache. I shall take a sleeping draught. Please see to it, Charlotte, that Henri delivers my card to Mademoiselle Bernhardt.'

Charlotte accompanied the Princess from the terrace and into her opulent bedroom. As the maid assisted her from her voluminous folds of black silk, Charlotte closed the shutters, plunging the room into shadow.

It would be seven o'clock before the Princess awoke and dressed in readiness for the evening's entertainment. In Monte Carlo, days were turned into night, nights into day. Though in her eighties, it was seldom earlier than four in the morning before Princess Yakovleva returned from her nightly *sorties* at the whist and *écarté* tables.

The maid placed a jug of iced water on the bedside table, carefully plumped the lace-trimmed pillows and adjusted silk sheets with their lavish monogram of the House of Romanov.

Discreetly they withdrew, the maid to attend to the Princess's evening gown; Charlotte to request the coachman to deliver the Princess's card to the Hotel de Paris.

Stepping out into the sunshine on the terrace, she hesitated. The sun was high in the sky. Monte Carlo was asleep. There could be no harm in taking the short walk to the hotel unescorted. Decisively she stepped back into the villa, perched a deliciously small hat of bows and feathers low over her forehead, picked up her parasol and quietly closed the door of the villa behind her. Even the Monégasques had taken refuge from the heat. Magnolia and hibiscus gave way to the narrow cobbled lanes that climbed the hills behind the casino and hotel. In the Boulevard des Moulins a handful of children played barefoot, laughing joyously.

The Princess had told her that when she had first come to Monte Carlo, in the early 1870s, the Boulevard des Moulins had been practically non-existent. Now, thanks to the success of the casino, fashionable villas spilled window boxes of strelitza and scarlet geraniums along its length. There were now hotels, too, their owners desperately vying with the long-established Hotel de Paris for the droves of Russian grand dukes who descended yearly to spend their gold at the gambling tables.

The hotel adjoined the casino. The children grinned impishly at her as she closed her parasol and stepped past them into a world they would never enter. A liveried bellboy discreetly approached her. Charlotte deposited the Princess's card on a small silver tray.

'For Mademoiselle Bernhardt from Princess Yakovleva,' she said, her soft smile making the bellboy her instant slave.

As she spoke, the hotel manager, resplendent in frock coat and with a gardenia in his buttonhole, hurried across the opulent lobby to greet a gentleman descending the crimson-carpeted stairway.

'I trust we will have the pleasure of accommodating you once again, Count Karolyi.' His bow was sweeping.

'I am afraid not,' a deep, rich-timbred voice replied. 'I have recently purchased Beausoleil and shall be remaining there for the duration of my stay.'

'Ah, yes!' The hotel manager clasped his hands together. 'A most beautiful residence, if I may say so, Count Karolyi. Perhaps I can persuade you to partake of some refreshment? Champagne perhaps, or brandy?'

'No. I came only to pay my respects to Mademoiselle Bernhardt.'

His eyes flicked past the hotel manager and rested on Charlotte. The expression in them changed from one of uninterest to one that was bold and black and frankly appraising. Charlotte turned away quickly, the blood rushing to her cheeks. For an insane moment she feared that he would recognise her but common sense quickly asserted itself. He had seen nothing but the flash of sun on the lens of opera glasses. He had no way of knowing that only an hour ago she had studied him with indecent intimacy, marvelling at the pain in his anguished eyes. There was no pain there now. His manner was one of almost arrogant self-assurance. His voice caused her nerves to throb. It was like the man, strong and dark, the voice of a man used to being obeyed.

Aware of his continuing gaze, her discomfort mounted. In her lightly accented French she wished the bellboy goodbye and turned to leave. The sound of galloping hoofs shattered the dignified calm of the hotel's richly furnished lobby.

From the narrow streets came shouts of alarm, the thundering rattle of wheels hurtling over cobbled stones. Hastily Charlotte hurried to the door, the bellboy and hotel manager following in her wake.

The bolting horse was petrified, eyes rolling; nostrils flaring; foam flecking its mouth. In the sturdy peasant cart being dragged in its wake a few sacks of grain rolled perilously from side to side. The children halted in their game, gazed at the oncoming fury and fled to press themselves against the nearest wall. All save one small boy who remained sitting in the dust, transfixed in terror.

Charlotte screamed. A sack of grain tumbled to the ground, bursting open in a golden shower. She could see the sweat on the horse's coat, feel the vibration of the hoofs.

The child cried out in fear; the hotel manager crossed himself and closed his eyes, and Charlotte flung her parasol to one side and darted in front of the oncoming horse. Her arm circled the child, lifted. Dust flew around her. She could feel the breath of the horse on her neck, see the flailing hoofs bearing down on her. Instinctively she raised her free arm in an effort to ward off the crushing onslaught. As she did so she was seized and hurled bodily across the boulevard. She thudded down on the ground, the child still clasped in her arms, the breath driven from her body. The horse snorted and whinnied and was gone. The child struggled from her grasp and ran into the beefy arms of a peasant woman, crying loudly. She tried to rise to her feet and failed.

Dazedly she was aware of the commotion around her, of strong hands grasping her as a blood-red mist clouded her vision.

'A brandy for mademoiselle,' the hotel manager cried, clearing a way as Count Karolyi swept her up into his arms and carried her away from the rapidly growing crowd of curious Monégasques and into the privacy of the hotel lounge. Her head was against his chest. She could feel the strong beating of his heart, smell the faint aroma of cologne. Count Karolyi was carrying her with consummate ease past the bronze equestrian statue of Louis XIV, and into the Hotel de Paris' lounge. Her cheeks flamed at the indignity; at the turbulent emotions that threatened to rob her of coherent thought or speech.

The manager proffered the brandy again and Charlotte declined it, wondering where the striding Count was taking her with such indecent familiarity. At last, to her intense relief, he halted. She felt herself lowered gently, felt the comforting support of a velvet upholstered sofa. Overcome with confusion, she raised her eyes to his. He was standing over her, regarding her with an unfathomable expression.

Her hat had been dislodged, bowling down the boulevard with the flying grains of wheat. Her elaborate chignon had come undone and her hair tumbled around her shoulders in wild disarray. Her cheeks smarted and pressing her fingers to her face she felt a trickle of blood. The turquoise satin gown that had been her pride and joy was covered in dust and dirt, the hem torn.

She tried to speak, to regain some semblance of dignity, but her breath was ragged and her limbs shook.

'I think it best if you drink the brandy, Mademoiselle,' Count Sandor Karolyi said firmly.

She pushed her hair away from her eyes, humiliatingly aware of her dishevelled appearance.

The brandy was proffered once more, this time by a

strong, olive-toned hand. Not daring to do otherwise she took it and drank, coughing as the unfamiliar spirit burned her throat. Above her, her rescuer suppressed a smile.

He was well aware of her discomfort but had no intention of putting an untimely end to it. She was still trembling with shock and her grazed cheek would need attention before she could leave the hotel.

'That was an extremely foolish and courageous thing to do, Mademoiselle . . .'

'Grainger,' Charlotte said, not daring to lift her eyes to his, wishing with all her heart that he would excuse himself and allow her to compose herself and tidy her hair and attend to her face and dress.

He frowned. He had meant to chastise her for risking her life so heedlessly and occasioning him to risk his own, but the sight of her lying so vulnerably on the sofa with her hair tumbling around her shoulders filled him with compassion. She looked little more than a child. Her eyes were a soft, smoky green, thickly lashed; her cheekbones were high; her mouth full and soft and generous. The shining mass of her hair was a rich copper that glinted gold in the morning sunlight. She was, Count Karolyi observed, outstandingly beautiful.

He turned to the hotel manager. 'Could I have a bowl of warm water and a sponge, please. Mademoiselle Grainger's face is in need of attention.'

'No!' Charlotte's mortified protest was torn from her throat.

Count Karolyi raised well-defined brows.

'It . . . would not be . . . proper,' she stammered. 'I can attend to my face myself.'

'A maid perhaps,' the hotel manager offered obligingly.

A hint of a smile curved Sandor Karolyi's mouth. 'Water and a sponge,' he reiterated.

Charlotte gazed helplessly at the hotel manager, but a

bellboy had already been sent to carry out the Count's orders.

'I feel quite rested,' she lied in vain, attempting to move from the sofa, seeking only to escape from his overpowering presence.

His hand restrained her firmly. 'You have sustained a very severe shock, Mademoiselle.'

The water was brought and as maids and bellboys gathered round at a respectful distance, Count Sandor Karolyi began to sponge flecks of blood from the graze on her cheek.

A Russian grand duchess, entering the hotel lobby with her retinue, halted in her tracks at the stupefying sight of Count Sandor Karolyi on his knees beside a semi-conscious young woman. Only a heavy whiff of smelling salts restored her and even then she had to be physically assisted to her room.

Charlotte thought she would die with humiliation. Her cheeks burned; her eyes painfully avoided his. At last her torment came to an end. Satisfied as to his ministrations, Count Karolyi rose to his feet and handed the bowl and sponge to a maid.

'There will be no mark,' he said reassuringly. 'If your carriage can be summoned, I will escort you to your destination.'

Charlotte gathered the last remnants of her pride. 'I have no carriage,' she said stiffly. 'I am companion to Princess Yakovleva.'

The interest in his eyes deepened. There was a hint of a smile around the abrasive lines of his mouth.

'Then you must allow me to put my carriage at your disposal, Mademoiselle Grainger.'

'I . . . No . . . I . . .' To protest was useless. Count Sandor Karolyi was a man accustomed to being obeyed. Vainly she scooped her hair into a loose knot at the nape of her neck, securing it with the few pins that remained.

To Charlotte's anguished eyes it seemed that the

whole staff of the hotel had congregated in the lounge as she allowed herself to be escorted by Count Karolyi towards his waiting carriage.

In the sunlight she became even more aware of her dust-covered and bedraggled gown. The carriage that had drawn up outside the Hotel de Paris's main entrance was drawn by white stallions with crimson cockades. The coachman was resplendent in full livery, the carriage door emblazoned in gold with the Count's crest.

From the windows of the hotel wealthy patrons watched with interest, a golden haired, feline-eyed woman with delight, as Count Sandor Karolyi helped her into the scarlet leather interior. Charlotte held her head high, blinking back the tears that threatened to overwhelm her. Soon her ordeal would be at an end. Soon the devastatingly handsome Count Karolyi would turn his attention elsewhere. To Mademoiselle Bernhardt; to one of the ravishing cocottes who haunted the casino. To a lady of his own rank.

Through narrowed eyes Sandor regarded her speculatively. She was certainly a different breed from the beauties he usually associated with. Her actions had saved a child's life. And, if it had not been for his own presence of mind, could have cost her own. Her shyness was touching; her dignity appealing. He continued to survey her in unnerving silence and a pulse began to beat wildly in her throat. He had saved her life and she had not yet found the presence of mind to thank him for his action. Was that why he was gazing at her with such disturbing intensity, his satanically black brows furrowed as if in displeasure?

Her throat felt dry, her hands twisted nervously in her lap.

'I would like to thank you for saving me from hurt,' she said in a voice little more than a whisper.

Something flickered in the back of his eyes. Was it amusement? 'You appreciation is accepted,' he said and it seemed to her that the hard lines of his mouth softened imperceptibly.

She looked away quickly, her heart pounding, staring blindly at mimosa and pine. For a split second of time she had been overcome with the immodest desire to reach out and touch him. Did he know the effect he was having on her? The answer came swift and fast. Of course he did. Count Sandor Karolyi was a professional lover; a man who amused himself with countless women, discarding them as lightly as the Princess did her gloves. No doubt his anecdote of how he had saved a lady's companion from death would entertain his friends vastly. As would the fact that the lady in question had fallen instantly in love with him. Her head lifted imperceptibly; her hands tightened. She would give him no such satisfaction.

The hill steepened. With relief she saw the warm ochre walls of the villa between the trees. Soon she would be free of his unwelcome presence. She would be able to bathe, brush her dishevelled hair and calm herself.

'It is a long time since I have seen Princess Yakovleva. I am looking forward to meeting her again,' Sandor Karolyi said, shattering her barely recovered composure. 'I trust she is well.'

'Yes, very.' Her voice was barely audible. It had not occurred to her that he would alight from his carriage at the Villa Ondine. She had hoped to enter the villa discreetly; to make no mention of the incident to the Princess. Now she saw that to do so would be impossible. Her agony was to be prolonged. The Princess would chastise her for walking unaccompanied to the hotel, she would probably be outraged at having her companion make a public exhibition of herself. Once again she was acutely aware of her dust-marked dress; of the rent in the hem; of a stubborn curl spilling free from the hastily gathered knot in the nape of her neck. She looked more like a peasant girl than companion to a princess of royal blood.

Hot tears stung the back of her eyes. She blinked them away rapidly. She had behaved impulsively but in no way that she need be ashamed of. Her chin tilted defiantly. Anger replaced humiliation.

Watching her, Sandor's amusement deepened. For a moment her lips had trembled and he had seen the brilliance of tears in her eyes. They had been swiftly suppressed but her mouth was still softly vulnerable. He wondered what it would be like to kiss and thought that it would be an exceedingly pleasant experience but one he would have to forgo.

Her demeanour was one of modesty and breeding. A light flirtation would be misunderstood, a liaison disastrous. His mouth tightened. All liaisons were disastrous, bringing nothing but agony and pain. He thought of Irina, marble-white and beautiful in death, and his knuckles clenched fiercely. Damn it to hell; would it always be so? Would he never find happiness? Would the burden he carried continue to darken his life and destroy the lives of those he loved? Irina had not understood and so, in a foolish gesture, had taken her life. She had been a delightful companion, gay and tender, yet he had known instinctively that she would have been unable to live with his secret as he lived with it. And so, unable to marry her, he had severed the relationship. And she had taken her life.

At his sigh of despair Charlotte turned her head. The winged brows were pulled together in a deep frown. The suggestion of a smile had vanished. His mouth was a tight, harsh line. His hair tumbled low over his forehead as if he had just run his fingers hopelessly through the blue-black curls. He looked forbidding yet curiously vulnerable. Her anger fled. Her first opinion of him had been correct. Count Sandor Karolyi was a spirit tormented. She wondered what dark thoughts caused him such anguish and remembered the Vicomtesse who had taken her life when he had spurned her.

The carriage had halted. The coachman had dismounted and opened the door and still Sandor sat, lost in his inner hell.

Charlotte cleared her throat hesitantly.

'Thank you for escorting me safely, Count Karolyi.'

He passed a hand across his eyes. The past was past. He was a fool to dwell on what could never be altered.

'The pleasure is mine, Mademoiselle,' he said, once more himself as he alighted from the carriage and courteously held out his hand to assist her.

At his touch she trembled slightly. His mouth curved into a smile. There was a smudge of dirt on her cheek. Her copper curls were rapidly escaping the remaining pins. He wondered if the Princess would be willing to give up Miss Grainger's services. The English girl was exactly the kind of young lady Zara needed for companionship.

At the thought of Zara his smile faded. She would be in Monte Carlo within days. There would be distant courtesies exchanged in the presence of her insufferable husband. All too short and infrequent furtive meetings in his absence. There were times when he wished neither he, nor she, had ever been born.

'Sandor!' To her alarm, Charlotte saw that the Princess had risen early and was walking towards them, black silk rustling, rubies shining blood-red. 'Whatever has happened? Charlotte! Your face! Your gown!'

'I had a mishap,' Charlotte said, hot with embarrassment. 'If you will excuse me, Your Highness . . .'

'Most certainly not!' The Princess thumped her cane smartly on the ground, her white-powdered face grim. 'What is the meaning of this, Sandor? Why is Miss Grainger's face grazed and her gown torn?'

Sandor took the Princess's hand and kissed it.

'Miss Grainger has been playing the part of heroine,

Princess Natalya. She saved a child from being trampled to death by a bolting horse in the Boulevard des Moulins.'

The Princess's thinly arched eyebrows rose. 'Is this true, Charlotte?'

'I . . . Yes . . .'

The Princess pursed her lips. There would be time enough to ask what Charlotte had been doing walking down to the hotel unescorted when Sandor had taken his leave.

'I trust the horse was not yours, Sandor?'

'It was not.' He had taken the Princess's arm and was escorting her to the chairs and tables on the terrace. Charlotte, undismissed, was obliged to follow unhappily in their wake.

'How long do you intend to stay in Monte Carlo?' the Princess asked as they sat down.

'Until it bores me,' Sandor replied easily.

'And how is that abominable cousin of yours, Povzervslay?'

'As bestial as ever.' The words were languid enough but there was an intensity of feeling behind them that shocked Charlotte. Was this the cousin whose crimes were crimes of blood?

The Princess's fingers tightened over the knob of her cane. 'I saw him at Marienbad last season and left the place immediately. He contaminates the very air. What is the matter, Charlotte? Surely you wish to change? Your hair looks like a peasant girl's.'

Charlotte's cheeks flamed. There was nothing she wanted to do more, and it was the Princess's fault that she had been unable to do so. There were times when, despite her fondness for Princess Natalya, she sympathised with her scores of predecessors.

'Yes, Your Highness. Please excuse me.'

Her eyes caught Count Karolyi's for a brief second and met undisguised amusement. Her own sparked with a flash of anger. Any man who derived such amusement from a lady's misfortune was contemptible. With her head held high she swept from the terrace and walked swiftly to the sanctuary of her room. Her vexation increased when she stood in front of her mirror. Her face was smudged with dirt. Her hair disarrayed. And so she had sat opposite the elegantly attired Count Sandor Karolyi for the best part of half an hour.

'Wretched man!' she said, wrenching at the small pearl buttons of her bodice. 'Wretched, detestable, *hateful* creature!'

She bathed her face, applied salve to the graze, grudgingly grateful that Count Karolyi had insisted on cleaning it and that it showed no sign of infection. She brushed her hair vigorously, smoothing the curls high into a gleaming chignon. The dust-blown gown was exchanged for a pretty creation in lemon with long, full sleeves gathered tightly at the wrists. The bodice was *cuirass*, accentuating her tiny waist and the gentle swell of her hips. When the Princess's maid knocked on the door and announced that the Princess required her presence on the terrace, she gave one last, hasty look in the mirror and was well pleased with what she saw. When she emerged into the late afternoon sunshine to find the Princess alone and the Count gone, her disappointment was acute.

Princess Yakovleva gestured to her to sit down and she did so, wondering why she had been so eagerly looking forward to being once more in the Count's disturbing presence. She had no time to come to a conclusion. The Princess was saying crisply,

'I congratulate you, Charlotte. You've achieved more than the Marquise Vermont achieved in a month.'

'I beg your pardon, Your Highness.' Charlotte tried to concentrate on what the Princess was saying to her and not on disturbing black eyes.

'Count Karolyi,' the Princess said with unconcealed

satisfaction. 'Ariadne, the Marquise Vermont, tried to attract his attention for a whole month at Bad Homburg. You attracted it within five minutes.'

'Not intentionally,' Charlotte replied tartly.

The Princess laughed. 'Maybe not, but you should be well pleased with yourself all the same. It's unlike Sandor to show such unnecessary civilities to anyone. He had no need to escort you all the way to the villa. He could quite easily have deposited you in the care of his coachman.'

'I believe he wished to see you, Your Highness.'

'He'll see me tonight, and every other night, in the casino,' the Princess said practically. 'Don't throw yourself before any more bolting horses, Charlotte. The turquoise silk is ruined and will have to be discarded.'

'The rent can quite easily be mended,' Charlotte began apologetically.

The Princess waved her hand dismissively. Charlotte had entered her employment wearing a serviceable and unbecoming gown and with only one other in her portmanteau. She had set about furnishing her with a suitable wardrobe and had taken great pleasure in doing so. Her only child was a son she disliked and seldom saw and Charlotte had become more like a daughter than a paid companion. She made a mental note to get in touch with her lawyer and have her will altered so that on her death Charlotte would be left with a suitable income.

'If Sandor is residing at Beausoleil, why was he at the Hotel de Paris?'

'He had been to call on Mademoiselle Bernhardt, Your Highness.'

The Princess nodded to herself, a smile playing on her wrinkled lips. 'Young devil. I should have realised it was La Bernhardt that had drawn him away from Paris.'

A strange emotion suffused Charlotte. One that she had never experienced before. Her heart felt as if a knife had been plunged into it and cruelly twisted. The Princess continued to talk but Charlotte no longer heard her. Why did she feel such sweeping desolation at the knowledge that Sandor Karolyi had come purposely to Monte Carlo to see the divine Sarah? Why did it matter to her who he escorted?

Her head pounded. The afternoon had been traumatic. It was no wonder she was reacting perversely. The sight of the child in the path of the galloping horse; her impetuous dash; the throb of the ground as the horse raced down on her; the strong arms that had hurled her to safety.

The Princess eyed her with concern. 'I think it would be best if you rested before dinner,' she said with a gruffness that disguised affection. 'Today is the tenth of the month and ten is my lucky number. I have great expectations of alarming Monsieur Blanc by winning repeatedly at the tables this evening.'

With relief Charlotte returned to her room and lay down on her bed. The day had started so calmly, so ordinarily, and had contained so much. She closed her eyes. It was still not over. Tonight she would accompany the Princess to the casino and surely there, among the glittering throng, would be Count Sandor Karolyi and the beautiful Sarah Bernhardt.

Sleep drifted over her in waves. She wondered if the beautiful Sarah knew of Sandor Karolyi's other face; the brooding, pain-filled face that he was so careful not to show in public. What occasioned his anguish? Past sins? Past loves? An inexplicable sadness engulfed her. Count Sandor Karolyi and Mademoiselle Bernhardt. Sandor and Sarah. And then, as sleep claimed her, Sandor and Charlotte. . . .

CHAPTER
TWO

THAT evening she dressed with extreme care, filled with a nameless excitement. Would he be in the Salle Mauresque when they entered? Would he pay her any attention? Her heart throbbed fiercely as she adjusted a camellia nestling in her hair. Of course he would not. She was Princess Yakovleva's paid companion. Why should Count Sandor Karolyi condescend to speak to her in a place as public as the Salle Mauresque? The full satin skirts of her gown swirled as she picked up her fan and turned her back on the mirror. Besides, she had no desire for such attention. She wished for nothing more than to forget the whole distressing incident.

She joined the Princess and allowed the coachman to assist her into the Princess's carriage. Eventually she would have to face the manager of the Hotel de Paris, but perhaps he would have the good manners not to embarrass her by making any mention of the near catastrophe. Fortunately, it had occurred at a time of day when very few people had been present to witness it. She could remember only Monégasques and the liveried bellboys of the Hotel surrounding her as Count Karolyi had carried her into the Hotel de Paris lounge. And startled faces at upper windows. Her fingers tightened on the ivory clasp of her fan. The occupants of the Hotel de Paris were *habitués* of the casino.

Her cheeks burned in the darkness of the carriage. Had her rash escapade been witnessed by Lord and Lady Pethelbridge and the Countess of Bexhall? Perhaps even by Princess Helena? She tilted her chin a defiant fraction higher. There was no way of rectifying the matter if they had. She could not have let the child be crushed by the flailing hoofs. Any gossip would just have to be lived with and ignored.

The Princess, guessing accurately that the pucker on Charlotte's brow was caused by memories of the afternoon, remained silent. While Charlotte was dressing she had summoned the manager of the Hotel de Paris to the villa and had heard a corroborated account of her companion's courage. She pursed her lips. She must settle the matter of Charlotte's future with her solicitor at the first opportunity. She would write to him immediately. It was impossible to think that Charlotte should be left unprovided for.

The casino flamed and shone by the sea, lit by hundreds of chandeliers. As they alighted from the carriage Charlotte could hear the monotonous surge of the waves merging with the distant voices of the croupiers, the rattle of gold, the click of ivory balls spinning round roulette wheels. This was the moment that normally filled her with pleasurable anticipation. Tonight, as she descended from the carriage and faced the brilliantly lit entrance, her pleasure was overcome with anxiety.

The doorman nodded deferentially as they entered. Monsieur Bertora, the casino's manager, greeted the Princess warmly, resplendent in frock coat and silk hat.

'I must warn you, Monsieur Bertora, that I feel exceedingly lucky this evening,' the Princess said, a fortune of rubies hugging her throat and arms.

He smiled. He liked the casino's patrons to feel lucky. When they did, they gambled recklessly and heavily. And, occasionally, they won handsomely. Such an event did not disturb him. Money won in the Devil's Palace was money only lent.

In the glittering room Charlotte caught a glimpse of Princess Helena, full-bosomed and full-hipped, her tiny waist corseted in diamonds, the rich satin of her gown flowing into a demi-train.

Lord Pethelbridge was talking to a Turkish pasha, a fat cigar in one hand, a glass of champagne in the other. Lady Pethelbridge was deep in a hand of *trente-et-quarante*, her corsage smothered in red roses.

A croupier, delicately ignoring the presence of the ladies, announced 'Gentlemen, eyes down' and Lord Pethelbridge took his leave of the pasha.

The gold plaques glittered and shone, rattling across the table. Lady Pethelbridge raised her eyes from the cards and nodded a greeting to Princess Yakovleva, her gaze flicking over Charlotte without interest. Charlotte breathed an imperceptible sigh of relief. Lady Pethelbridge, for one, had not witnessed the afternoon's events from the window of her room at the Hotel de Paris.

It was the Princess's custom to wander through the rooms, greeting friends and watching the play at the tables, before continuing upstairs to the Salon Privé and a hand of baccarat with other notable royals.

A Russian grand duke, his sparkling eyed *chère amie* on his arm, crossed the room to meet the Princess. The Princess ignored the exquisite curtsey of the duke's companion and conversing in Russian asked after the grand duchess and other family members.

The pretty Parisienne refused to be deflated and flashed Charlotte a smile. Three months ago she had been the companion of an English lord. Six months ago, when Charlotte had first arrived in Monte Carlo, she had been constantly on the arm of an American railroad tycoon. After the grand duke there would no doubt be a marquis or a count, a prince or a millionaire.

The boldness of the ladies of the *demi-monde* had at first disconcerted Charlotte. With plumes in their hair and daringly *decolleté* gowns of velvet and silk, they thronged the casino, laughing and chattering like a bevy of exotic birds. The titled friends of Princess Yakovleva paid little attention to Charlotte. The ladies of the *demi-monde* habitually smiled and exchanged a word of greeting. At first Charlotte had been apprehensive that this signified she had been mistaken for one of their ranks. But as time passed and this was clearly not so, she had begun to smile shyly and wish good evening in return.

The grand duke was taking his leave of the Princess. His companion slipped a lily-white hand once more through his arm, wondering why a girl as beautiful as the Princess's companion should be content only to watch and not participate in the many pleasures at the Devil's Palace. Surely she would prefer to play the tables rather than remain so decorously a spectator? And surely she would prefer the company of a rich and handsome protector to the formidable companionship of Princess Yakovleva?

The little Parisienne shrugged cream-smooth shoulders and turned her attention to the task of subtly guiding the grand duke in the direction of the roulette tables where the devastating Count Sandor Karolyi was staking high sums. The English girl did not look discontented, and as long as she was demurely dressed and constantly at the Princess's side, was not a prospective rival.

Charlotte watched the French girl glide across the vast room, drawing glances both envious and admiring. She knew full well that there had been sympathy as well as friendship in the china-blue eyes. She suppressed a smile. The sympathy was misplaced. She had no desire to be a cocotte, exchanging one lover for another as easily as a change of gown. Love was too precious to be treated so lightly. Perhaps one day she would discover it for herself. Unbidden came the memory of strong hands seizing her; of being carried with consummate ease into the shade of the Hotel de Paris' grand lounge; of narrow black eyes holding hers appreciatively.

'*Voilà!*' A melodic voice called out, silencing the

chatter in the room. 'It is you! Oh, how brave! How heroic!'

Charlotte gazed around, trying to see who had cried out and to whom the speaker was referring.

The roulette tables were stilled. Cards were laid down. Beflowered and bejewelled heads turned simultaneously as an unmistakable figure rose to her feet, arms outstretched.

Her hair was an abundant aureole of red-gold, her eyes the long-lashed, superb eyes of a beautiful animal. A choker of pearls clasped her throat. Her gown was a diaphanous creation of chiffon and lace, swirling around her as she moved forward, commanding the attention of every eye in the room.

It seemed to Charlotte that the great Sarah Bernhardt was intent on descending on the person standing immediately behind her. Quickly she turned her head. There was no one there except one of Monsieur Bertora's frock-coated lieutenants. Startled, she gazed all around to find that the entire room was stilled and gazing in her direction.

'I am honoured to make your acquaintance, Mademoiselle.' Sarah's voice held the rhythm and music of poetry. A wide, smiling mouth revealed perfect teeth. Deep, luminous eyes held hers as Sarah clasped her hand and fell into a curtsey at her feet.

Fevered whispers circled the Salle Mauresque.

'Bravo!' a male voice called out, the cry instantly taken up as the whispers spread.

'A child . . .'

'Risked her life . . .'

'A runaway horse . . .'

Charlotte stood transfixed. The greatest actress of the era remained at her feet. They were a tableau; an island in the centre of the room. Dazedly Charlotte heard the cheers; saw hands clapping; saw Lady Pethelbridge smiling across a vast sea of scarlet carpet; saw Princess

Yakovleva, ramrod straight, a proud smile on her face.

The sun-gold head lifted. 'You were magnificent, Mademoiselle,' Sarah said, rising gracefully. 'Superb.'

'I . . .' Charlotte tried to speak and could not. Other hands were claiming hers. Incredibly she heard Lady Pethelbridge saying in a carrying voice,

'What a brave child you are, Charlotte,' as though they were intimately acquainted.

It seemed that everyone in the room, Princess Helena and the Turkish pasha included, desired to meet her.

'Champagne,' the divine Sarah was saying. 'On such an evening we must drink champagne!'

'I'm afraid that I . . .'

'Nonsense,' Princess Yakovleva said, once more at her side, 'We will be most happy to join you for champagne, Mademoiselle Bernhardt.'

Charlotte gazed around her helplessly. Although the crowd was dispersing, the roulette wheels once more turning, every face was smiling, every eye trying to catch hers. For six months she had entered the casino at the Princess's side and been ignored. Now, in a dizzying, terrifying instant of time, everyone was eager to make her acquaintance.

Sarah Bernhardt's tawny eyes gleamed. She knew very well what she had accomplished in the matter of a few seconds.

'We must be friends,' she was saying as she led Charlotte and the Princess back to the roulette table she had been playing.

'I would love to be friends.' Charlotte's smile was soft and pleased.

A champagne cork exploded into the air. It seemed to Charlotte she was the centre of the most delightful party she could imagine. And then they were at the roulette table and the croupier was giving her a bow and the Princess was seating herself and Sarah was saying in her voice of magic and music,

'Darling Sandor, you are quite right. She is impossibly beautiful.'

There was unconcealed amusement in his eyes as he rose to his feet and greeted her. Once more her hand was trapped in his. This time he raised it to his lips and at the touch of his mouth on her flesh, her blood leapt.

Impossibly beautiful. Had Sandor Karolyi said that? And of her?

The champagne was poured.

'To Charlotte,' Sarah said, raising her glass high.

'To Charlotte,' the Princess and Sandor echoed.

Sandor was laughing. It had never occurred to Charlotte that he was capable of laughter. His teeth were strong and white. He turned, his gaze resting on Sarah, and Charlotte's surge of joy died. She had not been the source of his pleasure. Sarah was the enchantress who had dispelled his inner dark thoughts and made him laugh. The knowledge brought with it desolation. Yesterday Charlotte had been happy, her heart at peace. Today, ever since she had gazed through the glasses at his handsome, tortured face, she had been in turmoil. She had become infatuated with a man at least ten years her senior; a man of wealth and title. A man with a notorious reputation. A man referred to by the Princess as the Devil's spawn. A man who regarded her with mild amusement and nothing more.

She gazed at Sarah, so sparkling and ravishing, and was incapable of jealousy.

'Red number ten,' Sarah cried and Charlotte sank back, hands folded in her lap, once more a spectator as the Princess leaned across the table and the ball spun.

With difficulty Charlotte retained her outward composure. Her moment of glory was at an end. A fact for which she was not sorry. Mademoiselle Bernhardt might revel in public admiration, but Charlotte had found the moment when every eye had been turned on her excruciating. Now all attention was firmly riveted on Sarah as, blessed by the gods, piles of golden plaques were raked by the croupiers in her direction.

Occasionally Sandor Karolyi's dark eyes left the table and the captivating perfection of Sarah, and glanced across at her. Each time Charlotte quickly lowered her eyes to her lightly clasped hands. No doubt he was annoyed at her continued presence. She could still remember a mortifying evening when a Polish princess, an intimate of Princess Yakovleva's, had asked loudly and bad-temperedly why Princess Natalya felt obliged to bring her maid with her to the tables.

Princess Natalya had tartly replied that Charlotte was a companion—not a maid—and that her company was far preferable to that of the present players at the table. The princess had risen furiously, vowing never to sit in Princess Yakovleva's presence again.

Princess Yakovleva had been unrepentant and Charlotte continued to sit at her side.

From Count Karolyi's slightly raised brows whenever he looked at her, it was obvious he was expressing the same feelings as the Polish princess. She was *de trop*. She gazed steadfastly away from the gay, titian-haired Sarah; from the Princess; from Count Karolyi, and stared out across the brilliantly lit rooms to where the darkened terraces led down to the sea.

Exotic trees, shrubs and giant magnolias were silhouetted against the moonlit sky. She had an overwhelming urge to free herself from the brilliant gaiety of the gaming rooms and to escape into the secluded gardens. As if reading her thoughts, the Princess excused herself, declaring that she must get some air.

'Please do not be long, Princess Natalya,' Sarah said, her rose-red lips curving into a bewitching smile. 'Your presence has brought me luck this evening.'

It seemed to Charlotte that, as they moved away, the dark head and the gold moved closer together.

The light breeze from the sea was cool and reviving as

they stepped outside. In the distance the lights of yachts in the Port twinkled like fireflies against the moonlit sky. The air was sweet, fragrant with the perfume of velvet-petalled magnolias. Couples sauntered along the terraces, the gentlemen magnificent in their evening attire, the ladies with chinchilla and sable draped around their naked shoulders. There was laughter, low and seductive, as assignations were made.

'Mademoiselle Bernhardt has requested that you pose for a sculptured likeness to be taken by herself,' the Princess said as they walked at a sedate pace.

'Oh, but I couldn't . . .' Charlotte began in alarm.

'I think you could.' Princess Natalya's voice was firm, brooking no argument. 'It would be most rude to refuse such a request. Mademoiselle Bernhardt is an accomplished sculptress. A marble bust of her sister, Regina, has been exhibited at the Salon in Paris.'

Charlotte lapsed into unhappy silence. Events were taking a turn she could not possibly have envisaged. First the standing ovation from the Salle Mauresque; now her likeness to be taken by Mademoiselle Bernhardt. It was all too overwhelming.

The Countess of Bexhall stepped out from the shadows and towards them, an elegant young hussar officer in her wake. Pleasantries with the Princess were exchanged. The Countess, no longer young but exceedingly beautiful, requested an introduction to Charlotte. The hussar was also introduced and his eyes were attentive.

The English girl had about her an air almost as magical as that of Mademoiselle Bernhardt. Her hair echoed the vibrancy of the actress's, but was sleeker, smoother, darker. Nevertheless, even in the moonlight, it was possible to discern golden glints amongst the rich copper ringlets piled high at the back of her head. Her eyes were wide and lustrous, thickly lashed, charmingly shy. Yet the young man sensed a passion unawakened; a recklessness that had not only prompted her to risk her life for an unknown peasant child, but that would make her a delightful initiate into the art of love.

Justin, Comte de Valmy, bowed low.

'My pleasure, Mademoiselle,' he said, and his eyes, as they gazed up into hers, were blatantly admiring.

The Countess, unaware that her escort's attention was centred elsewhere, charmingly requested the Princess to introduce her to Mademoiselle Bernhardt. The Princess, aware that the Countess was indefatigable in her requests, sighed and led the way back into the thronged gaming room.

Justin allowed the Countess to continue ahead with Princess Yakovleva and remained at Charlotte's side as they stepped into the brilliantly lit room. Charlotte's skirts rustled seductively. He was aware of a light perfume emanating from her skin and her hair. He noted the swell of her breasts beneath the lilac satin of her bodice, the gentle curve of her hips beneath the drapery of her skirts, the incredible smallness of her waist. A surge of desire flooded through him. She would be flattered by his attentions. Honoured. The Count of Bexhall was due to return to Monte Carlo within days. The Countess would no longer be so accessible. A diversion with Charlotte would be exceedingly pleasant.

The gold plaques stacked in front of Sarah had risen higher and higher. At their approach Sandor raised his head and at the sight of Justin accompanying Charlotte in undue proximity, his eyes narrowed.

Charlotte felt a pulse at the base of her throat begin to throb. Was her presence so distasteful to him? His greeting of the Countess was curt and brief, his attention returning once more to the roulette wheel.

Charlotte forced herself to look away from him. He had wanted to monopolise Sarah, not share her with the Princess's acquaintances.

Resuming her place at the Princess's side, she reflected that no matter how accustomed he was to getting his own way, in this Count Sandor Karolyi would be disappointed. Sarah's witchery would never belong solely to one man; it belonged to the world.

Play commenced. The Comte was slightly disconcerted at seeing Charlotte so openly engaged in the part of companion. Did Princess Yakovleva never allow her to play the tables? But of course not. With what would she play? He smiled to himself, imagining her delight at being supplied with gold *louis* with which to indulge herself.

Charlotte was uncomfortably aware of his gaze resting on her with disquieting frequency; of the admiration in his eyes; of the intimate smile playing around his lips. He was in his early twenties, young and dashing. Exquisitely dressed ladies of the *demi-monde* tried repeatedly to catch his attention. It was fixed on Charlotte. He even declined to play so that he could enjoy the sight of her without interruption. Her silken hair was parted in the centre, looped softly over her ears, gathered high with a velvet ribbon and spilling in a cascade of natural ringlets. Her expression was as sweet as that of a madonna. The Countess, overcome by Sarah's presence, was oblivious that her escort's attention was centred elsewhere. The Princess had eyes for nothing but the ball as it spun and clattered around the wheel, bringing, as she had anticipated, fortune in its wake.

Sandor was not so unaware. Justin, Comte de Valmy, did not abide by the rules Sandor set himself, restraining his conquests to world-weary cocottes and sophisticated married ladies all too happy to enter into a liaison and stave off boredom. Justin's thoughtless conquests were all too often innocent virgins; young girls overcome by the honour of his attentions and speedily forgotten. The de Valmy estates were littered with his carelessly conceived progeny. In Justin's eyes the breathtakingly beautiful English girl would be just another amusing diversion.

'The whole of Monte Carlo is talking of your courageous action this afernoon,' Justin said as Sarah called for more champagne to celebrate her continuing good fortune.

'It was Count Karolyi who was courageous,' Charlotte said shyly in her lightly accented French. 'I acted only on impulse and my action would not have saved the child. It was Count Karolyi who did so – and who saved my life as well.'

'I had not realised you were the true hero of the hour, Sandor,' Justin said as his champagne glass was replenished.

'I was not.' There was a distinct edge to Sandor's voice and he did not condescend to look in the Comte's direction. 'I merely removed an exceedingly foolish young woman, and an even more foolish child, from the path of a horse to prevent the animal breaking its knees and having to be shot.'

Charlotte's cheeks burned. Sarah and the Princess were too engrossed in the spinning wheel to hear his remark.

The corners of Justin's mouth twitched. It seemed that Count Karolyi was exceedingly put out that the honours for the afternoon's escapade had fallen to the Princess's companion.

'But no doubt if Mademoiselle Grainger had not acted so promptly you would not have felt obliged to remove the child?' he asked smoothly, and was pleased to observe a thin white line around Sandor's mouth, signifying anger barely under control.

'Assume what you wish,' Sandor said curtly, wishing that the Countess and her lover would remove themselves elsewhere.

The flush of colour in her cheeks only emphasised Charlotte's gentle beauty. The Comte fought the desire to unpin her ribbon, sending her hair spilling about her shoulders in a shining mass.

The Countess, losing yet again, excused herself from the table and was immediately taken to one side by an elderly Russian with silver hair and unnervingly pale blue eyes. As the Countess declared how pleased she was to see him again, Justin took the opportunity he had been waiting for.

'I would deem it an honour if you would accompany me on a drive tomorrow afternoon,' he said in a low voice, and was well pleased at the disbelief his words aroused in her sea-green eyes.

'I am afraid that I cannot, Monsieur. My duties are to attend Princess Yakovleva.'

'I am sure that if I approach the Princess on your behalf, she will consent.'

Sandor swung away from the table so suddenly that Sarah cried out in alarm.

'You will kindly address your attentions elsewhere, de Valmy. Mademoiselle Grainger is Princess Yakovleva's companion and is not open to such requests.' There was a savagery in his features that silenced even Justin. Sandor Karolyi was not a man it was wise to cross. There was talk of more than one duel; of more than one death.

Anger flooded through Charlotte like a tide. Her suspicions had been correct. In Count Karolyi's eyes she was nothing but an appendage to the Princess. A menial of whom no consideration must be taken.

'If the Princess consents, I shall be delighted to accept your kind offer,' she said, her eyes flashing defiantly.

The Princess looked at her in astonishment. Had the attention that Sarah had brought to her gone to the child's head? Her raisin-black eyes flew from Sandor's grim face to the Comte de Valmy's furious one. Her bewilderment vanished. A suspicion of a smile tugged at the corners of her wrinkled mouth.

'A carriage ride would make a welcome diversion for Charlotte,' she said and was rewarded by the Comte's flashing smile and Sandor's blazing anger.

The Russian departed. The Countess returned her attention to Justin, unaware of the assignation her lover had just made. She took her leave of Sarah and the Princess, bade Charlotte a charming goodnight and murmured to Justin that she had a headache. He patted her hand, aware that she had no such thing but that she was anxious to leave the casino and enjoy his company in private. There would be no such opportunities when her husband returned.

'Shame on you, Sandor,' Sarah chastised, tapping him lightly on the arm with her ostrich-feathered fan. 'Why should not Charlotte accompany the Comte for an afternoon carriage ride?'

'Indeed,' said the Princess, 'why not?'

Charlotte gazed at her employer in disbelief. She had expected the wrath of heaven to fall on her for her forwardness. Instead, the Princess seemed positively buoyant at the prospect of being deserted the following afternoon. Her head whirled. Why had the Comte made such a request? Surely he was aware of the difference in their social status? And why had the Princess acceded to it?

Sandor's face was taut with fury, his eyes blazing. He, at least, was well aware of the incongruity of her being escorted on a carriage ride by Comte Justin de Valmy, Charlotte thought bleakly.

Sarah's gaiety dispelled the tenseness that had descended on the table. The wheel continued to spin. The Princess continued to play, forsaking her usual game of baccarat in the Salon Privé. To Charlotte the night seemed endless. Sandor Karolyi's anger, though controlled, was patently not dissipated. The sun-bronzed face was hard and uncompromising. A pulse throbbed threateningly at the corner of his jaw. She averted her gaze from his downturned head and surveyed the sparkling throng milling in the room. The little Parisienne who had smiled at her so warmly was ecstatically scooping up a pile of gold plaques, the grand duke watching indulgently at her side. A wave of apprehension flooded Charlotte. Had the Comte mistaken her for a cocotte? Was that the reason he had so surprisingly asked her to accompany him? The heat in the room seemed insufferable. She longed to walk the terrace and feel the breeze from the sea cooling her face. No such mistake could have been made. Princess Yakovleva had made it perfectly clear that Charlotte was her companion.

A member of the royal house of Serbia entered the room, a bevy of plumed and jewelled ladies in his wake. A crowd was congregating around a *trente-et-quarante* table as the bids rose astronomically. Monsieur Blanc was striding from table to table. The Countess of Bexhall had been delayed in her exit by Princess Helena. The Comte was at her side, his thick, fair hair gleaming beneath the lights of the chandeliers. Charlotte averted her gaze swiftly. Why had she accepted his invitation? She had not the slightest desire to ride with him.

In turning her head from the Comte's direction her eyes inadvertently met Count Karolyi's. The harshness in his expression made her feel faint. She had accepted the Comte's invitation because he had paid attention to her and Count Karolyi had not. The hard glitter of his eyes was unnerving.

'If you will excuse me, Your Highness, I would like to take some air.'

The Princess turned her head sharply. Charlotte's face was unnaturally pale.

'Would you like me to accompany you, child?'

'No thank you, Your Highness. That will not be necessary. I shall only be a few moments.'

The Princess nodded and Charlotte excused herself with relief, her skirts rustling as she walked hurriedly across the Salle Mauresque and out on to the terrace and into blessed coolness.

There were too many couples promenading for her to

feel at ease and she ran lightly down the terrace steps and on to a lower, less populated terrace. Pots of verbena and marguerites shone palely in the moonlight. A high bank of rhododendrons concealed her from the view of those above. She halted against a marble statue of Venus and gazed out over the silk-black sea. She had behaved foolishly, allowing Count Karolyi's uninterest to goad her into accepting an invitation she had no desire for.

The night air was fresh. From above she could hear subdued laughter and the murmur of voices but there was no one on the lower terrace to disturb her privacy. She leaned her cheek against the coolness of the marble, reluctant to return to the heat and dazzle of the Salle Mauresque.

There was the sound of a footfall. The leaves of the rhododendrons were brushed aside and a dark figure descended the steps. She picked up her skirts, intent on leaving now that her privacy had been invaded. His silhouette was unmistakable. Thick curling hair, broad shoulders, narrow hips, and an air of negligent sensuality that sent the blood pounding in her veins. Helplessly she looked around for a way of escape, and found none.

'I would like a word with you, Mademoiselle Grainger,' he said, and there was a hint of menace in his words.

'I think not,' she retorted bravely, aware that her voice held an underlying tremor. 'If you will excuse me.'

She moved towards the steps purposefully but he barred the way.

'I feel obliged to point out to you that if it had not been for the events of this afternoon and Mademoiselle's Bernhardt's attention, the Comte de Valmy would have paid you no regard at all.'

'I don't see of what interest that is to you, Monsieur.' Her eyes sparked dangerously.

He seemed to hesitate and for a moment Charlotte thought he was going to step aside and allow her to ascend the steps. Instead, he said with a depth of feeling that startled her,

'If I had not saved your life earlier today, you would not have been able to accept the Comte's invitation. Therefore I feel a measure of responsibility for you.'

'Let me assure you, you have no need! I have given you my thanks for . . ' Anger and humiliation choked her, '. . . for . . . *hurling* me to safety. There is no need for you to feel any responsibility for my future actions.'

· She was so near that he could smell the clean perfume of her hair. He cursed inwardly. What the devil was it to him whether de Valmy seduced her or not?

'And now, Monsieur, if you will excuse me?' Her lips were parted and trembling.

'De Valmy has only one motive in seeking your company, Mademoiselle Grainger, and it is not an honourable one.'

She gasped. 'How dare you imply that . . . that . . .' She struggled to find the right words and failed, '. . . that he is without honour!'

The broad shoulders shrugged carelessly. 'Because it is a truth known throughout Europe.'

'As is the truth of your own reputation, Monsieur!' she flared, her breasts heaving.

His eyes narrowed, holding her prisoner. 'My reputation is none of your concern, Mademoiselle!'

'And my actions are none of yours, Monsieur!'

There was a sudden flexing of muscles at his jaw line as they glared furiously at each other.

'Then you still intend to keep your assignation with him?'

She tilted her head defiantly. 'I am looking forward to it exceedingly.'

Something deep inside him, long suppressed, exploded.

'Then *this* is what you are looking forward to, Mademoiselle!'

His hands shot out, grasping her wrists. She tried to wrench them away but he held her easily, drawing her in one swift movement into the circle of his arms.

'No! Please! *No!*' Her protests were in vain. His mouth came down on hers in a hard, silencing kiss.

Her hands pushed purposefully against his chest. His lips claimed and demanded, searing hers, hot and sweet.

She twisted her head but there was no escape. His hands burned through the silk of her gown. Heat surged through her body as if she were in the grip of a fever. His mouth parted hers and she could summon no resistance. Weakness flooded through her and she swayed helplessly against him, held upright only by the strength of his arms.

His kiss had lost its savagery. It was long and slow and expert, shocking in its effect on her. Her hands no longer pushed against him in protest. Instead her fingers opened and closed helplessly and then clutched despairingly at his shoulders, sliding upwards of their own volition to the warmth of his neck as her senses reeled.

For a lifetime his mouth held hers captive and then very gently he released her, looking down at her with a strange expression in his devil-dark eyes.

'Charlotte . . .' His voice was unsteady, scarcely recognisable. She was panting for breath, suffused with shame, her emotions in turmoil. She struggled to speak and when she did so the words were ragged and thick with suppressed tears.

'You . . . are . . . despicable.'

Falteringly she backed away from him.

'Charlotte, please . . .' The harsh planes of his face looked almost Arabic in the moonlight.

Her voice rose, edged with hysteria. 'Don't touch me . . . don't ever touch me again!'

His nearness, his masculinity, were overpowering. She had to move, had to be free of his presence. His hand reached out for her and she struck it blindly away.

'You are hateful! Detestable! I never want to set eyes on you again!'

Her hand rose again, slapping him full across the face and then the tears that had been held back for so long scalded her cheeks as she whirled away from him, running along the terrace and up the steps, as if the Furies themselves were at her heels.

He didn't move. His face had hardened into an impenetrable mask. As she disappeared from sight he cursed softly and then, his eyes bleak, followed slowly in her wake.

She paused at the entrance of the Salle Mauresque, struggling to regulate her breathing. Charlotte. He had called her Charlotte. And he had behaved infamously. She pressed her hands against her scalding cheeks. She was trembling violently, her heart racing. Captured in his arms she had felt no revulsion, only a wild, fleeting joy. She had wanted to remain there, to hear the thud of his heart against hers; to feel the strength of his body; the heat of his hands. The blood surged through her veins in a hot tide. She was shameless; little better than the Parisienne who flaunted herself on the grand duke's arm. She took a deep, shuddering breath and stepped once more into the laughter-filled room.

The Princess eyed her curiously. Unless she was very much mistaken, Charlotte's cheeks were unduly flushed and there was a suspicious glitter of unshed tears in her eyes. She felt suddenly tired. Perhaps she had been unwise in allowing Charlotte permission to accompany Justin de Valmy. Certainly a proposal of marriage would not be forthcoming from such a venture. De Valmy was not a young man who would be so rash as to align himself to a girl of no social status.

'I shall be enchanted to join you for supper tomorrow evening, Mademoiselle Bernhardt,' she said as she prepared to depart.

Sarah's almond-shaped eyes danced. 'I have much to

show you, Princess Natalya. My paintings, my sculptures, my animals. They travel everywhere with me.' In a graceful, fluid movement she rose to her feet and kissed the Princess goodbye. 'Will you be brave enough to play with my pet cheetah tomorrow, Charlotte? He is as brave and beautiful as yourself. Naughty Monsieur Bertora will not allow me to bring him into the casino. Yet my cheetah is not so wild as some who pass through his door!'

Despite her anguish, Charlotte laughed. Sarah's blatant joy of life was infectious.

'That is better,' Sarah chided. 'You were made to smile and laugh, my dear Charlotte, not to look so inexplicably sad.'

Her acolytes surrounded her, eager to gain attention. Sarah ignored them and announced her desire to bathe in the sea.

The Princess walked without her usual sprightliness through the gilded rooms. 'I feel unusually fatigued,' she said as she entered her coach.

'You won splendidly.'

A hint of Princess Yakovleva's zest returned. 'I did, didn't I? I told you today was a lucky day for me.'

Charlotte remained silent. It had not been lucky for herself. It had been momentous; traumatic; nearly tragic. But it had not been lucky.

Twelve hours ago she had been unaware of Count Sandor Karolyi's existence. Her lips burned with the memory of his kiss. It had been the first she had ever received. Were all kisses so inflaming to the senses? She thought of the Comte, dashing and appraising. Her pulse remained steady. Her heart did not beat in long, thick strokes as it did when her thoughts dwelt on the handsome Hungarian. If Justin de Valmy kissed her, would she feel the same, shameless response? It was a question that would go unanswered because she had no intention of permitting such liberties. She had every intention of pleading a headache and not accompanying him at all.

The carriage swept through the stone, lion-flanked gateway and Maria, the Princess's maid, hastened from the lamplit villa to divest the Princess of her sable wrap and to assist her to bed. Charlotte walked slowly to her own room.

Dawn was already tingeing the sky a dull gold. She removed her dress and took the camellia from her hair. If it had not been for Sandor Karolyi's presence, the evening would have been the most memorable of her life. For one heady moment every eye had been turned in her direction.

Her nightdress was cool as she slipped it over her head. And if it had not been for Sandor Karolyi she would not have been alive to experience it. In that, at least, he had spoken the truth. She lay on the bed, vivid images burning against her closed lids.

Sandor Karolyi gazing down at her with an unfathomable expression in his eyes as she lay semi-conscious on the sofa in the Hotel de Paris; Sandor Karolyi regarding her discomfort with amusement as the Princess chastised her for looking like a peasant girl. The coldness of his expression in the casino when the Comte de Valmy had treated her as a social equal. The hard glitter of his eyes as he had faced her on the terrace. She closed her mind against further memories, unable to endure them. She would think of Sarah instead. Sarah; so magical and full of life. She wondered if Sarah had been teasing about the cheetah or if it were true.

Sleep edged nearer and nearer but her last thought was not of Sarah but of Sandor Karolyi and the strange note in his voice as he had called her name and she had run, leaving him alone on the darkened terrace.

CHAPTER
THREE

THE NEXT morning Charlotte woke with a sense of disquiet. She lay for a few moments, gazing at the sunbright ceiling. The Comte was calling for her at eleven. The little French maid who did tasks too menial for Maria, came in with a cup of morning chocolate. She sipped it, wondering yet again why the Princess had countenanced such an expedition. She achieved no answer. The Comte had made his request, been accepted, and now she had no alternative but to make herself ready for his arrival.

The Princess was still asleep and would be until long after the Comte had called for her. Reluctantly she dressed in a gown of watered green silk that emphasised the colour of her eyes. The neckline was demurely high, small pearl buttons running from the base of her throat to her tiny waist. Her nonsense of a hat, with a wisp of veiling and a feather, was perched on the top of her abundantly waving hair, the ringlets tamed into a smooth, upsweeping chignon. White net gloves covered her hands. Her parasol was edged with lace. She gazed at herself in the mirror and knew that anyone seeing her would assume her to be a lady of quality. A slight smile curved her lips. If the Comte de Valmy had seen her before she had entered the Princess's employ, he would certainly not have asked for her company. The memory of serviceable dimity gowns in lack-lustre colours made her run her fingers appreciatively over the fullness of her silk skirts. The Princess had been kinder to her than anyone save for her beloved parents.

The sound of hoofs and the rattle of a landau permeated her thoughts. Her fingers tightened around the handle of her parasol. He had come. Never in her life had she driven alone with a gentleman. What was she to say to him? What did he expect of her?

'There is a gentleman for you,' Maria said, disapproval registering in her velvet brown eyes.

Panic seized Charlotte. The whole affair was improper. Cocottes rode alone with their gentleman friends. Married ladies, too, saw no reason to be accompanied by anyone other than a footman or a maid when indulging in a promenade or a carriage ride with gentlemen other than their husbands. But they were accustomed to the laxity of Monte Carlo society. Charlotte was not. She had been brought up quietly and with reserve. She enjoyed being a spectator to the dazzling, glamorous pageant surrounding her, but it had never occurred to her that she might be a participant. Her position had precluded any such aspirations: until last night.

A flare of anger sparked her eyes. She was only suffering thus because of Sandor Karolyi. If he had not goaded her, she would never have accepted the Comte's invitation. 'Damnable man,' she said aloud, giving vent to her feelings in a way that would have shocked her father inexpressibly. Then, head high, she marched across the room to face Justin, Comte de Valmy.

If Justin had entertained any doubts as to the wisdom of escorting a paid companion in public, they vanished the moment Charlotte stepped towards him.

Her beauty was stunning and effortless, arousing his protective instincts as well as his admiration. Within hours, news of his morning's outing would have reached the Countess's ears, but he was uncaring. He would teach her that he was not a plaything to be taken up and discarded at will.

'You look very beautiful,' he said, deep blue eyes holding hers unnervingly.

Charlotte blushed. She was unaccustomed to such

attention and it was occurring to her that the eligible young man assisting her into the landau was doing more than flirting with her. It was almost as if he was embarking on a courtship.

'Thank you,' she murmured, and lowered her eyes as the coachman flicked his whip and the horses began to trot out through the Villa Ondine's open gates and up and away from the casino and the villas huddling the Port.

'Have you been long with Princess Yakovleva?' he asked, determined to do what so far he had only considered doing. He would make the sweet-faced English girl his mistress for the summer. She would accompany him to Paris and then to his château in Brittany. Unfortunately, from September, the liaison would have to be conducted more discreetly. In September he was to marry.

'Six months.'

'And are you happy in her employ?'

His ease of manner had relaxed her. 'Exceedingly,' she smiled, and the effect was like warm sunlight.

He was sitting opposite her, elegant in the uniform of an officer of the *Chasseurs à Cheval*. His jacket was of light blue, decorated lavishly with silver braid. His tight fitting trousers scarlet; his boots polished to mirrored brilliance.

'But not so happy as you would be outside it.'

Her expression was one of puzzlement.

He laughed, reaching out and taking her hand.

Dismayed, she withdrew it hastily, noting that they were already a disturbing distance from the villa. The vine-clad hillside fell steeply to the sparkling blue of the Mediterranean, clouded in mimosa and the purple haze of jasmine.

He laughed, bewitched by the shyness he was about to overcome.

'You must surely guess the reason for my seeking to

speak to you in private, Charlotte.' His voice was caressing. Heat smouldered at the back of his eyes.

'I am afraid that I gave it no thought, Monsieur,' she said in confusion.

Was he going to make a proposal of marriage to her? The idea was stupefying. They had only met the previous evening. He was wealthy and titled. It was beyond belief that such a man could have fallen instantly in love with her. Yet his eyes told her differently. They were warm and flattering.

'Charlotte.' He reached once more for her hand and this time she did not withdraw it. 'It cannot have escaped your attention that I am most deeply attracted to you . . .'

He *was* going to propose. Her heart began to beat light and fast.

He was young, no more than twenty-five, undeniably handsome with his sleek fair hair and startling blue eyes. She would be a Comtesse. She would no longer have to live in fear of the future. She would have a home of her own. Children. The prospect was intoxicating; impossible. She was not in love with the Comte. The touch of his hand sent no reverberations down her spine. The prospect of his kiss aroused no desire in her. Sadly she sought the words to refuse him without hurting his feelings.

'I am leaving Monte Carlo within days for Paris. Come with me, Charlotte.' He raised her hand to his lips and kissed it fervently.

She stared at him. 'I am afraid that I do not understand. I . . .'

As the landau rocked gently along the dusty track his arm circled her waist and he pressed feverish kisses on her neck.

'You shall have everything your heart desires, my love . . .'

She shrank away from him, comprehension flooding

her shocked eyes. 'Are you asking that I . . . that I become your *cherie amour*?' she asked, the words strangling in her throat.

He laughed, the heat in his eyes hotter. 'But of course. It will be a whole new world for you, Charlotte. You will have a maid of your own: Paris gowns, jewels . . .'

'Tell the coachman to stop! Instantly!' She was shaking, overcome with mortification.

He did as he was bid, imagining she wanted to enter his arms and enjoy his embrace without the diverting motion of the carriage.

The second the horses were reined to a halt, she leapt to her feet and opened the carriage door.

'Charlotte! What is the matter? Where are you going?'

He sprang to his feet, starting after her. The carriage door slammed sharply on his hand and he screamed in pain. Charlotte was uncaring. Tears stung her eyes and choked her throat. Twice in the space of a few hours she had been treated as a lady of loose virtue. She began to run, heedless of Justin and his shouts. Never before had she felt so lonely; so isolated. She fitted in nowhere. Not with the society the Princess kept, nor with the pleasure-loving cocottes. Yet if she left Monte Carlo and the Princess's employ, where could she go? Her heart beat rapidly as she ran down the dusty track. Her haste was unnecessary. No carriage tried to overtake her. Justin, furious at the damage done to his hand and the insult of her reaction to his proposal, had bad-temperedly ordered his coachman to continue on his way. The girl was foolish and deserved to live and die at the beck and call of cantankerous elderly females.

Fearfully Charlotte glanced over her shoulder. There was no one in pursuit. Gasping for breath she reduced her pace to a walk, wondering what to say when Princess Natalya enquired about her morning's outing. She would tell the Princess nothing of the Comte de Valmy's shameful behaviour. It would only arouse the Princess's wrath and the thought of being the centre of attention of another scene was almost more than she could bear.

Hot and tired she stumbled down another incline and entered the Villa Ondine's exotic gardens. The Princess was still in her room and Charlotte escaped thankfully to her own, sponging her face and drinking a calming glass of iced water. By the time the Princess summoned her for her afternoon promenade, she had regained her composure. The Comte would not trouble her again. He had made an error of judgment, as had she in consenting to drive with him. The incident was over: past. She even permitted herself a wry smile at the thought that she had believed his intentions were honourable and that she had been on the verge of receiving a proposal of marriage. Albeit one she had no intention of accepting.

The Princess still felt uncommonly fatigued and did not enquire after Charlotte's carriage ride with the Comte. She had a pain in her right arm and a tightness in her chest that occupied all her attention. Seeing that she was unwell, Charlotte suggested that they remain at the villa, but the Princess tapped her cane impatiently, insisting that she had never in her life missed her daily walk and that she had no intention of beginning now.

The Yakovlev carriage which transported them from the villa to the boulevard overlooking the Port was summoned. The Princess entered it with difficulty, her breath rasping. A worried frown puckered Charlotte's brow. The Princess's exact age was a well-kept secret but she was almost certainly an octogenarian. The ruby collar she wore only emphasised her pallor. For once she was disinclined to talk. Charlotte quietly asked the driver to take extra care and to ensure that the horses did no more than walk at a sedate pace.

White lilies nodded their heads gracefully as the carriage passed. The twin-domed towers of the casino could be seen in the distance, golden in the sunshine. A yacht, flying the red ensign, was making for the harbour, waves creaming around its prow.

'Are you sure you feel well enough to walk?' Charlotte asked anxiously as the coachman stopped at his accustomed place.

'Of course I am,' the Princess snapped irritably. 'A little breathlessness never hurt anyone.' Another twinge of pain shot up her arm and she clenched her teeth. She couldn't be ill now. Not until she had returned to St Petersburg and put her affairs in order.

She dismissed the coachman, sending him on to the Hotel de Paris with a message for Mademoiselle Bernhardt.

The palm-shaded boulevard was a favourite walking place of many of Monte Carlo's rich and royal visitors. Today it was sparsely populated. Two ladies, delicately frilled parasols disguising their identity, strolled leisurely some distance away. An elderly gentleman puffed wreaths of cigar smoke into the air and studied the amethyst sea with contentment.

'I think,' the Princess said heavily, 'it is about time that I saw Victor again.'

Victor was the Princess's son: a gentleman rarely mentioned.

'I am sure that is a very good idea,' Charlotte said. She hated to see divisions in families and was sure the Prince was not as boorish as the Princess had led her to believe.

The Princess paused and stared unseeingly at the sea. 'He is not so far away. He winters in Nice and this year has remained there.'

Charlotte felt a stab of shock. Nice was only a carriage ride away and yet the Prince had not once visited the Villa Ondine.

'Perhaps tomorrow, when I feel stronger, I will make the journey and see him.'

'If you really feel so unwell, Your Highness, could not a message be sent . . . ?'

The Princess lurched heavily against her. Charlotte cried out, taking her weight.

'Charlotte . . .' The breath rasped in the Princess's throat. She was no longer able to stand unaided. A wizened hand clawed at the collar of rubies, as if trying to wrest them from her throat. 'Charlotte. . . I . . .' Her knees buckled and Charlotte was no longer able to hold her upright. She pitched forward, black silk billowing around her frail figure.

With a moan of horror, Charlotte knelt at her side, removing the necklace with trembling, fevered fingers, loosening the bodice of the Princess's gown at the throat, gazing frantically around for help. The two ladies were no longer discernible: the gentleman had gone.

'Charlotte . . .' The raisin-black eyes in their whitened mask held Charlotte's.

'Charlotte . . . Thank you . . .' The breath gurgled in her throat. She choked, tried to speak once more, and then her head fell back against Charlotte's arm and she was silent.

Help. She must get help. Tenderly she lowered the Princess's head on to the unrelenting ground, and scrambled to her feet. It could be an age before the Yakovlev carriage returned. There had to be someone, somewhere, who could take the unconscious Princess speedily to a doctor.

She began to run along the boulevard in the direction of the Port. The white stallions trotted towards her, resplendent in scarlet harness, a spanking landau bowling in their wake. She almost sobbed in relief. Frenziedly she ran towards them.

'Stop! Oh, please stop!'

There was a startled oath and then a command. The coachman reined in obediently.

'Oh, thank goodness!' The horses snorted and pawed the ground. Gasping, she almost fell against their sides.

A lithe figure leapt from the coach and seized hold of her shoulders. 'What the devil is the matter?'

Once more Count Karolyi's face was only inches from hers. 'The Princess,' she panted. 'She has collapsed . . .'

In the heat haze, on the ground, the black silk shimmered. 'Into the carriage,' Sandor said tersely. 'Quickly, Alphonse.'

His coachman did not need to be told twice. He flicked the reins and within seconds Sandor was kneeling at the side of the inert Princess.

'We must get her to a doctor!' Charlotte's eyes were large and bright.

Without speaking, Sandor scooped the pathetically small figure into his arms and strode back to his landau.

'Doctor Deslys,' he ordered. 'Fast!'

Charlotte leaned back against scarlet leather upholstery, feeling as if she were in the grip of a nightmare. The Princess's head lolled against Sandor's arm grotesquely. The landau sped heedlessly over the cobbles, between narrow lanes of golden-stoned houses, their balconies thick with bougainvillaea, their walls covered in jasmine. A brass plate decorated the residence of Dr Deslys.

Alphonse rapped on the door.

'For God's sake, man. Walk straight in,' Sandor commanded tersely, a frightening expression on his face.

Alphonse did as he was bid. A maid hastened towards them and was brushed aside. An elderly, bespectacled gentleman hurried from his study and at the sight of Sandor with the Princess in his arms, opened his surgery door wide so that they might enter.

Sandor laid Princess Yakovleva on the doctor's leather examination couch. Charlotte remained by the door, terrified of getting in the way, her hands pressed tightly against her chest, a prayer on her lips.

The doctor felt the Princess's pulse, opened the lid of

one closed eye and sighed heavily. Almost without haste he adjusted his stethoscope and listened intently to her heart. Then he raised his head and shook it.

Fear drowned Charlotte. 'What is it? A heart attack? A stroke? She's going to be all right, isn't she?'

'I am afraid, mademoiselle, that the lady is dead.'

Charlotte gazed disbelievingly from him to Sandor and then back to the lifeless figure on the couch.

'No!' The word was torn from her throat. 'No! She can't be dead!'

'A brandy for mademoiselle,' the doctor was saying. Sandor was moving towards her but she was uncaring. Her eyes were riveted on the ethereally calm features of Princess Yakovleva.

'No! There must be a mistake!' She stumbled forward and felt a strong hand support her arm. 'Princess . . . Your Highness . . .' The ruby ringed hand she took in hers was still and already cold. She sank to her knees, pressing it against her cheek, weeping unrestrainedly.

The brandy was proffered and ignored. Through a sea of grief she heard Dr Deslys ask Sandor if the deceased had been her mother. A serviceable masculine handkerchief was thrust into her hand. Gently, strong hands raised her to her feet.

'There is nothing more you can do for her, Charlotte.' He was looking down at her compassionately.

'I loved her,' Charlotte said helplessly, her eyes bright with pain.

His arm circled her shoulders. 'I know, and the Princess knew. It is all that matters.'

Her head was cradled against the frilled linen of his shirt. Incredibly, she was content to let it stay there, crying in a way she had not cried since the death of her parents.

His strength seemed to surround and protect her. His arms were a haven she had no desire to leave. She could hear the strong beat of his heart and was aware that he was holding her with astounding tenderness.

She leaned against him, grateful for the comfort of his presence as he led her away from the surgery. The door was closed on the dead Princess. Maria, brought swiftly from the Villa Ondine by Sandor's coachman, was standing in the hallway, ashen faced.

'Oh, mademoiselle,' she cried and Charlotte left Sandor's arms and grasped Maria's outstretched hands.

She remembered very little of the journey back to the villa. She had lost the person dearest to her in the whole world. There would be no more acid-tongued conversations; no more kindnesses; no more laughter. She was once more alone in the world. Penniless in an environment where paupers had no place. Where respectable employment was almost impossible to find. Only hours ago she had been offered the only financial safety a girl without family could hope to find in Monte Carlo. She had refused it then and she would refuse it now. Whatever happened, she would not abandon her honour and become a cocotte. She would return to England. Find employment in a respectable house. The prospect sank like lead on her heart. Respectable employment as a governess or companion in England was worlds away from the sun and the society to which she had grown accustomed in Monte Carlo. Her dazzling, brilliant world would have to be abandoned. There would be no more evenings in the glittering Salle Mauresque; no more hours of excitement as fortunes were staked in the Salon Privé.

She rose bleakly to her feet. A return to England would cost money. She had travelled to Monte Carlo at the Princess's expense. Her gowns had been generously paid for by the Princess, as had every other item she owned. She had had no need of her salary and the Princess had retained it for safekeeping. Now there was no one she could approach who had the authority to pay her what was due. Her head ached. What would happen to the Princess's body? Where would it be buried; and by whom?

Maria stepped out on to the darkened terrace.

'Count Karolyi wishes to speak with you, mademoiselle.'

Charlotte turned to enter the lamplit room but he was already striding towards her.

In the moonlight his black hair had a blue sheen. The firm jaw and finely chiselled mouth were strangely comforting.

'I have sent word of the Princess's death to Prince Victor in Nice. I have also seen to it that the newspapers in London, Paris and St Petersburg are informed.'

'Thank you.'

She looked up at him with sad, vulnerable eyes and he felt a surge of pity for her.

'I have also arranged that the Princess's body be brought to the villa to lie in state. The Princess expressed a wish many times to be buried in Monte Carlo and I am assuming that Prince Victor will accede to her request. Therefore I shall go ahead with the necessary arrangements.'

'Yes. Thank you.' There was so much she wanted to say and could not for the tears that choked her throat.

'You need rest,' he said abruptly, the darkness hiding the concern in his eyes.

'Yes.'

She had determined never to speak to him again but that had been before his kindness in Dr Deslys' surgery. Now he was being kind again, offering to take the burden of the Princess's death from her shoulders.

'Goodnight.' He could stay no longer. If he did so he would be unable to maintain his cool politeness. There was something at once innocent and paganly beautiful about her. She needed loving and cherishing and the temptation to undertake the task almost overcame him.

The abrasive lines of his mouth were bitter as he

restrained himself. The imprint of her fingers had taken a long time to fade from his cheek and he had no desire to add to her distress by pressing on her attentions that were so patently unwelcome; attentions that could lead to nothing but disillusion.

Abruptly he took his leave of her, wondering as he did so what had taken place on her carriage ride with the Comte de Valmy. A deep frown furrowed his brow as he stepped into his carriage. Damn it to hell. It was none of his affair.

'Madame Santillinos',' he rasped.

'Yes sir.' Obediently the coachman flicked the reins and the carriage pulled away from the Villa Ondine to Monte Carlo's most notorious brothel.

Hours later, as dawn broke, he emerged from Madame Santillinos' opulent and luxurious house of pleasure, his white frilled shirt open at the neck, his hair tousled, his eyes bleak. Dear God in heaven. Did the future hold nothing more for him? Was he condemned to spend the rest of his life seeking transitory affection from women who cared only for the gold in his pocket?

'Faster!' he urged the driver as the carriage sped along the perilous coast road. 'Faster!'

The sins of the fathers are visited on the children, but it was not his unknown father's sin that weighed so heavily on his heart and mind. It was the sin of his gay, foolish mother. The sin of the wife of Count Istvan Karolyi. He groaned, leaning back, eyes closed as the horses galloped at a suicidal pace. Istvan Karolyi had loved his erring wife. Had refused to let her endure the world's censure. Instead he had accepted his wife's bastard son as his own, and, with all the generosity of his great heart, had come to love him as if he were a son of his flesh. But not Sandor's sister, Zara. Zara had been handed to the childless Prince and Princess Katzinsky and brother and sister had been parted for all their childhood.

On her deathbed his mother had been overcome by guilt and remorse. Not until then had he been aware that he had a twin sister: that he was not Count Karolyi's son but the son of a handsome, flashing eyed, wandering gypsy. His agony had been terrible. Even to think of it caused beads of perspiration to dampen his forehead. To know he was not the son of the man he loved. A man he had called father from his youngest day. Not the rightful heir to Karolyi land, to the magnificent castle overlooking the carp-filled lake. He had thought he would die of grief and shame. Instead, his pretty, heedless mother had died and it was by her deathbed that he met his sister, Zara.

Her bewilderment, her anguish, was as deep as his and, drawn by bonds of love and circumstance, they had clung together and in her dependence on him he had gained strength.

Zara. She had kept her secret as he had kept his. She had married and lived in fear that her husband would discover the truth of her parentage. Within days she would be in Monte Carlo: the one person in the world who knew him for what he was. Her love was the bed-rock of his life.

Pebbles flew as the beating hoofs raced perilously along the barely discernible track. The carriage rocked on its springs. Sandor was uncaring.

He had pleaded with Count Karolyi to be allowed to forsake the name that was not rightfully his. Istvan Karolyi had adamantly refused. He had no sons—Sandor had become his son. He had taught him to ride, to fish, to shoot. His lands would pass to Sandor. The alternative was unthinkable.

All through his youth Sandor had determined that, when the moment came, he would do the honourable thing. He would disclose to Istvan Karolyi's next of kin, Count Povzervslay, that he was the true heir to the Karolyi lands. Only with maturity had he realised why the noble-hearted man who had reared him had desired otherwise.

Jozsef Povzervslay was a debaucher and a sadist of the worst kind. His thousands of tenants lived in fear of him. Blood flowed freely on his land. Emperor Franz Josef refused to receive him at court. Countess Povzervslay committed suicide. His daughters lived in abject fear, pale and dull-eyed.

Povzervslay blood had been tainted for generations. His father had displayed the same perverted vices and Istvan Karolyi had been well aware that the son had followed in the father's footsteps. It was his dying wish that Karolyi land and tenants would never come under the stewardship of such a man. Sandor had promised. Istvan Karolyi had died and Sandor, son of an unknown gypsy, had inherited his title and his wealth.

The lathered horses clattered into the drive of the Villa Beausoleil. Sandor flung himself from the carriage, throwing his cloak at the footman who hurried deferentially forward, striding into the lamplit salon and pouring himself a large brandy.

There had been a time when he believed he could live with the secret. That he could marry, raise sons of his own, exercise just stewardship over his tenants. Those dreams had faded as he had embarked on his first love *affaire* and realised that, though such a secret could be kept from the world, it could not be kept from the woman who would share his heart, his life, his bed. And never yet, among the princesses, countesses and cocottes had he met a woman he had known would love him just as passionately when she knew that the object of her affections was not the son of Count Istvan Karolyi, but the bastard child of a nameless gypsy. That if Jozsef Povzervslay's son grew up without the tainted blood of his father, the vast Karolyi estates would be handed over to him when his father died. That, marrying a man of wealth and title, their days could be concluded married to a man stripped of his name and bereft of his wealth. Such a woman did not exist and Sandor had long since abandoned the search for her. At thirty-two he indulged only in countless *affaires* with ladies safely married.

He drained his glass, lifting the decanter again, pouring generously. Irina, Vicomtesse de Salbris, had not been married. She had been a pretty young widow and before he had been aware of it she had fallen in love with him – and died.

He hurled the still-full glass across the room, shattering it against a mirror, golden droplets drenching the carpet..

God in heaven. He had had no option but to break off the *affaire*. And he could not indulge in another, especially with an English girl with lustrous lashed green eyes and a mouth made to be kissed.

He roared for his valet to pull off his boots. Why the devil he had kissed her in the first place he did not know. Nor why, once kissing her, he had wanted to continue more than anything else he had wanted in his life. His eyes glittered. Princess Yakovleva's affection for Mademoiselle Grainger had not been misplaced. Charlotte's grief at the death of her elderly and often querulous employer had been genuine and deep. She was a young lady of many commendable qualities. Not only was she undeniably beautiful, she was courageous, and her heart was warm and loving. As no doubt Justin de Valmy had already discovered.

He dismissed the valet irritably and sank into a leather winged chair, staring moodily through the window at the dark shapes of pines. He was still there when the night sky pearled to dawn and the sea began to take on the first warm hints of day.

When the Count left, Charlotte walked back into the villa and shivered. The rooms were empty and desolate. She felt like an intruder, yet she could not leave. Not until the Princess was buried and not until she had been paid the money owing to her. How long would it take Prince Victor to arrive from Nice? One day? Two? Heavy hearted she went to bed and lay for long hours, open-eyed in the darkness.

CHAPTER
FOUR

SHE OPENED her eyes to the unmistakable sound of
Sarah's voice. Hurriedly she slipped from the bed and
slid her arms into her silken négligé. Maria was already
knocking on her door.

'Mademoiselle Bernhardt for you, Mademoiselle
Grainger.'

'Tell Mademoiselle Bernhardt I shall be with her
instantly.'

Feverishly she brushed her hair, knotting it loosely on
top of her head. There was no time to dress. Sarah's
golden voice was coming closer and closer. Another
second and she would be in the bedroom.

Charlotte flung open the door and hurried along the
corridor and down the broad sweep of the staircase.

'Charlotte!' Sarah stood at the entrance of the main
salon, poised on tiptoe as if halted at the very moment
she had been about to mount the stairs and invade
Charlotte's room.

She was in mourning, the corsage of her ebony-black
dress softly draped like that of a Grecian goddess,
accentuating her ethereal slenderness. Around her
shoulders a cape of chinchilla trailed the ground.

'Charlotte!' She held her arms wide and Charlotte was
clasped in a warm embrace. 'What a tragedy! What a
catastrophe!'

She drew away from Charlotte, surveying the pale
face and the shadows, dark as bruises, beneath Charlotte's eyes.

'How you have suffered, little one. You were exceedingly fond of Princess Natalya, yes?'

'Yes,' Charlotte said, feeling another onrush of tears prick the back of her eyes.

'I shall be at her funeral service,' Sarah said, drawing Charlotte into the salon, ordering refreshments from an overawed maid as if the villa were her own. 'Spenser's "Sleep after toil, port after stormy seas, ease after war, death after life, does greatly please" will be the most suitable I think.'

Charlotte sank back against the cushions on the sofa as Sarah seated herself. Had she slept? It didn't feel as if she had.

'And what of your position now, my little Charlotte?' Sarah asked, reclining on a chaise longue, unutterably elegant; unbelievably beautiful.

'I shall return to England.'

Sarah's pencil thin brows disappeared under the shower of her gold-red hair. 'To England? So cold and so damp.' She shivered expressively.

For the first time since the Princess's death, Charlotte smiled.

'It is my home, Mademoiselle.'

'Sarah,' Sarah corrected, waving a long, thin hand. 'One's home is where one chooses to make it, my little Charlotte. There is the home of our birth, and there is our spiritual home.'

The maid set down a silver tray of coffee and brioches, still warm from the oven.

'For myself, the Comédie-Française is my spiritual home. For you . . .' The limpid pools of her eyes were questioning. Charlotte thought of the gold and velvet plush of the Salle Mauresque: the excitement of the Salon Privé. In her heart of hearts she knew where her spiritual home was, yet it was one grossly unsuitable for the daughter of a churchman. One she could not admit to, even to herself.

'I do not think I have yet found my spiritual home.'

'It is in the sun, my brave, beautiful Charlotte. Not in

the greyness of England.'

Sarah consumed a brioche with relish and demanded that the maid take out a plate of those remaining and feed them to the wolfhound unhappily deserted in her carriage.

'Has Prince Victor been informed of his mother's death?'

'Count Karolyi did so yesterday afternoon.'

'Ah. Count Karolyi.' Sarah's feline eyes took on a dreamlike haze. 'So tall; so handsome; so . . . *dangerous.*'

Charlotte's hand shook as she placed a china cup and saucer back on to the delicate low table. She had no desire to discuss Sandor Karolyi. Nor to think of him. Yet think of him she must. She had still not thanked him properly for his prompt assistance; for his kindness in taking the burden of informing the Princess's son of her death.

Sarah rose to her feet. 'Do not grieve too deeply for Princess Natalya, Charlotte. She lived life zestfully. She died without pain. It is all any of us can hope for.'

She kissed Charlotte on the cheek, enveloping her in an exotic fragrance and then, her furs sweeping the ground, she made her exit and through the open window Charlotte could hear her lovingly chastise her barking dog, promising it the finest steak the chef at the Hotel de Paris could offer.

She returned to her room and was immediately faced with a dilemma. The Princess, declaring that Charlotte was too young to be dressed in black, had omitted anything suitable for mourning from Charlotte's wardrobe. There was a day dress of heavy pearl-grey silk. She stepped into it, fastening the tiny pearl buttons of the bodice and cuffs.

All through the morning there was a succession of callers bearing cards of condolence for the still absent Prince Victor. Lord and Lady Pethelbridge, the Countess of Bexhall, Princess Helena, the pasha. The friendliness with which they had treated her the previous evening was politely lacking. She was once again Miss Grainger, companion. No word of sympathy or kindness was extended to her.

The Princess's body was brought in full regal dignity from the home of the doctor to rest in state in the boudoir displaying the Romanov crest. Flowers arrived in unending succession, surrounding the death bed in fragrant profusion. Charlotte, unable to compete with the lavish confections from the Kings of Serbia, of Sweden, of Spain, placed a small wreath of forget-me-nots on the satin pillow and a posy of the Princess's beloved Parma violets in her hand.

The Princess's face, so wizened in life, was serene and full of peace. The afternoon wore on and still the procession of those coming to pay their respects did not abate, and still the Prince did not arrive.

Monsieur Bertora paid his respects, as did the manager of the Hotel de Paris. The grand duke the Princess had spoken to the previous evening came, followed by another grand duke, and yet another. As dusk approached Charlotte sought refuge on the terrace.

The twin bulbous domes of the Devil's Palace glowed softly in the approaching twilight. The Princess would not enter those walls again. Charlotte's heart tightened in her chest. And neither would she. When Prince Victor arrived and remunerated her for her services to the Princess, she would have to turn her back on the Devil's Palace and the glittering blue sea for the last time. Through the trees that scattered the hillside she could see the road winding down towards the Port.

Count Karolyi's landau and white stallions were unmistakable. As was the abundant upsweep of sun-gold hair of the lady at his side.

She turned, stifling the rush of conflicting emotions that threatened to swamp her. When the Prince arrived she would excuse herself from the Villa Ondine, thank Count Karolyi personally and correctly, and dismiss him from her mind forthwith.

The Prince arrived late that evening in a Victoria drawn by two greys. Other equipages carrying his valet and household staff followed. He was stout, flush-faced, flamboyantly dressed and displayed none of the Princess's caustic charm.

In the dimly lit hallway Charlotte was barely discernible as his valet removed his cloak. Apprehensively she stepped forward.

'Miss Charlotte Grainger, Your Highness. I was companion to Princess Yakovleva.'

Small, almost feminine lips pursed. 'And where is . . . Princess Yakovleva?'

There was no outward sign of grief. He seemed rather to be annoyed at the fatigue of his journey.

Dutifully Charlotte led him through the luxuriously furnished rooms to the flower-filled boudoir where Princess Yakovleva lay in state, candles at her head and feet.

The Prince did not enter the room, merely slapped his doe-skin gloves repeatedly in the palm of his hand and then turned away, demanding a brandy and a cigar.

Charlotte remained at the open door of the room aghast. She had known that there was little love between Princess Yakovleva and her son, but surely he could have at least spent a few moments in silence and prayerful thought at her side. The Prince was talking to a sombrely dressed gentleman Charlotte assumed was his secretary.

'The body must be transported by *wagon-lits* to Petersburg at the earliest opportunity.'

Shock numbed her into action. Softly she closed the door on the candlelit room and hurried towards them.

'Excuse me, Your Highness. Princess Yakovleva expressed the wish to be buried in Monte Carlo . . .'

As the Prince turned on her she faltered. His pale blue eyes were icy in their frostiness.

'I do not believe I addressed you, Mademoiselle,' he said crushingly.

Charlotte's cheeks burned at the uncalled for reprimand. 'But Your Highness . . .'

Prince Victor was already turning his back on her. Were Princess Natalya's last wishes to be ignored? Her chin tilted defiantly.

'The Princess's wishes were expressed on paper as well as verbally,' she said to a back upon which the rich material of the jacket stretched dangerously.

Prince Victor stiffened but did not deign to turn around. 'Remove her,' he said to his pale-faced secretary.

Charlotte felt as if the ground were yawning in a chasm at her feet. Within minutes she had antagonised the one person whose good will it was in her interests to keep. There was the money owing to her; carefully documented in the Princess's own handwriting in her personal ledger. Without benefit of it she had no way of returning to England. And only the Prince had the authority to remunerate her.

'Your Highness, you must allow me to speak with you.' There was a note of barely concealed desperation in her voice.

Slowly Prince Victor turned while his secretary quaked. The Prince surveyed Charlotte thoughtfully. He had paid her little attention on entering the villa. His thoughts had been elsewhere; on the bad taste his mother had shown in expiring only a stone's throw from the notorious Devil's Palace; on the vulgar scene his current mistress had exhibited on being told he would not be returning to her; on the financial implications of his mother's death.

He saw, to his surprise, that his mother's last companion was devastatingly different from those who had preceded her. She was extraordinarily beautiful. Her dress was demure enough, the gown fastened high at the throat with small pearl buttons, but delightfully rounded breasts were clearly defined beneath the grey silk of her bodice. Her waist was minuscule, her hips a seductive curve. He raised his eyes to her face; to the creamy soft skin, the lustrous eyes, the mouth of rose petal softness. A familiar gleam heated the ice in his eyes.

'Indeed you must speak to me, Mademoiselle Grainger. But later. When I have rested.'

He turned, walking quickly from the salon, his retinue hurrying in his wake.

Charlotte felt a flood of relief. He had been curt because he had been distressed. Once he read the Princess's private papers he would acquiesce to the funeral she desired. And if he did not, perhaps Count Karolyi would speak to him. At the thought of the Count she was overcome with fresh anxiety. He had done so much for her. It was thanks to him that the Princess had not lain for far longer in the ignominy of the boulevard. It was thanks to him that a doctor had been reached so speedily, albeit in vain. It was thanks to him that Prince Victor had been notified, that the Princess's body had arrived in full splendour to be laid in state. And her barely coherent thank you of the previous evening when he had startled her on the terrace, was insufficient. Good manners demanded that she thank him properly.

The next morning Prince Victor's household staff received the steady stream of visitors and Charlotte was freed of the tasks she had carried out since the Princess's death. Prince Victor had declared his intention of resting. Her absence would not be noticed.

Count Karolyi was residing at Beausoleil, a magnificent villa overlooking the Port. She donned a black mantilla over her hair, exchanged her customary white day gloves for black ones and slipped from the villa. The Princess had allowed her the use of the landau any time she desired. She hesitated in the villa's courtyard. The road to Beausoleil was steep and the sun was already hot. With the Princess dead she had no longer any authority to use a Yakovlev carriage. She turned her back on the landau and horses, her skirts whipping around her ankles as she walked swiftly out of the luxurious grounds and headed in the direction of Beausoleil.

Tall pines shimmered in a heat haze. Fields of rosemary stretched out on either side of her, thick with clusters of myrtle and arbutus. Occasionally she paused, looking down at the far distant boulevard, the casino and the sea. Beausoleil had no near neighbours. It stood magnificently alone among orange trees and thyme.

Hot and tired she rang for admittance. The footman was liveried in green and gold. The hall was floored in pink marble. An exquisite bronze by Gouthiere decorated one corner; a Boucher tapestry the other.

After some moments' absence the footman returned and led her into a drawing room so unlike those to which she was accustomed that she gasped. The walls were white, the carpet was white; pale lilac and jonquil sofas were thickly endowed with cushions. The vast windows overlooked the curving rock of Monaco, the yacht-clustered port, the fairytale twin towers of the casino.

Sandor had just returned from his morning ride. His white ruffled shirt was opened to reveal a firmly muscled chest and a pelt of crisply curling dark hair. His breeches fitted snugly about his narrow hips. His boots gleamed. His masculinity was overpowering, taking her breath away.

He surveyed her silently, making no move towards her. She fought down a rising sense of disquiet.

'Excuse my calling on you uninvited, Count Karolyi. I thought it only proper that I . . .' Hesitantly she began to thank him for his kindness.

Sandor regarded her through narrowed eyes, oblivious to what she was saying.

So, with Princess Yakovleva dead, Mademoiselle Grainger was without a protector. And, as so many others had attempted to do in the past, she had come to him in the hope that he would be so moved by her beauty, her vulnerability, that he would take pity on her.

He remembered the kiss on the darkened terrace of the casino. Safe in the Princess's care, she had shown all too clearly what she thought of his advances, yet here she was, only days later, offering herself to him almost as a gift.

His handsome, satanic features darkened. His disillusionment was acute. In Charlotte Grainger he had thought he had discerned the exception to the rule. A young lady neither mercenary nor shallow. In the casino she had been delightful, charmingly shy, breathtakingly lovely – a welcome change from the flaunting, forward ladies of the *demi-monde* and the brittle society beauties. When the Princess had died her grief had been genuine, she had wept unrestrainedly, uncaring of his presence or her appearance. He had liked Mademoiselle Charlotte Grainger exceedingly, and now . . .

His eyes lingered on her mouth. If he did not become her lover, no doubt Justin de Valmy would. Or had she already been there and been refused? He doubted it—de Valmy had been obviously infatuated with her. But de Valmy was not as rich as he, Sandor Karolyi was rich. And that was why Mademoiselle Charlotte Grainger was now standing before him, her hands clasped disarmingly, her mantilla of mourning accentuating the rich chestnut of her hair.

The most curious longing swept through him. She was not what he had hoped and yet she was still entrancing, still sufficiently different to arouse in him instincts both primeval and protective.

Charlotte faltered. Why was he looking at her so strangely? It had not occurred to her that he would take such exception to her visiting him unaccompanied. After all, he knew of her circumstances. She had no female relatives; no maid.

Slowly, almost languidly, he moved towards her. The whipcord muscles rippled beneath the linen of his shirt. She lowered her eyes, averting them from the lean, tanned contours of his body, aware of her pulse leaping, the blood surging into her face.

On the white, deep-piled carpet, black hessian boots faced petite high-buttoned ones peeping from silken skirts.

He hooked a finger under her chin and tilted her bewildered face to his. 'Set your mind at rest, Mademoiselle Grainger. Your immediate future is assured. And after me . . .' He shrugged and there was bitterness in the lines of his mouth. 'There will, no doubt, be others.'

'I'm afraid I do not understand. I . . .'

She tried to step away from him but his eyes hypnotised her. She was aware of hints of gold in the near-black pupils, of the indefinable smell of his maleness, of the fact that, in some strange way, she had aroused his anger.

His hands caught hold of her wrists. 'You understand perfectly, Mademoiselle Grainger,' he said, his voice dangerously soft. 'Your mission is accomplished. Let us have no more false modesty.'

She tried to free herself of his grasp but his fingers were pressed so tightly it seemed he would crush the bones rather than release her.

'I am sorry . . . There has been a mistake . . .' Even to her own ears her voice sounded high and strained.

White teeth flashed in a mirthless smile.

'There has been no mistake, Mademoiselle.'

The expression that flamed in his eyes sent the blood pounding along her veins. Slowly, almost languidly, he drew her towards him.

'No,' she whispered, feeling her wrists released and her waist imprisoned. 'No. Oh, please. No.'

Her protests were silenced as his mouth came down on hers in swift, unfumbled contact.

Heat swept through her like a forest fire. She swayed against him as he kissed her slowly at first and then harder, his hands bending her in to the hardness of his body. For a terrifying moment time seemed to be suspended. She was aware only of a need so primeval that it robbed her of coherent thought. Her hands had slid up and around his neck for she could feel the tight spring of curls against her palms. His mouth took and took and she trembled convulsively, yielding without protest. Then his hands cupped her breasts, caressing and arousing over the silk of her gown. She heard herself moan and was aware of strong fingers unbuttoning her bodice. The feel of his fingers against her naked flesh shook her into sanity.

Violently she began to struggle, aware of her body's betrayal, of its yearning to succumb utterly to the intoxication of Sandor Karolyi's hands and lips. He chuckled, restraining her with ease, bruising her mouth, her throat, her shoulders with fiery kisses.

Tears scalded her cheeks. She had asked to see him merely as a courtesy and she had allowed him to think that his advances were welcome. Hating herself for lack of judgment, hating her body for its weakness, she fought like a wildcat. At last the wetness of her tears permeated Sandor's consciousness and he released her with a look of baffled surprise in his coal-dark eyes.

'Is no woman safe from you?' Charlotte panted, running for the door, grasping the porcelain doorknob for support. 'First the casino! Now this! Do you accost women in the streets, Count Karolyi? I am surprised that you did not force your attentions while the Princess lay dying! You are unbelievable! Beyond contempt!'

With a look of stunned incredulity he strode towards

her but she wrenched open the door, pushing past a
startled footman, running, running as she had never run
before in her life. The breath hurt in her chest. She
dropped her mantilla and didn't pause to retrieve it.
Pines, hibiscus, myrtle, merged and swam before her
eyes. The road wound dizzily. The sun blinded her. Her
heart pounded, her breath coming in harsh gasps.

There came the sound of trotting hoofs and a carriage
and she turned in terror but it was only a lady of the town
out for an afternoon drive. Cockades of pink carnations
decorated the horses' bridles. The lady lolled back
against satin upholstery, a lavishly frilled parasol
sheltering her flawless skin from the sun, her lips crim-
soned prettily with rouge, her eyes rimmed in kohl.

As the carriage drew alongside her, Charlotte heard a
husky voice command the coachman to rein in the
horses.

'You appear to be in distress, Mademoiselle. May I be
of assistance?'

Charlotte turned her head and found herself gazing
into the eyes of the pretty Parisienne who had smiled at
her on her last evening in the casino. The carriage door
was opened invitingly.

'Please, Mademoiselle. The sun is hot and the pebbles
are hard.'

Gratefully Charlotte stepped into the open caleche.
The Parisienne's eyes were mischievous. 'Are you going
to tell me why you are so distressed and dishevelled,
Mademoiselle? Is a gentleman responsible?'

'No gentleman!' Charlotte said so vehemently that the
Parisienne laughed delightedly.

'Allow me to introduce myself. I am Louise de Remy
and you, I know, are Mademoiselle Charlotte Grainger,
companion to Princess Yakovleva.'

'The Princess died yesterday.'

Louise's china-blue eyes clouded. 'But how sad. Monsieur Blanc will have lost one of his best patrons and you

will have lost a lady I think you were inordinately fond of.'

'Yes.' The painful racing of Charlotte's heart was subsiding.

Louise's quicksilver brain flew from sympathy to practicality. 'What will you do now, Charlotte? Have you finances? A family?'

'No.' Incredibly Charlotte felt a wry smile touch her lips. 'No, Louise. I háve nothing.'

'But what will you do?' Louise's delicately featured face was perturbed.

'I shall return to England. There is money owing to me—sufficient for my fare.'

A small frown furrowed Louise de Remy's brow. Money owing was all too often money never paid. She twirled her parasol. 'I shall gamble for you this evening, Charlotte. If I win, my winnings shall be yours.'

Charlotte felt a rush of warmth towards her new-found friend. 'That is exceedingly kind of you, Louise, but I shall be able to manage. Prince Victor will honour the Princess's debt to me.'

Louise de Remy's frown deepened. Prince Yakovlev was not a man likely to part with a single *louis* without gratification in return. Gratification it was obvious Charlotte was unwilling to provide.

The horses cantered into the elegant boulevard that ran past the entrance to the Villa Ondine. It suddenly occurred to Charlotte that she was riding with one of Europe's grande cocottes; that if she were seen her reputation would be ruined. She was uncaring. Friendship had been extended and Charlotte did not care that the source was unacceptable in polite society. Polite society had spared her little sympathy. Neither Lady Pethelbridge, the Countess of Bexhall, or any of the other ladies who had paid their respects to the dead Princess had concerned themselves with her welfare. Louise's long-lashed eyes held genuine concern.

As the carriage approached the stone lion-flanked gates of the villa the horses reined to a standstill.

'You will not take exception, Charlotte, if I tell you there is no need for you to return to England. No need for you to suffer financially.' The parasol twirled. 'The life I lead is one of comfort and leisure. It is one you could live on as grand a scale. You understand my meaning, Charlotte? You do not take offence?'

Charlotte shook her head. 'No. I do not take offence, Louise. I know that you are only trying to help me, but I could not be happy as a cocotte.'

'It is very easy, Charlotte,' Louise laughed. 'Delightfully easy and delightfully pleasurable. If you should change your mind, please contact me.' She handed Charlotte a gold embossed card. 'And take care. No more compromising situations with gentlemen who are not gentlemen and . . .' Louise de Remy leaned forward, '. . . no man is a gentleman when alone with a beautiful woman.'

Charlotte smiled. Louise reclined once again against the satin upholstery. The posies of pink carnations bobbed in the sunlight as the horses once more began to trot in the direction of the Boulevard des Moulins and the splendid apartment where the grand duke waited impatiently.

Charlotte began to walk between the Villa Ondine's immaculately kept flower beds. The bronze knocker on the front door was draped in black crepe. The curtains and shutters at every window were drawn. To ask at such a time for money seemed to Charlotte to be the height of bad taste, yet what else could she do? She could not remain at the Villa Ondine now that there was no function for her to perform. And if she waited for a more suitable time to approach the Prince, it might well prove to be too late. The Prince had given no indication of how long he was staying in Monte Carlo. He could disappear at a moment's notice and she would be left destitute.

Heavy-hearted she entered the sombrely shadowed villa, filled with a presentiment of disaster.

Maria approached her, her face white and strained.

'Prince Victor would like to speak with you, Mademoiselle. He is in the main salon.'

'Thank you, Maria.' She had hoped to be able to bathe and change before facing the Prince. Now, not only would she have to face him in a gown dust-blown from her hasty flight, but she would also have to explain her absence. An absence he had given no permission for.

She knocked lightly on the satinwood door. On no account must she allow herself to be intimidated. The reimbursement she was about to ask for was reimbursement due to her. Without it, she could not return to England; could not survive.

'Enter.'

Charlotte did so. The salon had been the Princess's favourite room. In it she had lain on the Louis Philippe *chaise longue* while Charlotte had read to her. In it she had sat, eyes clouded with memories, reminiscing to Charlotte about the days of her youth. Charlotte felt her stomach turn and tighten at the sight of the empty *chaise longue*. There would be no more such happy moments. The atmosphere in the villa had already changed. It was as if the very rooms were no longer so warm, so light. With a shock she saw that the Princess's personal stationery, her gold embossed pen, her crystal paperweight, had all been removed from the desk. Photographs, too, were missing. The Grand Duchess no longer smiled from her silver frame on the secretaire. Within hours the room had been robbed of the Princess's presence.

Prince Victor was sumptuously attired in military uniform. He had a weakness for gold braid and tasselled epaulettes. His military uniforms were splendid and various, and all entirely honorary. As he rose from the gilded chair behind the desk the scarlet of his jacket tightened dangerously. The Prince refused to accept his portliness and instructed his tailor to make all his jackets for a man of a lesser size, believing that the effect was complimentary. His hair was fine, effeminately soft, pale in colour. His moustaches were sparse and though grown long at either side of his mouth in order that they could be dashingly twirled, remained limp and drooping, no matter how much care was expended on them.

He was fifty-four. There had been a wife but she had died. He couldn't remember when or where. She had been a whey-faced creature who had given no satisfaction in bed and had not even had the courtesy to produce an heir. He would marry again. At his leisure. A girl of rank and wealth and tender years.

Prince Victor seldom exerted himself over any female over the age of fifteen, but the girl in front of him was an exception. He surveyed her appreciatively. 'Please be seated, Mademoiselle Grainger. I have ascertained that there is money owing to you.'

Charlotte breathed a deep sigh of relief that was quickly quelled as the Prince sat himself disconcertingly close beside her.

'And your family, you are no doubt desirous of returning to them?'

'I have no family.'

'Ah . . .' The Prince moved slightly. A bulging thigh pressed against Charlotte's skirts.

'I know that the time is not fitting to discuss financial matters,' Charlotte began, painfully aware of his unwelcome weight and of the Princess's body only rooms away, 'but my position is . . . difficult.'

Prince Victor observed the long, slender fingers, the almond tipped nails.

'Whilst in Princess's Yakovleva's employ I had little need of my salary and the Princess kept it in her care.'

Prince Victor's pale blue eyes gleamed. It was going to be even easier than he had anticipated. The girl had no money. She was entirely dependent on him. The seduction of a virgin of good breeding was always titillating. The seduction of a girl who had been in his mother's employ even more so, especially if that seduction were carried out only yards from where his mother lay in state, candles at her head and feet.

His hand moved up and clasped her shoulder.

Charlotte's eyes widened. She drew as far away from him as politeness would allow. His kindness was disturbing and his manner of showing it unwelcome.

'And so, I must ask you if you will kindly pay me the money owing to me,' she said with a rush. 'The amount is written in the Princess's account book. The book is in the top, right-hand drawer of the secretaire . . .'

'Do not worry yourself on account of the money,' the Prince said, and there was a tone of unmistakable heat in his voice. 'I shall take exceedingly good care of you, my little Charlotte.'

Charlotte trembled. What had happened to the world? Was every man a lecher?

'I will get the account book now, Your Highness.' Perhaps she had misunderstood the Prince. Perhaps his manner was merely unusual—European. She tried to rise to her feet and a hot, avaricious hand circled her waist.

'We must become better acquainted, Charlotte. I am a generous man, a . . .'

Charlotte pushed his chest violently, sending him falling backwards against the *chaise longue* as she sprang to her feet.

'I want none of your generosity, Prince Yakovlev! I want only that which is due to me . . . My salary!'

Her skirts whipped around her ankles as she marched across the room and pulled open the drawer of the desk. The Princess's leather-bound account book was in its accustomed place. She seized it, flicking through the pages with a trembling hand.

'Here!' She held out the open book. 'Here is the amount owed to me in the Princess's own handwriting. I ask that you honour that amount now, Prince Yakovlev!'

Prince Yakovlev was not a man accustomed to having his dignity insulted. Or to having his attentions spurned by those of lesser birth. A button had sprung from his jacket. A thin lock of hair had fallen across his forehead. He rose to his feet, breathing harshly, his face suffused an ugly dark red.

Viciously he snatched the book from her hand. Instinctively she stepped back.

'*That* for your demands,' he said, ripping the page from the book, screwing it into a ball and throwing it into the waste basket.

'But you cannot!' Charlotte's eyes were horrified.

'I can.' There was sweat on his brow and an ugly tic had appeared in the lid of one eye. 'Until you come to me with an apology, Mademoiselle, you will not receive one penny. An apology and *compliance!*'

Charlotte pressed her hand against her mouth to stifle her choked cry. Blindly she rushed from the salon. Reaching her own room she turned the key in the lock, leaning her head back against the door, her fingers splayed against the wood, tears coursing down her cheeks.

In the space of twenty-four hours her world had turned into nightmare. Count Sandor Karolyi had treated her as a woman of loose virtue. Comte Justin de Valmy had assumed she would be only too happy to live as his mistress, and, now, Prince Victor Yakovlev was demanding physical favours from her before he would pay her the salary owing to her. The salary that stood between herself and destitution.

She had no one to turn to. No friends—no family. She could not remain at the Villa Ondine. Despair engulfed her. Slowly she moved from the door and sat down on the bed. It was not true that she had no friends. Louise de Remy had declared herself her friend: and so had the great Sarah Bernhardt. She already knew what Louise's answer would be to her problems. She would go to Sarah. Perhaps Sarah would intercede on her behalf and speak to Prince Yakovlev.

Sandor strode across his vast, white-carpeted room and watched as Charlotte hurtled from the villa, running heedlessly down between banks of roses and magnolia.

Where the devil was the Yakovlev carriage? Charlotte continued to run, down between Beausoleil's flower-banked driveway and out through the gate. Tersely he rang for a footman.

'Was a carriage waiting for the young lady at the gate?'

'I think not, Count Karolyi.'

'Then find out.'

The footman hastened to do as he was bid.

Sandor remained at the window, already knowing the answer. With Princess Yakovleva dead, Miss Charlotte Grainger would not think it proper to continue using Yakovlev *equipages*. She had walked the tiring distance from the Villa Ondine to Beausoleil. Not for the reason he had so foolishly assumed, but because her innate code of etiquette demanded that she did so. She had come to thank him and he had barely listened to her. Now, painfully, her words came back.

'. . . your kindness. . . . much appreciated.'

He smashed a fist hard into the carved wood that surrounded the window. The wood splintered. Blood spurted.

God's teeth! How could he ever have been such a fool as to imagine she would offer her body in exchange for shelter? He staunched the blood with a handkerchief and continued to stare broodingly at the road that led through orange and lemon groves towards Monte Carlo.

The footman knocked and was admitted.

'There was no carriage, Count Karolyi. The young lady arrived on foot.'

'Then send one after her!'

'Yes, Count Karolyi.'

It would come back unused. Savagely he turned from the window and with his uninjured hand poured himself a glass of brandy. What would happen to her now Natalya was dead? She obviously had no financial resources of her own, so what other employment would she find? He thought of the cocottes who flaunted themselves so provocatively every evening in the Salle Mauresque. The brandy seared his throat. Charlotte Grainger would not become a cocotte. She would starve first. Nor a mistress. The decanter clinked against his glass as he poured more brandy. De Valmy's bed would not be warmed by Charlotte.

He rang for his secretary. A young gentleman entered, noticed the bloodstained handkerchief that was wrapped around his employer's hand and discreetly ignored it.

'I want to know the financial position of Mademoiselle Charlotte Grainger, companion to the late Princess Yakovleva,' Sandor said curtly. 'I want to know her movements, her future plans, you understand?'

François nodded dutifully. Count Karolyi's barely controlled rage was evident. Yet rage at what? The English girl had arrived at Beausoleil uninvited and of her own volition. Surely she had expected nothing else but an amorous advance from a man with his employer's reputation. Yet she had fled in obvious distress and Count Karolyi's knuckles were clenched white, his winged brows meeting in a satanic frown. Why? Surely a rejection of his advances by an insignificant English girl could not have disturbed him so deeply? True, it would be the first time any woman had been known to do so, but pride was not one of Count Karolyi's besetting sins.

He collected goatskin gloves and a cane and summoned the carriage that Count Karolyi had placed at his disposal. An English girl. He shook his head in despair. In Monte Carlo Count Karolyi was surrounded by the most beautiful Frenchwomen in the country and he had allowed an English girl to consume his thoughts. It was beyond the Frenchman's understanding.

Stoically Charlotte set out on yet another tiring walk. This time to the Hotel de Paris. The sun was losing its heat and a gentle breeze fanned her face. The beauty of the flowers, the lushness of the orange groves and the amethyst blue of the sea soothed her nerves. Her spirit was not one that inclined naturally towards despair. Prince Yakovlev had assumed she could be easily taken advantage of: that she had no one to speak in her defence. He had been wrong. Tomorrow, thanks to Count Karolyi's intervention, the Princess would be buried in Monte Carlo. The day after, suitably remunerated, she would begin her long journey to England.

Bright red geraniums crowded the window boxes of the first of the houses in the pretty, tree-lined avenue. A monkey-puzzle tree cast its shadow across her path. Clumps of wild orchids grew lushly.

Even if Prince Yakovlev refused to honour his mother's debt, she would not be defeated. English ladies were constantly travelling from England to Monte Carlo. She would approach each and every one of them until she found one in need of a companion and so work her way back home.

Comte Justin de Valmy had intended no offence in expressing his desire that she become his mistress. Therefore she would take none. He was a pleasant young man who had misjudged her.

Prince Yakovlev had misjudged her too, but she could feel no tolerance for *his* behaviour. It had been unforgivable. Her brow puckered. No wonder the Princess had had such little contact with her son. A shiver of distaste

ran down her spine at the memory of his sweetly cloying
cologne, his hot, avid hands. It would be a long time
before she would be able to forget the hideous scene in
the sun-filled salon of the Villa Ondine.

As for Count Sandor Karolyi . . . Warmth spread
through her like a fire. His every touch, his every glance,
aroused in her a desire that was shameless. A desire she
would never capitulate to: never allow him to be aware
of. Desire that seemed to ignite even further when
compounded with the furious anger his actions aroused.
To have *twice* treated her as a harlot! And for her twice
to have responded as one!

Her eyes stung. There would not be a third occasion.
She would *not* see Count Karolyi again and she would
not feel grief at the prospect. Head held high, she
stepped smartly into the lobby of the Hotel de Paris and
asked for Mademoiselle Bernhardt to be informed of her
presence.

The staff were apologetic. Mademoiselle Bernhardt
could not be disturbed. Charlotte fought her fatigue and
declared her intention of waiting until Mademoiselle
Bernhardt *could* be disturbed.

The Hotel de Paris' manager was summoned from his
office, a rosebud in his buttonhole, a silk cravat exquisitely tied.

'Mademoiselle Grainger, I am afraid it is not possible.'

'It is of the utmost urgency, Monsieur. If Mademoiselle Bernhardt is resting then I shall wait . . .'

The manager saw the determined tilt of her chin, the
flash of her eyes, and sighed. The English—always so
stubborn.

'Mademoiselle Bernhardt is entertaining a guest,
Mademoiselle.'

'Then I shall wait.' Charlotte reiterated, ignoring the
painful throb of her feet.

'Mademoiselle Grainger,' the Frenchman lowered his

voice to an intimate whisper, leaning towards her so that she could hear. 'I am afraid it is not so simple. The guest is a gentleman . . .' He spread his hands out, palms uppermost, expressively.

Charlotte was beyond shock. She simply said once again, 'I shall wait in the lobby, Monsieur. I cannot possibly make my journey a second time today and it is of urgency.'

The manager sighed. With any other lady he would have been stern and curt, but the child the English girl had saved the previous day had been the child of his chef. A debt of gratitude was owed. Seeing the determination in Charlotte's eyes he knew that only the truth would suffice.

'Mademoiselle Grainger,' he said in a voice little more than a whisper. 'Mademoiselle Bernhardt's guest is Baron Renshaw!'

Clearly Charlotte was meant to be impressed. She was not. She had not heard of the gentleman.

'If I could just sit a while, Monsieur . . .'

The Frenchman raised his eyes to heaven. Why were the English so unsubtle? Gently he took her arm.

'Mademoiselle Grainger. "Baron Renshaw" is the pseudonym of the Prince of Wales.'

Charlotte stared at him transfixed. The hotel manager gave a Gallic shrug.

'The Prince would not be pleased if he knew I had allowed someone to wait while . . . while . . .'

'No. Of course not.'

Charlotte struggled to collect her scattered wits. Clearly she could not speak to Sarah today. Tomorrow, no doubt, Sarah would attend the Princess's funeral. Perhaps then she would have the opportunity to ask for an appointment to see her. She swayed slightly and the Frenchman saw the lines of fatigue on her delicately boned face, the blue shadows darkening her eyes.

'I think, Mademoiselle Grainger, you need rest and

refreshment before returning to the Villa Ondine. Jacques!' He snapped his fingers commandingly. '*Timbales de sole Grimaldi* for Mademoiselle Grainger. followed by *mousse Monte Carlo* and a bottle of Hiesdeck Monopole.'

Weakly Charlotte allowed herself to be led into the dining room, deserted in the hours between afternoon tea and dinner. Only when the *Sole Grimaldi* was placed in front of her did she realise how hungry she was. How long ago had been her last meal.

The fillets of sole were served with truffles and small crayfish topped with butter and cream and cheese and wrapped in a deliciously light pastry case.

The *mousse Monte Carlo* was a meringue and Chantilly cream mould sprinkled with crystallised violets and tasting delicious. Though she protested that she never drank champagne, neither Jacques nor Monsieur Fleury would hear of serving lemonade to their guest and she found the Hiesdeck Monopole restored and revived her.

When she had finished her meal, the hotel manager said kindly, 'And now, Mademoiselle, a *barouche* for your return journey.'

For a fleeting moment Charlotte wondered if she dared reveal her predicament to the kind Frenchman. Perhaps he would allow her to remain beneath the Hotel de Paris' roof? The thought of returning to the Villa Ondine filled her with horror. She stifled the impulse. The hotel manager had been more than kind. She could not impose on him any further. Besides, this one last night it was her duty to remain at the villa with Princess Natalya's body.

She entered the villa quietly, fearful of encountering the Prince. Maria hastened towards her and Charlotte pressed a finger against her lips.

'Hush, Maria. I have no desire for Prince Yakovlev to know of my presence.'

Maria's pretty face was bitter. 'There is no fear of that, Mademoiselle. The Prince,' the words were spat viciously, 'is occupying himself with a *putain.*' The adjective for a lady of the streets was the most vile Maria was capable of.

'Then you and I will sit vigil by Princess Natalya tonight,' Charlotte said, beyond shock or distress.

'And then, Mademoiselle? You will leave?'

Charlotte nodded. 'Yes, Maria. I will leave and return to England.'

'And I,' Maria flashed with venom, 'will return to Nice. I will not stay one more day in the household of that . . . that *animal!*'

Charlotte was grateful for the night's vigil. The room was full of peace and serenity. The candles flickered at the head and foot of the catafalque. Maria's rosary beads slipped rhythmically between her fingers. Charlotte intermittently opened the pages of her Bible and sought comfort from the words she had often heard her father quote.

In the morning Prince Victor's eyes met Charlotte's in frustrated, vindictive fury. Her rejection of him had only inflamed his lust. Damnation, but he would have her. She would not receive a single franc until he did so.

A crucifix was placed in the Princess's marble-white hands. Charlotte, in a borrowed black dress of Maria's, felt suitably attired. The pall-bearers arrived. Every church in Monte Carlo tolled its bells as the cortege moved from the Villa Ondine, first to the Church and a Requiem Mass, and then for the long funeral procession to the cemetery.

The hearse led the mourners at a slow pace, the horses' black plumes swaying gently. Edward, Prince of Wales, would have preferred his second day in Monte Carlo to have been spent in a more entertaining pursuit than attending a funeral, but etiquette demanded that he did so. Besides, he had enjoyed the Princess's sharp wit

on many occasions. He was flanked by a gallery of
Romanovs. By Polish nobility. By French. Lady Pethel-
bridge was swathed in black tulle. The Countess of
Bexhall in black sable despite the sun.

Sarah was draped in a dress of black brocade, a black
chiffon ribbon, its wide ends floating loose, tied a bunch
of white lilac to her breast. Her long, slender neck
emerged from the high lace collar *à la* Marie Stuart, her
turbulent hair veiled in fine black silk.

Count Sandor Karolyi was clearly discernible, standing head and shoulders above those around him, his dark
eyes brooding, his handsome face forbidding.

Charlotte, following the titled mourners at a distance
with Maria and other members of the household staff,
averted her eyes from him, painfully aware of his presence.

Prince Victor, to all outward appearances, was a man
bowed down by grief. Charlotte wondered where the
putain of the previous night now was.

A large assortment of carriages waited to take the
mourners away from the graveside and back to their
respective hotels and villas. Charlotte began to make her
way towards Sarah and then faltered. A broad-
shouldered figure was at Sarah's side. Sarah was leaning
prettily against him.

The King of Belgium and the King of Serbia departed.
The Prince of Wales entered his carriage. Grand dukes
and grand duchesses dispersed. Sandor was assisting
Sarah into her *barouche* and followed her, sitting beside
her. Charlotte stood by helplessly. Her chance was lost.
She would have to make another visit to the Hotel de
Paris. The hotel manager would lose patience with her
and, far worse, by so doing she would very likely come
face to face with Sandor Karolyi once again.

Justin de Valmy saw her standing on the fringe of the
cemetery, surrounded by household servants and curious Monégasques. Her dress was of cheap, black

cotton; the dress of a peasant. She looked indescribably lovely and utterly alone. He excused himself from his companions and began to walk purposefully across to her.

The Bernhardt carriage followed the long line of those with royal emblems. Sandor Karolyi saw Justin de Valmy halt; saw Charlotte stare up at him with eloquent eyes; saw them turn together as de Valmy ushered her into his carriage.

A wave of jealousy surged through him. She was in need of help and by his own actions he had ensured that he was the last person on earth to whom she would turn. His mouth set in a grim line and even Sarah dared not intrude on his thoughts.

CHAPTER
FIVE

'MY CONDOLENCES and my apologies,' Justin said, removing his gleaming silk top hat and bowing. 'My carriage is at your disposal, Charlotte. I promise there will be no repetition of the previous incident when you consented to ride with me.'

His eyes were sincere, concerned. She was unbelievably tired. The all-night vigil by Princess Natalya's side had taken its toll. As had the long, hot walk to the cemetery.

'Thank you, Comte de Valmy. I should be most grateful to ride with you back to Monte Carlo.'

A slight smile touched Justin's lips as he took her arm and escorted her to his landau.

'As we are now friends, and no longer mere acquaintances, I would be grateful if you would address me as "Justin". To be addressed always as "Comte" is too reminiscent of my creditors.'

The long line of carriages before them moved off at a suitable sedate pace. The Princess was left behind. Her final resting place, high above the town she had loved so passionately. It was even possible to see the distant twin domes of the casino. Charlotte's mouth softened. The Princess would have been pleased. Perhaps she had known of the view when she had so firmly stipulated where she was to be buried.

'It is the first time I have had the pleasure of seeing your future sovereign. He looks like a man who knows how to enjoy life.'

'I am sure that he does, Monsieur le Comte . . . Justin. And that he is also diligent in his duties.'

Justin's eyes sparkled. It was obvious Charlotte knew nothing of her future sovereign's private life; of the beguiling Mrs Edward Langtry who had succeeded in becoming Edward's mistress, acknowledged not only by his long-suffering wife, but even by Queen Victoria.

Not, Justin reflected as the carriage began to pick up speed, that the Jersey Lily was much in evidence in Monte Carlo. The Prince of Wales's nature was not one of faithfulness, be it to wife or mistress. When in France he sought fresh diversions. No doubt he had visited Paris before journeying to Monte Carlo and he had certainly wasted no time in securing the company of the magical Sarah.

As the carriages in front of them wound their way down to elegant villas and hotels, the sun gleamed on the polished harnesses of the horses, on the glazed hats of the *cochers*, their florid faces sweating beneath the weight of their tiers of capes.

Monte Carlo lay golden in the sun. Madame Blanc's beds of exotic flowers were a riot of colour surrounding the casino. In the Port the white sails of yachts were brilliant against the azure blue of the sky. The air was heavy with the fragrance of flowers and the hum of bees. All too soon the stone lions flanking the gates of the Villa Ondine were discernible between the trees.

Justin leant forward, about to ask his coachman to halt the horses.

'No!' The word sprang to her lips instinctively.

Justin paused, looking at her strangely.

She tried to cover her confusion. She could not confide her difficulties to the Comte de Valmy. His solution would be to renew his attentions. To try and persuade her to leave Monte Carlo and live with him as his mistress.

'I . . . I am not returning to the Villa Ondine. Not for the moment.'

Justin leaned back and surveyed her with curiosity.

'Then where would you like to be taken, Charlotte?'

'To the Hotel de Paris, if you please.' Her eyes shied away from his. What would she say if he asked her what her mission at the hotel was? She had never been able to lie. She could not begin now.

Justin did not query her explanation. To him it meant only that he would have her company for an extra quarter of an hour.

'The Crown Prince of Germany is expected in Monte Carlo shortly. I believe he is not over-fond of his uncle.'

'His uncle?' Charlotte's thoughts were far away from those of society.

'The Prince of Wales.'

'Oh.' Charlotte lapsed into silence. She knew nothing about the relationships between the members of the royal houses of Europe. Her thoughts were taken up with far more mundane matters. On how to return to England and fresh employment; on the necessity of living from one day to the next.

As the landau halted at the hotel's main entrance and Justin alighted to assist her from the carriage, his hand held hers too long for necessity.

'If you should need me, Charlotte, I shall be only too happy to be of assistance.'

She hesitated, but only momentarily. To seek assistance from Justin, Comte de Valmy, would be to lose her honour—and to a man she did not love.

The commissionaire's eyebrows rose. Mademoiselle Grainger's visits to the hotel were becoming increasingly regular. At the desk Charlotte asked charmingly that Mademoiselle Bernhardt be informed of her presence. The staff were apologetic. The shy-mannered English girl with the gentle, soft smile had won all their hearts. But they could not help her.

Mademoiselle Bernhardt had arrived only minutes ago. She had changed hastily from mourning into attire more suitable to that of a companion to a Prince, and had speedily left in a cloud of perfume and furs on the arm of Charlotte's future sovereign.

Charlotte refused to be defeated. It was becoming increasingly obvious that while Edward, Prince of Wales, was in Monte Carlo, it was going to be virtually impossible to speak to Sarah. Therefore she must fall back on her second plan. She would approach Lady Pethelbridge and ask if she might accompany her as a companion back to England.

Lady Pethelbridge had stared at her footman in astonishment at being informed that Miss Charlotte Grainger wished to speak with her. The funeral had tired her exceedingly. She hated funerals and only attended because etiquette demanded it. Vaguely she remembered that Miss Grainger had been companion to Princess Yakovleva and that she had behaved extraordinarily in throwing herself beneath the hoofs of a horse. To what purpose Lady Pethelbridge could no longer remember.

'Send her in,' she commanded bad-temperedly, adjusting her lorgnette.

'It is most gracious of you to see me, Lady Pethelbridge, especially today.'

Lady Pethelbridge wasn't quite sure why the day was different from any other and then remembered the funeral.

'Yes,' she demanded impatiently. 'What is it you require?'

Charlotte remembered the smile Lady Pethelbridge had bestowed on her in the casino when Sarah had proclaimed to the world Charlotte's bravery. It was sadly absent now. Charlotte doubted if Lady Pethelbridge even remembered her identity.

'Since the princess died my position has become . . . precarious,' she began.

Lady Pethelbridge was fast losing interest. She had hoped the girl was bringing her a memento that perhaps Princess Natalya had bequeathed to her.

Charlotte continued undeflected.

'Prince Yakovlev is unwilling to pay the salary owing to me, and so I have no means of returning to England. I wondered if perhaps . . . If it would be possible . . .' She took a deep breath. 'I wondered if I could accompany your ladyship as companion when you return to England.'

Lady Pethelbridge stared at her in astonishment. 'Are you asking me for *employment*, young woman?'

Charlotte's voice was low but firm. 'Yes, your ladyship.'

Lady Pethelbridge rose indignantly. 'When I require staff *I* employ them! I do not expect them to solicit *me*!'

'No, your ladyship, but the circumstances . . .'

Lady Pethelbridge was uncaring of the circumstances. She rang the silver bell at her side.

'Miss Grainger is leaving,' she said to the footman who entered.

The interview was at an end. Charlotte's eyes held Lady Pethelbridge's for a long second and her ladyship felt inexplicably uncomfortable. Then, head held high, her back straight, Charlotte left the room.

Princess Helena was no kinder. She was indifferent as to Charlotte's circumstances. And she needed no companion.

'A maid?' Charlotte asked desperately.

The princess required no further maids.

The young Frenchman in reception, on being asked by Charlotte what other English ladies were in residence in Monte Carlo, informed her that a lady of no rank but enormous wealth was residing at the Villa Grimaldi. That the Countess of Bexhall was in residence at the hotel. That a marchioness was the guest of Prince Charles of Monaco.

The Countess was uncaring of Charlotte's plight and had no intention of returning to England—ever. The lady of no rank was elderly and helped herself generous-

ly to Vichy pastilles from a jewel-encrusted candy box as
Charlotte stated her case, and then informed her she had
no need of her service.

Entry to the palace and the marchioness proved impossible.

It was late afternoon. She had not slept; not eaten.
She had no alternative but to return to the Villa Ondine
and once more face the detestable Prince Yakovlev.

She was footsore and weary. Fashionable carriages
passed her without a second glance. To the occupants
she was indistinguishable from the peasants in her cheap
black dress of mourning.

Charlotte recognised many ladies who had, only hours
previously, been dressed in the deepest of mourning for
the Princess's funeral. The mourning had been quickly
discarded. The funeral had been only another social
occasion. The Princess was not a relative. Black was not
becoming.

It was late afternoon, the customary time for carriage
rides along the boulevard. Charlotte observed the
leisurely salutes from carriage to carriage of the ladies,
their huge hats shading their eyes. Men lifted their
gleaming silk toppers with one dove-grey gloved hand,
and adjusted their monocles with the other.

What did they know of a life without financial means?
Of a struggle for respectability without employment or
family?

A debonair phaeton drawn by a pair of high-steepers
with pink roses in their bridles passed her so closely she
had to step hurriedly out of their way. Driving them was
a queen of the *demi-monde*. A deliciously wicked creature dressed in matching shades of pink from her buckled shoes to her feather boa.

She, too, could drive a carriage of her own, be dressed as
exquisitely, if she became Justin de Valmy's mistress.
She sighed and continued her walk. Love was too pre-

cious to be given in exchange for a carriage and Paris gowns.

A peasant girl in *sabots* hurried noisily past her. Two worlds, rich and poor, living side by side and never meeting. For a time, thanks to Princess Natalya, she had been a spectator to the life of the rich. Now she must return to reality.

She pressed a hand to her throbbing temple and continued her walk, oblivious of the landau some distance behind her. The horses' bridle chains were of silver; the driver and footmen wore gold embroidered liveries. The occupant was a curious Frenchman who had watched her ever since she had entered the Hotel de Paris, who had followed at a discreet distance as she walked to the Villa Grimaldi; to the gates of the palace.

François regarded Charlotte's back with growing admiration. Her appeal, her beauty, was undeniable. His only regret was that she was not French.

As Charlotte approached the Villa Ondine he ordered the driver to halt the horses. Then, after a suitable length of time, he approached on foot and asked for Maria, handing her a handsome sum of money and returning to the carriage. His vigil, for the moment, was over. The maid would inform him of whatever took place inside the Villa Ondine's ochre coloured walls. He wondered if he had time to make a visit to one of the ladies of the town, but decided against it. Count Karolyi's temper was extremely volatile, no more so than at the present moment.

Victor Yakovlev had had plenty of time to smart under Charlotte's refusal of his advances. He had seen her at the funeral, standing at a suitable distance with the other servants, dressed in a cheap black dress that should have destroyed her beauty but did nothing but enhance it. Charlotte Grainger's allure was not dependent upon fancy clothes and jewels. It was an innate part of her nature. In the way she held herself; in the long, lovely line of her throat, the unknowing sensuousness of her smile, the lustre of her thick-lashed eyes. She possessed a radiance that seemed to illuminate her. A radiance *he* wanted to possess.

Feverishly he had waited for her to return to the villa and she had not. His disappointment had been so acute that he had felt physically ill. Where had she gone? And with whom? When he heard her voice greeting Maria in the mosaic-tiled hall, he fumblingly lit a cigar, his hand shaking, so great was his relief.

Returning to her room Charlotte changed from the dress she had borrowed from Maria and into a lavender silk gown. Slowly she began to collect her personal possessions and lay them on the bed. A simple locket on a slim gold chain that had been her mother's. The Bible her father had carried everywhere. A tortoise-shell-backed brush and mirror. A slim volume of poetry. The dresses and shoes and parasols that the Princess had given her she left in the giant mahogany wardrobe. They had been for her to wear in the Princess's service. She would take nothing, save the dress on her back, that she had not arrived with.

Her pathetically few possessions were soon gathered. She would eat, sleep, and then she would go. Her head ached. Where? How? She still did not know, but one thing was clear. She could not remain at the Villa Ondine.

Maria knocked on the door and entered. 'Prince Victor wishes to see you, Charlotte.'

Charlotte felt herself tremble. 'Thank you, Maria.'

This was her last chance. She had to make Prince Yakovlev aware of his obligations. To her unspeakable relief the Prince's attitude seemed to have altered when she entered the main salon. He greeted her with civility.

'I fear that last evening my intentions were perhaps . . . misunderstood.'

Charlotte remained silent. She had misunderstood nothing. The Prince had made improper advances to her and had been rejected. And he had categorically refused to pay her the salary owing to her.

The Prince took out a large silk handkerchief from his pocket and mopped his perspiring brow.

'I had not understood then how . . . devoted . . . you had been to my mother.'

Charlotte waited, her heart pounding. He had reconsidered. He was going to reimburse her after all.

'I have studied my mother's accounts and you are quite correct in that there is money owing to you.'

Charlotte put a hand out to a nearby table to steady herself.

'I think that, by tomorrow morning, my secretary will be able to settle your account.'

'Thank you, Your Highness.' She felt dizzy with relief. There had been no scene. No angry words.

'In the meantime,' Prince Victor's paunch strained at the buttons of his waistcoat as he paced from the desk to the window and back again, 'I would be most grateful if you would accompany me to the casino this evening.'

Carlotte stared at him, her eyes rounding. The casino! On the very day he had buried his mother!

'There is no need to appear so shocked,' the Prince said hurriedly, reading her mind. 'My mother lived and practically died in the casino. She would certainly not take such a visit this evening as a mark of disrespect.'

What he said was true, but Charlotte had no intention of accompanying the Prince anywhere. 'I am afraid I shall not be able to do as you ask, Your Highness.'

The Prince halted in his pacing, his pale blue eyes hot and fevered. 'Why, I have already explained to you that . . .'

'Yes, Your Highness. It is just that it would be impossible for me to accompany you to the casino at any time.' She strove for the right words. She must not antagonise him. He had still not given her the money. He could change his mind at a moment's notice. She forced a small smile. 'I was merely companion to the Princess, and . . .'

'Damn what you were employed as,' the Prince exploded testily. 'You accompanied my mother to the casino every evening. You will accompany me.'

Charlotte stared at him helplessly. If she did not he would almost certainly alter his instructions to his secretary. And if she did, he could not possibly behave improperly. They would be surrounded by too many people.

'Yes, Your Highness,' she said at last, unhappily.

The Prince mopped his brow once again. For one hideous moment he had thought she was going to refuse.

'And now if you will excuse me, Prince Yakovlev.'

The Prince excused her, hardly able to contain his rising excitement. The English girl had only entered the casino as companion to his irascible mother. She had never known the headiness of playing the tables, of feeling gold slip through her fingers, of the intoxication of champagne. Once she had experienced such pleasures she would be unable to turn her back on them. Especially when he made it clear that such pleasures could be hers for the asking. Already he had arranged that a small, private, upstairs room was put at his disposal. By the time they had arrived at the Devil's Palace that evening, champagne would be chilling. He would indulge her at the tables in the Salle Mauresque and then take her upstairs for dinner à deux; for more champagne, for caviar—for the delight of seduction.

'You mean she has nothing?' Sandor rasped at his secretary, frowning fiercely. 'Not a sou? And that reptile, Yakovlev, tried to seduce her?'

The secretary flinched at the savagery in his employer's voice. 'The maid was adamant that Prince Yakovlev demanded certain favours if the lady in question was to be paid.'

'Damn him to hell, but he'll regret the day he was born!'

'Yes, sir.'

The secretary waited obediently as Sandor strode the room, his handsome face contorted with anger. 'That pot-bellied lecher will learn his lesson once and for all. As for Mademoiselle Grainger . . .'

'Yes, sir.'

Sandor cursed, his eyes narrowing. Zara would be in Monte Carlo within days, perhaps even hours. Zara would take care of Charlotte; she could approach Charlotte without his name even being mentioned.

'I want Mademoiselle Grainger to be informed that Lady Beston will be arriving in Monte Carlo before the end of the week and that she is desirous of hiring her as a companion for her journey back to England. Allow Mademoiselle Grainger to believe that a member of the English fraternity has spoken with Lady Beston and that Lady Beston has instructed a room to be set aside for her at the Hotel de Paris until her arrival.'

'Yes, sir.'

Sandor rounded on him, 'At *once*, François!'

Sensing the fury barely under control, François hastened from the room. Sandor swore viciously. Not a sou to her name and reduced to going to those uncaring bitches of high society and asking for employment. Employment they could easily have given her – if they had cared. He could imagine the air of dignity with which she had approached them, carrying herself straight and tall and with effortless grace. Damn them all to hell. The whole lot of them were not worth a hair of her head.

His jaw tightened. He would not leave Beausoleil

until he knew she was safely installed at the Hotel de
Paris.

Unable to curb his turbulent emotions, he ordered
that his horse be saddled and stormed to his room,
changing into riding breeches and a cream-coloured silk
shirt with a high Russian neck. He dismissed his valet
curtly, pulling on riding boots of soft Spanish leather,
picking up his riding crop, marching to the stables, his
brows pulled together demonically.

'But today of all days!' Maria gazed aghast at Charlotte.

Charlotte sighed wearily. 'I know, Maria. But the
prince insists it is no disrespect to his mother and, to tell
the truth, I think that perhaps he is right.'

'But what will people say?'

'In Monte Carlo?' Charlotte shrugged. In Monte Carlo the most outrageous behaviour went unnoticed.

'The Prince will want you to wear a suitable gown,'
Maria said doubtfully. 'Something *décolleté*.'

'I shall wear the gown I am wearing now. It is as near
to a mourning gown as I possess. Monte Carlo may have
forgotten the Princess the minute the funeral was over,
but I have not.'

Maria nodded in agreement. 'I will dress your hair
with fresh rosebuds. That is all the adornment you will
need.'

Already dusk had fallen. Maria summoned the undermaid to bring large jugs of hot water to fill Charlotte's
bath and then set to work, pressing the lavender gown
while Charlotte bathed.

Later, as Charlotte sat at the dressing table and Maria
brushed the thickly waving chestnut hair high on the
back of Charlotte's head, arranging it in a natural fall of
ringlets, she thought that, despite her tiredness, Charlotte had never looked so lovely.

'The carriage is waiting, Mademoiselle Grainger,' a
Yakovlev footman said, his eyes vaguely troubled.

'Thank you.'

Unwillingly Charlotte rose to her feet. Tonight would be her last night in the Devil's Palace. She had not thought to enter it again. Certainly not in such company. Always before she had set off for the evening amongst the glitter and the gold with a heady sense of excitement. Now she felt only reluctance.

The prince was waiting for her in the villa's magnificent entrance hall. His silk cravat was tied flamboyantly, a large diamond glittering in the intricate folds. His cut-away coat was expensively tailored but did nothing to flatter his portly figure. It was heavily embellished with black silk facings and a footman deferentially adjusted a scarlet-lined opera cloak around his shoulders.

For a moment the Prince was about to protest at the simplicity of Charlotte's dress, but seeing the wilful set of her chin he decided against it. Besides, she looked ravishing. He took her hand, kissed it, and complimented her lavishly on her appearance and then led her out into the soft night air.

Charlotte stepped up and into the carriage. Prince Victor followed, his physical presence overpowering her. A footman slammed the door shut and jumped on to the box. The coachman cracked his whip. Charlotte looked steadfastly away from Prince Victor who was devouring her with his small, protruding eyes, and prayed that the evening would come to an early end.

Victor Yakovlev was not a man accustomed to feeling out of his depth but there was something about Charlotte's gentle dignity that unnerved him. It was as if his rank, his wealth, meant nothing at all to her. She was young and indescribably beautiful. Surely being at his mother's beck and call had been hateful to her? Surely she must have longed for such an evening? A rich escort, gold *louis* to play the tables, champagne, caviar? Why then was she not teasing him with one of the smiles she bestowed so freely on Maria, on the footman—on anyone who performed the slightest task for her? Without his favour she would be destitute and yet she was not making the slightest sign of seeking it.

He strove for patience. He would wait until they had entered the casino. Till she had experienced the thrill of the croupiers pushing their wooden shovels of gold plaques in her direction. Till the champagne made her heedless and reckless.

He stroked his wispy moustache. She had been high and mighty the previous day when he had made advances to her, but that was before she had realised how utterly dependent upon him she was. Tonight would be different. Tonight he would teach her how to be grateful. He smiled in the darkness as the carriage rattled towards the casino and its myriad blazing lights.

Heads turned, shocked and disapproving, as Charlotte entered on the Prince's arm. She held her head a fraction higher. It was not she who had chosen to show disrespect to Princess Natalya. It was her son. What did the ladies and gentlemen at the tables know of her dilemma? What did they care?

Her skirts swirled softly as she continued to walk by the side of Prince Yakovlev, her eyes fixed firmly ahead of her, greeting no one. The rococo mirrors reflected her appearance. Duplicated it. The soft lavender of her gown intensified the golden highlights in her hair. Dressed in utter simplicity the Parisian-gowned and jewelled ladies of high society paled into insignificance beside her.

Dowagers in tiaras nodded acknowledgements to the Prince and pointedly ignored his ill-chosen companion. An elderly French marchioness, her face garishly coated with rouge and white powder, her hair henna-ed in a pathetic attempt to retain beauty long-since fled, froze Charlotte and pointedly turned her velvet-clad back.

Lady Pethelbridge raised horrified eyes and turned

quickly away, the train of her gold-embroidered turquoise silk dress swirling on the lushly carpeted floor.
The Countess of Bexhall followed suit. Back after back
turned, fans flicking, indignant whispers rife.

Twenty-four hours ago they had clapped and applauded her. Charlotte's eyes were overly bright. Maria,
a Monégasque peasant, was worth far more than the
titled, wealthy ladies thronging the Salle Mauresque.
Then, across the brilliantly lit room, a pair of eyes met
Charlotte's, china blue and mischievous. Louise de
Remy was on the arm of her Russian grand duke, her
dress white satin and covered in seed pearls, diamonds at
her throat, her wrists, her ears. She raised a hand, white
gloved to the elbow, pressing it lightly against her lips
and blew a kiss across the room in Charlotte's direction.
Charlotte's smile was instant and spontaneous. Louise
had misunderstood the situation entirely but what did it
matter? She had halted her carriage for her when she
was in distress. Her friendship was sincere and did not
depend on Charlotte's popularity or unpopularity.

The Prince ignored the frozen glances cast in his
direction. If society had expected him to remain in
mourning, then society was going to be disappointed.
Charlotte's hand rested on his arm so lightly it was like
the touch of a butterfly. He could feel the rhythm of her
graceful, swaying walk at his side. He thought of the
room upstairs already prepared. The opulent divan, the
chilling champagne. A rush of blood flooded his face. He
must not hurry things. He must take it step by step, so as
not to frighten her away. First she must experience the
feel of gold in her hands. With a flourish the Prince
seated her at a crowded roulette table, his hand caressing her shoulder proprietorily as he did so. Charlotte
flinched.

'Red or black, my dear?' the Prince asked, leaning so
near to her that his moustache brushed her cheek.

'I do not wish to play, Your Highness.'

'Nonsense!' The Prince's joviality held a note of desperation. If she was going to be awkward so early on in the evening, then there was little hope for his other plans.

'Black,' a male voice said behind them, 'for mourning.'

The Prince flushed and turned angrily. The English milord behind him merely smiled, bowed and moved away. Charlotte felt a rush of shame. What must they think of her, her fellow countrymen and women who took mourning so seriously?

'Red,' the Prince said heavily, turning his attention to the table. 'Red number nine, for the lady.'

The roulette wheel whirred, the ivory ball clicked slower and slower and then, miraculously, dropped into red nine.

The Prince was jubilant.

'And this time?' He was leaning so close to her that she could smell the sweat beneath the sweetness of his cologne.

'Number six.' She had to escape. She should never have come. The Prince was patting her hand, her arm, his small body pressed indecently close to hers. She was uncaring of where the ivory ball would fall. Her eyes searched the room in the hope of seeing Justin, of seeing Sarah. Instead they met the blazing dark eyes of Sandor Karolyi. With a gasp she swung her head away, staring sightlessly at the roulette wheel. Red number six had proved unlucky.

The Prince urged her to double up her previous winnings and place them once again on red nine. She did so, her distress barely under control. His gaze had held such hostility that for a second she had thought her heart would cease to beat. Vaguely she was aware that red nine had proved lucky again. She was trembling. What right had he to censure her so? Surely, of all the people in the Salle Mauresque, Count Sandor Karolyi was the

one whose opinion of her should bother her the least?
The play continued. Occasionally, whenever she raised
her mortified eyes, she would see in the expression of
those around her the belief that she had made the
transition from companion to the mother to mistress of
the son. Contempt, except from the ladies of the *demi-
monde*, was obvious.

The Prince's hand now circled her waist. Beside them,
a cocotte with creamily bared shoulders and near-naked
breasts leaned laughingly against her escort. Charlotte
was well aware of the intimacies exhibited so carelessly
by the ladies of the town and their titled lovers. Of the
caresses, the overt teasing of long-lashed eyes over
feathered fans. Now she, too, was being treated as such.
The heat of the Prince's hand seared the silk of her
gown. Squeezed and pressed. She could endure it no
longer. In her innocence she had thought that he had
wanted her companionship to ease the burden of his
loss. She now knew that Prince Victor Yakovlev felt no
sense of loss at his mother's death: no grief. He was
incapable of such honourable emotions.

'Please . . . excuse me . . . I must leave . . .'

Already she was rising from the crowded table. Her
winnings had been enormous. Prince Victor rose willingly. Now for the *coup de grace*

'A change of play, I think,' he said as their places were
taken at the table.

'No.' Charlotte felt faint. Though she had not dared
to look in his direction again, she knew that Sandor
Karolyi's eyes had never left her. That they were fixed
burningly on her even now.

The Prince's hand covered hers with unpleasant
firmness. 'We shall leave . . . soon. But first . . .' He
indicated a flight of stairs leading to the upper rooms and
the Salon Privé.

Charlotte had often accompanied the Princess there,
for it was reserved for those of royal blood, those who

preferred a little privacy as they staked and lost fortunes. Baccarat would be the game in progress. She could not play baccarat, therefore, for a time at least, she would be free of the Prince's touch. She could sit to one side as she was accustomed to doing, the Prince could indulge himself at the table, and then they would leave.

She nodded unhappy acquiescence and a triumphant Prince Yakovlev led her towards the gilded staircase.

Sandor's eyes narrowed, his fingers tightening around the curve of his brandy glass. She had gone reluctantly, but she had gone. Had he been so wrong about her? Was it possible that his judgment had been in error?

His fury when François had returned and informed him that his message concerning Lady Beston could not be passed on to Mademoiselle Grainger because she had left for the casino with Prince Yakovlev had been white-hot. The Charlotte he knew would never have consented to accompany Prince Victor Yakovlev anywhere. He had stormed from Beausoleil, ordering his coachman to drive the horses to the utmost in his haste to be swiftly on her heels.

He had seen her the minute he had entered the room. Small pink rose-buds nestled in her hair. Her gown was the gown she had worn when she had visited Beausoleil. She was the only woman in the room whose shoulders were modestly covered. She was the only woman in the room that he had eyes for. He saw her every movement: the stiffening of her body as Yakovlev touched her, the anguish in her eyes as he treated her publicly as a cocotte. Then, to his utter disbelief, he saw her rise and accompany Yakovlev up the sumptuous staircase. Sandor was well acquainted with the private rooms ostensibly used for supper *à deux* and in reality retreats for seduction.

He held himself taut, every line of his body rigid. Was she going to sell herself to Yakovlev for a handful of gold *louis*? A blood-red mist swam behind his eyes. A pretty vicomtesse approached him, spoke and was ignored. An English duke exchanged a word of greeting and was similarly treated.

He should have marched over to the roulette table the minute he entered and saw her sitting there. He should have forcibly removed her from Yakovlev's side. A nerve throbbed at his jaw. She would not have gone with him. He had destroyed for ever any faith she might have had in him. All he could hope to do was to shield her from Yakovlev until Zara arrived. That was, if she wanted to be shielded.

The crystal shattered in the tightness of his grasp. One of Monsieur Blanc's minions hastened forward. The glass was swept swiftly and discreetly away. A handkerchief staunched the blood from his already scarred hand. Sandor stood oblivious as the ministrations were carried out, his eyes fixed on the head of the staircase. How long had she been gone? Two minutes? Three? If she remained voluntarily with Yakovlev in the private supper room upstairs, then he knew nothing would ever be the same. Any belief he had in inherent goodness would have gone for ever.

Charlotte paused bewilderedly. They were not heading towards the Salon Privé. Were there other gaming rooms: rooms she had no knowledge of? Triumphantly Prince Victor opened the door of the room he had so carefully reserved, and ushered her inside. She stood for a moment, uncomprehending. There were no green baize card tables, no elegant gentlemen, cigar smoke wreathing their heads, no tiara-crowned ladies. Only a supper table laid for two, a divan heavily showered with soft cushions, champagne chilling in a silver ice bucket.

She swung around, her eyes flashing with realisation and revulsion. 'This is no gaming room, Prince Yakovlev!'

'I thought supper, *à deux* . . .' Prince Victor's voice

was sharp. She was not being amenable. She had not even counted the gold plaques she had won at the roulette table. She had refused all offers of champagne.

'I thought you needed companionship this evening, Prince Yakovlev, to ease your grief. That is the reason I accompanied you. I did not realise that the companionship you required was that of a . . . a . . . *putain*!'

Prince Victor goggled at her vocabulary, struggled for speech and failed. She swept past him, eyes blazing.

'Keep your gold, Prince Yakovlev! Your champagne! Your *hospitality*!'

She was out in the corridor, shaking, fighting to control the tears of rage and humiliation that threatened to engulf her.

Prince Victor felt the veins in his neck swell and throb. He rushed after her, seizing her wrists.

'Where the devil do you think you are going?'

'To the villa!' She wrenched herself free of his grasp. 'I shall collect my belongings and I shall leave.' She marched away from him, her skirts swishing.

'You shall not! Not unaccompanied!'

Charlotte paused and turned, her eyes withering in their contempt. 'Are you concerned for my virtue, Prince Yakovlev?'

'No, by God! My reputation!'

Charlotte laughed, the unshed tears stinging her eyes. 'Of course. How foolish of me. It would be damaging to your reputation if I were to be seen publicly leaving alone, wouldn't it? Well, I am afraid you will just have to live with that humiliation, Prince Yakovlev.'

'*Never!*' He had hold of her wrist again. He was panting, his eyes fevered. If she left in the mood she was now in, the news would spread through the casino like wildfire. He would be a laughing stock. A Prince rejected by a paid companion. His sweating fingers tightened their hold. 'Remain with me in the Salle Mauresque for five, ten minutes. Then we will leave together.'

'No!' She pulled away from him, half running towards the head of the stairs.

Gasping for breath he caught hold of her again. 'Your salary. Do as I ask and I will pay you your salary.' It was a pittance. He would take it from her winnings. Winnings he had no intention of allowing her to keep.

'Five minutes.' Her voice was tight with defeat. If she rushed unescorted from the casino she would have to face the long walk to the villa in the dark and alone. And where would she go when she reached her destination? Where would she take her pathetic belongings? She had endured much. Surely she could endure another five minutes and leave with a semblance of dignity?

Her satin-slippered feet hurried down the broadly sweeping stairs, Yakovlev following in her wake, his protruding blue eyes glazed with the fury of a man defeated.

Smoothly Sandor crossed to the foot of the stairs, his relief incalculable. She had not stayed to receive Prince Yakovlev's amorous advances. He remembered the Princess's love of baccarat and her frequent card-playing in the Salon Privé. No doubt that was where Charlotte had believed she was being led.

He wanted to take hold of her, chase the misery from her eyes, reassure her, comfort her. He could do none of those things because she would misunderstand his intentions. He could not even ask that she return with him to Beausoleil and wait there for Zara's arrival. She would not believe in Zara's existence. She would think it yet another ploy to rob her of her virtue.

His eyes slanted under their winged brows. There was only one way of achieving her safety. A cruel, heartless way, and yet if he did not act soon—tonight—she would be gone.

'Good evening, Mademoiselle.'

She sprang back from him as if he were the devil incarnate.

'Good evening, Prince Yakovlev.'

Prince Yakovlev had no desire to converse with Count Sandor Karolyi, yet Karolyi was a man it was wise not to snub. He accepted the Count's condolences on the loss of his mother and felt a surge of adrenalin in his veins as Count Karolyi suggested a hand of poker. To be seen seated with the notorious Sandor Karolyi would restore some of his lost self-esteem. It would also ensure that he did not have to make a hasty and undignified exit with Charlotte.

For a panic-stricken moment Charlotte wondered whether she should abandon all dignity and simply run from the Salle Mauresque and out into the night. Common sense asserted itself. Whilst the Prince played cards with Count Karolyi he could not touch or molest her. By remaining with him in the casino, she would have carried out her part of the bargain.

Aware that Sandor Karolyi's eyes were resting on her with disquieting frequency, she kept her own lowered as they crossed the room to a card table. An unopened pack of cards was brought across to the two gentlemen, was ceremoniously unwrapped and cut. Play commenced.

Charlotte, seated at the Prince's right-hand side, was only feet away from Count Karolyi. She could not help but be aware of his disturbing nearness, of the thick black hair, springy as heather. Of the high, lean, cheekbones, the amber flame burning deep in his eyes, the bandaged hand. She wondered if he had cut it, burnt it. How? Where? She tried to direct her thoughts elsewhere but it was impossible.

The first hand fell to the Prince. A corner of Sandor's mouth curved in a crooked smile. Play commenced again. Two further hands fell to Prince Yakolev. Count Karolyi was known as a card player to fear and yet it seemed to Charlotte that he was playing with almost negligent carelessness.

The Prince, buoyed up by the skill he was displaying, increased his bets. Socialites wandering the salon paused to watch the play. Again Count Karolyi lost. Again Prince Yakovlev was gleeful.

Sandor's eyes rose from the green baize of the table and caught Charlotte's unaware, holding her prisoner. The desire he aroused in her flooded through her so that she could hardly bear it. She tore her eyes away from his, her heart slamming painfully.

The idle bystanders had increased in number. A lady's sable brushed Charlotte's shoulder. A gentleman asked *sotto voce* what the devil Karolyi was playing at.

Three kings. A flush. Again Sandor lost and as his mouth curved into a smile and he picked up the cards in front of him, Charlotte was filled with sudden disquiet. He was losing on purpose. Luring Prince Victor into a state of euphoric self-confidence.

A strange tightness began to grow in her throat, making it difficult for her to breathe. He was doing more than luring Prince Victor into parting with his gold. In that instant of time when their eyes had held, she had read something unfathomable in their depths. Something that both frightened and exhilarated her.

Again he lost to the Prince. This time, when he raised his eyes to hers she held them. A brief smile touched his mouth. Time wavered and faltered. In that moment she knew why the Vicomtesse had taken her life for love of him. A tremor ran through her body. No other man would have the power over her that Sandor Karolyi had, yet she would not yield to it. She would not become another in his long line of conquests. Her defiance shone in her eyes. His smile twisted, his mouth setting in a tight line.

This time the Prince lost to the Count. Charlotte was too overcome with the tumult of her heart and mind to care. She must not look at him. Must not remember the feel of his mouth on hers. The feel of his body as he held her with such easy strength. Unseeingly she stared at the bodices of the ladies surrounding the table: at corselettes of diamonds, of swathes of tulle and brocade.

Another hand went down to the Count. Perspiration was beginning to break out on Prince Victor's brow. The audience surrounding the table made it impossible for him to call a halt to the game. Honour demanded that it be continued.

Charlotte strove to dismiss the Count from her mind. In the morning she would leave the Villa Ondine as soon as she had been paid. She would travel by carriage to Nice and then by wagon-lit to Paris. Surely there would be enough money for her to make the journey in reasonable comfort? In Paris she would rest overnight and then continue by road to Calais. In Calais she would take a ship to Dover.

His eyes were on her again. She would not turn her head. In Dover she would . . .

Cards were expertly shuffled and dealt. Covertly she slid her eyes across to his lowered head. He looked disturbingly commanding. In full control of the game he was playing.

Again the Prince lost. Lazily Sandor suggested that the stakes be raised. Unable to lose face, Prince Victor agreed. With almost insolent ease Sandor took Prince Victor's full house with a running flush. Excitement around the table was palpable. Victor Yakovlev's wealth was not vast, despite his rank. He had relied upon his mother for his finances and doubt had been expressed as to whether or not the Princess had left her fortune to her son.

Sandor Karolyi's wealth was indisputable. With utter assurance, hand after hand fell to the Count. Sandor continued to play, showing not the slightest mercy to his victim. Too late Victor Yakovlev realised that his judgment had been clouded from the moment he had first sat at the table. He had been seething with fury at the

English girl's rejection of him. His initial wins had restored his self-esteem. Now, thanks to his foolishness, he was a broken man. He had nothing left to stake. Monsieur Blanc would not extend credit to him. Credit had been extended too often in the past—and not repaid.

Savagely he rose from the table. He dared not continue to gamble on the strength of his mother's will. That document was still unread, languishing in the offices of her St Petersburg solicitor.

'One moment,' Sandor leant negligently back in his chair, regarding Victor Yakovlev with a curious expression in his eyes. 'I do not think the game is yet at an end.'

Victor Yakovlev glared at him with hatred. They were surrounded by half the crowned heads of Europe. Was Karolyi going to add to his humiliation?

'It is at an end,' he said curtly. 'I have nothing left to stake.'

On the table between them lay a ransom in gold and bank notes and letters of promise.

'I think, Prince Victor,' Sandor said lazily, 'that perhaps you have and are not aware of it.'

Prince Yakovlev halted. There was complete confidence in the Hungarian's voice.

Around the table the conversation ceased. News of Prince Yakovlev's loss had quickly circulated the salon and even the roulette wheels stilled as the curious walked across to the table where the two men faced each other and tried to obtain a view over dinner-jacketed and naked shoulders.

For several minutes Sandor did not put the Prince out of his misery. Then he leisurely lit a cigar, blowing a haze of blue smoke into the air and said carelessly, 'Stake your companion, Yakovlev. It will add spice to the game and, who knows, if you win you will not only retain the delightful lady but also recoup the money you have lost.'

For a second there was a stunned silence and then

slowly Prince Yakovlev sat down and reached for the cards. If he lost Charlotte he had lost nothing. Meanwhile, he stood to win a great deal.

'My companion,' he said, and his smile was one of malicious pleasure. 'Your deal, I believe, Count Karolyi.'

CHAPTER SIX

CHARLOTTE felt as if she were drowning. The breath had frozen in her throat, her heart had ceased to beat. It could not be happening. She had misheard—misunderstood.

'Prince Yakovlev has staked his mistress to Karolyi!'

The shouts went from table to table. Winning hands of cards were put down uncaringly. The whirr of roulette wheels ceased. The whole attention of the room was centred on the two men facing each other across the green baize table. And on Charlotte, standing immobile at Prince Yakovlev's side, her hand to her throat, her eyes disbelieving.

The crowd around her jostled and pushed.

'Where's the girl?'

'Surely she was Princess Natalya's companion?'

'What the devil is Karolyi up to?'

Words, sentences, permeated her brain. She tried to turn and run but could not for the crowd that hemmed her in.

No longer did Sandor Karolyi seek to hold her eyes with his. His glossily dark head was bent intently over the cards in his hand, his face taut with concentration. The langour, the carelessness, was gone. He was a man playing for high stakes. Stakes he had no intention of losing.

No wonder that harsh mouth had held a suspicion of a smile as he had looked up at her. He had known all along what he intended to do. He had been savouring the moment of her humiliation—enjoying himself at her expense.

She felt sick and giddy and if it had not been for the press of bodies surrounding her, would have fallen.

Princess Natalya had been more accurate than she had known when she had referred to him as the Devil's spawn. Prince Victor triumphantly laid down two pairs. Count Karolyi topped them with a full house. Prince Yakovlev mopped his perspiring face with a handkerchief. Sandor remained unperturbed, his mouth quirking in a humourless smile as Prince Yakovlev's distress grew more apparent.

Too late Victor Yakovlev realised he was no match for a man of Sandor Karolyi's cold, calculated expertise. He laid down the last of his cards. Three aces and two kings. The atmosphere round the table was electric. Sandor surveyed the cards in his hand and then, very slowly, laid them down.

Four queens. The room erupted around Charlotte. There were male shouts of 'Bravo Karolyi!' and the popping of champagne corks. Prince Victor stumbled to his feet. He had entered the casino intent on a night of pleasure. He was leaving it a broken man. Dementedly, he pushed past Charlotte. He had publicly staked and lost her as if she were a chattel, and he did not spare her a cursory word.

Champagne exploded and fizzed. Glasses were lifted in toast to the victor. Slowly Sandor raised his eyes to Charlotte's, saw the burning shame and humiliation in her face and felt a knife twist and turn in his breast. There had been no other course of action open to him. By the morning she would have fled with her pittance and her pathetically few belongings. He would never have seen her again, never have known if she had accomplished the journey to England in safety. Now she would be in his care, hating and despising him.

He ignored the back-slapping, the champagne, the fortune lying on the green baize. He rose to his feet and faced Charlotte. She could smell the clean, starched linen of his evening shirt, the faint aroma of cologne.

'And now, Mademoiselle Grainger, I think it is time that we left the casino.'

The lines of her jaw were tense with the effort she made to appear calm. She would not give him the pleasure of seeing her distress.

'I think not, Count Karolyi,' she said, her voice trembling. 'The entertainment is over. Your winnings are on the table. Goodnight.'

She turned, tall and slender, heartbreakingly dignified.

His hand closed around her wrist. There could be no explanation. He could not say he had won her in order that he might take care of her. She would never believe him and besides, to make such a statement would be to say far more. That she aroused and inflamed him as no other woman he had met. That she brought out in him feelings of love and tenderness he had previously believed himself to be incapable of. He had alienated the one woman in the world who might have accepted him for what he was: illegal inheritor of the Karolyi wealth, bastard son of a Hungarian gypsy. His own actions had destroyed any such chance of happiness. Since the night on the terrace when he had treated her so insultingly, kissing her against her will, she had regarded him with nothing but contempt and distaste. He didn't blame her. He felt only contempt and distaste for himself.

'We will leave together, Mademoiselle.'

Her barely held self-control snapped. Her green-gilt eyes flashed with revulsion. 'The charade at the table was meaningless, Count Karolyi! I am no man's to be lost or won at the turn of a card!'

She was only inches away from him. The nearness of her sent his blood coursing through his veins.

'You are mistaken, Mademoiselle Grainger. I won you and I intend to keep you.'

Charlotte gasped and drew back her free hand to

deliver a stinging blow to his cheek. He caught her wrist in a steel-like grip.

'You are only adding to your entertainment value by such behaviour.'

Stunned she glanced around. In her fury and indignation she had forgotten the casino patrons who had surrounded the table with such interest and were now regarding the altercation between herself and Sandor with unconcealed delight.

'We will leave.' It was a command. Forcefully Sandor pushed his way through the throng around them, Charlotte in his wake, her wrist still tightly held in his strong grip.

'Just where do you think you are taking me, Count Karolyi?' she demanded in low, raging tones.

They had gained the ornate entrance hall. Their procession through the room had been watched with shocked expressions by ladies of title, by envious lechery on the part of their escorts, and with amusement by the ladies of the *demi-monde*.

'To Beausoleil,' he said curtly. 'Where else?'

'To my home,' she flashed, struggling to free herself from his grasp and failing.

He pivoted on his heel, seizing her shoulders so savagely that she cried out in pain. 'You have no home! Would you return to the Villa Ondine and a man who would lose you at cards without a backward glance?'

'No! Neither will I accompany a man who won me in such a manner!'

They glared at each other fiercely.

'You have no option, Mademoiselle.' There was a cruel edge to his voice that chilled her. The Karolyi white stallions had cantered to a halt outside the casino's blazing entrance. The carriage door was open.

'No!' Her protest lacked conviction. Where else could she go? Her fate was sealed. The Prince's treatment of her in the casino had branded her publicly as a lady of loose virtue. No one, now, would ever believe otherwise. Louise de Remy would help her, but only in securing her a rich lover. Justin de Valmy would help her, but only by making her his mistress.

The carriage door slammed shut. She was alone in the darkness with Sandor Karolyi. Despairingly she raised her hands to her eyes and began to weep.

He surveyed her with pain-filled eyes. He had had no wish to cause her distress but his action had made it inevitable. His mouth compressed in a hard line and the skin tautened across his cheekbones as her slender figure was wracked by sobs.

Gently he reached across and laid his hand comfortingly on her shoulder. She sprang away from his touch as if it had been fire, huddling in the corner of the carriage, staring at him with the huge, frightened eyes of a trapped doe.

Ice entered his heart. Had it come to this? That her anger had dissolved into fear of him?

'Your fate is not so bad as it would have been if I had not intervened,' he said, and his voice held an underlying throb that was far distant from the cruelty of his tones in the casino.

Charlotte willed herself to look away from him but could not. The darkness of the carriage had cast him into deep shadow but she could still see the blue sheen on the midnight-black hair and his eyes pinned her in place like live coals.

'You . . . shamed . . . me,' she whispered, wondering how it was that a man who could be so cruel one minute could emanate a sense of comfort and safety the next. His jaw tensed and small white lines framed his mouth.

'No one could shame you,' he said curtly.

She brushed the tears from her cheeks but they continued to flow. She should not be even condescending to speak to him. He had humiliated her, taken her captive.

Any kindness was nothing but a figment of her imagination.

He leaned towards her, and through the heavy silk of her skirt his knees brushed hers. Heat flooded her face and she was grateful for the concealing darkness.

'Charlotte.' His voice was deep and caressing. Panic welled up in her. How could she hold on to her rage, her fear, when he had only to change the tone of his voice for her to feel faint with longing?

He made no move to take advantage of the intimacy of the carriage. Instead, very slowly, he held his hand out to her, palm upward, his eyes never moving from her face.

The carriage lurched and swayed as the horses began to climb the hill to Beausoleil and Charlotte stared at him, mesmerised.

'I would not have willingly distressed you,' he said quietly.

Her heart pounded so that she could hardly breathe. She could no longer think clearly. She could see only his eyes, hear only his voice, gentle and coercing.

Hesitantly she inched her hand forward, slipping it tentatively into his. His fingers locked over hers tightly and she gave a gasp that he mistook for grief.

In one swift easy movement he was beside her and as his arms circled her shoulders she began to cry again, but for far different reasons than Sandor imagined.

His eyes darkened and he stroked the top of her head, marvelling at the thickness and softness of her hair. Perhaps, when Zara arrived, Charlotte would understand the reason for his actions. Zara. The love he felt for his sister and could never publicly show, tore at his heart. Wryly he reflected that if Monte Carlo society believed Charlotte was his mistress, it would make meetings with Zara far easier. And for once Monte Carlo society would be wrong. Charlotte would not be his mistress. She would never condescend to become so.

He had hurt her too deeply. Humiliated her beyond forgiveness.

He leaned his head back against the padded upholstery, his dark eyes bleak. His whole life was a lie. Povzervslay was Count Istvan Karolyi's true heir. His sister was believed to be the daughter of Prince and Princess Katzinsky and as wife of Lord Beston, she could do nothing more than exchange meaningless pleasantries with him when they met. His heart could be given to no woman, for no woman would accept him once she knew the truth. Or . . . His eyes rested broodingly on the woman in his arms. Only a very rare woman. A woman who would risk her life for a child, whose grief for an elderly lady was deep and genuine. A woman who spurned the easy option of becoming the mistress of a count or a prince, preferring to seek work even as a maid if it would enable her to retain her honour. A woman to whom he had brought nothing but unhappiness and distress.

The lights of Beausoleil gleamed between the pines. As the carriage halted Sandor released her, alighting in silence. When his hand took hers to assist her from the coach, Charlotte shuddered.

His touch flared through her like a flame. Her inner fight had been in vain. The tears glistening on her cheeks were tears of shame at the knowledge that she felt only relief that the man about to take her to his bed was not the loathsome Prince Yakovlev nor even the pleasant-faced Comte de Valmy. Shame at the passionate desire he aroused in her, at the fever that was possessing her, rising higher and hotter as he strode with her into the chandelier-lit entrance hall of Beausoleil.

Would he be forceful? Tender? Why was he not speaking to her? Not looking at her? A moment ago he had held her in his arms. Her head whirled and she felt sick with anticipation.

'Mademoiselle Grainger will be staying at Beausoleil

indefinitely,' he told the maid that hurried forward. 'See to it that a bath is drawn for her. She has had a tiring evening. Also, that the bed in the yellow room is aired.'

'Yes, Count Karolyi.' The maid bobbed and scurried away to give orders to the undermaid to fill the swan-shaped bath in the room adjoining the yellow boudoir.

A valet removed Count Karolyi's discarded gloves. A footman hastened forward with a silver tray bearing a glass of brandy.

'A drink for Mademoiselle Grainger, Georges. A lemonade I think. The evening is hot.'

'Yes sir. At once, sir.'

'Jeanne!'

Another maid hurried forward.

'From now on you will act as Mademoiselle Grainger's personal maid. Please see to it that she has everything she requires.'

His voice caught and deepened as he turned once more to Charlotte. 'I trust you will be comfortable, Mademoiselle. My goodnight.' He spun on his heel, knowing that if he stayed in her presence a moment longer he would be unable to control his raging desire for her.

She stared after him, uncertain and bewildered.

'This way, Mademoiselle.' The little maid indicated that Charlotte follow her. Numbly Charlotte moved forward. A small cap of lace perched delicately on the maid's neatly upswept hair. Her dress was black and of good material, expensively cut. Her wisp of an apron was lace-edged.

She led the way up a magnificent staircase that wound in a delicate curve. The room behind the door she opened was already being tended. A footman was lighting candles. A maid was turning down the sheets on the chiffon-draped and canopied bed.

'Your bath will soon be ready, Mademoiselle.'

Lemonade and biscuits were brought on a tray. No

curiosity was displayed by the maids or the footman. Perhaps Count Karolyi often brought home young ladies possessing neither bags nor baggage and installed them in his bedroom. She looked around her. The room bore no masculine overtones. There was no sign of Sandor's occupancy.

The undermaid entered from the adjoining bathroom, bobbed deferentially, and announced that a bath had now been drawn. Charlotte wondered what army of servants had carried jugs of hot water so quickly up the back stairs. Jeanne began to assist her with her dress and Charlotte stood uncomfortably. She had never had a personal maid before. It felt strange to be so waited on. To her relief she was left to enjoy the luxury of the fragrant scented bathwater in privacy.

What would she do when she emerged from the water? She had no nightdress. No négligé. Would Sandor be waiting for her in the satin-sheeted bed?

His face burned against her mind. She was his without reservation. Did he know it yet? What would be his reaction when she entered his arms of her own volition? Her body felt as if it were on fire, throbbing with an excitement she had never previously known.

Thick, soft towels were at her disposal. She wrapped herself in them and with her heart thudding in her throat, slowly entered the bedroom. The giant bed dominated the room. Candlelight cast soft shadows on the walls and the heavy velvet curtains. A nightdress and négligé were laid across the bed-foot. Soft silk slipped over her head and shoulders, rippled around her hips. She gazed at herself in the mirror. The candles behind her silhouetted her slender body, the soft roundness of her breasts, the gentle swell of her hips. Would he find her pleasing?

Her green-gold eyes held her reflection in the mirror. Was this really her, Charlotte Grainger? Was she really about to take as a lover a man who had barely bestowed one kind word on her? A man who had mocked her with his eyes? Gained amusement at her expense; humiliated her? Where was the Charlotte Grainger of a week ago? Was she really no better than the cocottes of the casino? Than Louise de Remy and her host of jewelled, perfumed friends? She did not know. She knew only that she had fought against her desire for him with every fibre of her being and that she had lost the battle. The Charlotte Grainger who had arrived in Monte Carlo six months ago had died with the Princess. Another Charlotte faced her in the mirror. A girl willing to risk everything to know fleeting happiness with a man who would possess her heart until it ceased to beat.

She crossed the room and climbed into bed. The sheets were cool to her fevered body, the room a warm glow in the soft light. Five minutes passed and then there came the sound of footsteps outside her door. She closed her eyes tightly, hardly daring to breathe as the door opened and he stepped into the room. He was walking towards the bed. She could sense his presence, smell the faint aroma of cologne. His shadow fell across her and she dug her nails deep into her palms and forced her eyelids open.

He stood looking down at her, his jacket discarded, his lace-frilled evening shirt slashed open at the throat revealing crisply curling dark hair. He seemed suddenly taller, more broad-shouldered than ever. She could see the ripple of strong muscles beneath the soft linen of his shirt, and was burningly aware of the leanness of his hips and the sleek fit of his trousers.

She lifted her eyes to his, her cheeks flaming at the indecency of her thoughts. The candlelight cast flickering shadows across the harsh planes of his face. His eyes were impenetrable. Dark lakes in which she could read nothing. The terrified excitement that had held her enthralled reached crescendo pitch. She longed for his touch. For the heat of his body next to hers. A small

pulse began to beat wildly at her throat. He was frowning slightly, turning away from her. Was he about to
leave her?

She gave a little inarticulate cry and stretched her
hand out, restraining him. He halted, staring down at
the trembling hand that covered his own. A muscle
twitched at the side of his jaw and then he groaned,
grasping her hand tightly in his, staring down at her with
an expression that rocked her heart.

So he had looked when he bathed her cheek, when he
had comforted her after Princess Natalya's death. So he
looked at her now as with the utmost delicacy his finger
softly traced the line of her forehead, down her nose to
her mouth.

Charlotte gasped, and as if it were the most natural
thing in the world, kissed the fingertip that rested on her
lips. Time hung suspended. She felt as if she were
drowning in the depths of his eyes and then he was on the
bed beside her and she was in his arms, her lips parting
willingly beneath the fierce onslaught of his. Delight
engulfed her as his strong hands moved down her body,
caressing her throat, her shoulders, releasing her breasts
from their light covering of silk.

She gave a soft, yielding moan and her fingers clutched convulsively at the thickness of his curls as with the
gentleness of absolute love his head moved down, kissing the hollow of her throat, the rose-pink nipples held
captive in his hands. She arched her body against the
hardness of his, the love she felt for him flooding through
her so that it seemed as if she would be consumed by it.

'Charlotte . . . Charlotte . . .' His voice was naked
with desire and longing as the weight of his body imprisoned her beneath him.

He had come into the room only to assure himself that
she was no longer distressed. The sight of her gold-red
hair cascading over the pillow in thick, undulating waves
and the tantalising outline of her slender body beneath

the silken sheets had held him enthralled. He had been capable of no other movement than to go forward. Standing by the bed, looking down at her, he had been stunned by her beauty, by the intensity of the emotions she awoke in him. Nevertheless, he had been determined to do nothing other than wish her goodnight. Until her hand had covered his with the light touch of a butterfly and his iron self-control had melted as if in a furnace.

His mouth was once more upon hers, the fever possessing him rising higher and hotter and then he heard her cry out, not in pain but in capitulation, and he halted, struggling for control. To possess her now would be madness. Their whole future would be tarnished by the knowledge that he had brought her to Beausoleil against her will.

Was that why she was responding to him with such sweet abandon? Because his behaviour had led her to believe that she had no choice?

Exercising almost superhuman control he hauled himself away from her, his eyes burning like live coals.

'Goodnight,' his voice was a harsh rasp over the beating of his heart. He could not see the bewilderment on her face for the red haze that clouded his vision. He had to be free of her. To stay a moment longer would be to succumb utterly.

With the blood pounding in his ears his hand wrenched at the smoked-glass knob of the door. For a terrible second he hesitated and then the door rocked on its hinges as he slammed it shut and strode, dark-visaged, down the corridor.

Charlotte knelt in the centre of the rumpled bed, her hair cascading around her shoulders, staring after him in disbelief. 'Sandor . . .' It was a tremulous plea that carried no further than the room.

She remained in motionless disarray and then the enormity of what had taken place overcame her. Shame descended like a tidal wave. She had behaved like a trollop. A *putain*. What would he think of her? How would she ever summon the courage to face him again?

Desolation swept over her and her cheeks were still wet with tears as the night sky imperceptibly lightened to presage dawn.

Downstairs Sandor sat in a high-winged leather chair and stared unseeingly into the flames of a log fire. Not until tomorrow would he know if she had responded to him out of love or fear, or if her response had been nothing but a figment of his fevered imagination, brought about by his overpowering desire for her.

And if it had? He passed a hand across his eyes. He would tell her that Lady Beston was desirous of having her as a companion. That no further amorous advances would be made to her under Beausoleil's roof. To kiss her again would be madness.

He swirled the brandy around in the glass and drank deeply. If she did not want him the sooner she left for England with Zara the better. She had destroyed his desire for all other female companionship, even that of Sarah. Wearily he rose to his feet and made his way to his vast, opulent and lonely room. It occurred to him that he had walked out of the casino leaving a fortune on the card table. No doubt François would have safely retrieved it. He was uncaring. He cared only for Charlotte. Restlessly he threw himself on his bed, tossing and turning, longing for the dawn, yet dreading it in case it brought disillusionment in its wake.

The next morning Charlotte awoke in a sunlit room, wondering where she was. Then memory came flooding back and her cheeks scorched. In nervous haste she sprang from the bed and dressed herself with trembling fingers. As she was pinning her hair there was a knock at the door and Jeanne entered with a tray bearing a cup of hot chocolate.

'Oh, I am sorry Mademoiselle. I had not expected you to rise so early. You should have rung for me . . .'

'It is all right, Jeanne,' Charlotte struggled to keep her voice steady, 'I am accustomed to dressing myself.'

'But Count Karolyi expressly wished that I . . .'

At the sound of his name Charlotte felt a pain like that of a knife between her shoulder blades.

'Where is Count Karolyi?' she asked stiffly.

There was a curious throb in the voice of the gentle-faced English girl. Jeanne was confused. What had her master done to enrage her so?

'He is in the breakfast-room, Mademoiselle. He . . .'

'Thank you, Jeanne.'

Forcing herself to move, she walked swiftly past the startled maid and along the corridor. She had disgraced herself once but she would not do so again. Her heart hammered painfully as she descended the stairs.

A footman hurried forward and she said with all the dignity she could summon, 'Count Karolyi, if you please.'

'Yes, Mademoiselle. This way, Mademoiselle.'

Charlotte followed him, her head high, determined not to stay a second longer than was necessary beneath Count Karolyi's roof.

Charlotte entered the room bravely, but the sight of him sitting in careless negligence almost robbed her of her good intentions.

He had obviously been riding. He was wearing a Russian-styled high-necked silk shirt that emphasised the Slavic lines of his face, and his riding breeches were tucked into glossy black knee-high boots. A whip had been tossed carelessly onto a nearby chair and he was at breakfast. He was cutting himself a slice of cheese and he paused as she entered, balancing the cheese on the edge of his knife. She stared at the sharp blade, noticing how long his fingers were, how well shaped.

She clenched her nails into her palm. She must not

think of his hands, his body. She had to forget her madness of the previous evening and make quite sure that he did not believe she had been acquiescent and willing.

'Count Karolyi, I insist on an apology for your behaviour last night.' Her voice was trembling. What if he cruelly pointed out to her that it had been her own hand that had detained him? She held on to the back of a chair for support as their eyes held and Sandor's brows drew together in a deep frown. The desperate hope that he had nursed throughout the night died. She had not come to him this morning with eyes shining with love. He could not clasp her in his arms and kiss her and tell her that he loved her more than he had ever dreamed he could love anyone or anything in the world. She had come to him demanding an apology. Any willingness on her part the previous night had been occasioned only by fear. With great difficulty he controlled his voice.

'Please be seated,' he said, rising from the table, and pulling back a gilt and monogrammed chair.

'No. I demand an apology. I . . .' She dared not look at him for the shame she felt. Surely he knew how willing she had been? How eager?

Sandor dismissed the footman and maid and fought the disappointment that was crushing him. His dream had been fragile enough and he had been a fool to think that it could withstand the light of day.

'Please be seated,' he repeated, cold with terror at the thought that she might leave Beausoleil, that he might lose her forever.

Hating herself for her weakness, Charlotte obediently sat.

'You appear to be distressed.' He was pouring a cup of coffee for her.

'Distressed?' Charlotte stared at him incredulously. 'Distressed? You barter for me as if in a funfair, take . . .

take indecent advantage of me and then accuse me of being distressed?'

'Excuse me,' he said, the underlying throb in his voice barely controlled. 'But *I* did not barter. The bartering, if that is the correct word, was made by your escort.'

Sparks flared in her eyes. 'You were party to my humiliation!'

Their eyes met across the breakfast table. She knew that he knew of the hideous little supper room, of the champagne, the divan. She fought to hold on to her anger but was aware of nothing but his nearness.

'Nevertheless, I demand an apology.' Her voice was low and he knew that it was not the cards and spectators and the bright lights of the Devil's Palace that she was referring to.

Time spun out in a long moment, and then he said, his voice rich and dark, 'I give it, Charlotte. Freely.' A bitter smile twisted his mouth. 'Perhaps you would listen to one or two suggestions I have for your future safety.'

Her safety? What did Sandor Karolyi care for her safety? Mistrustfully she stared at him.

'If you will consent to stay at Beausoleil for the next few days I can promise you a safe and escorted return to England.'

Her eyes widened in disbelief. 'As your mistress?' she flared indignantly. 'I could have returned as such with the Comte de Valmy!'

His hand shot out, lean and strong, encircling her wrist. 'Not as a mistress, Charlotte.'

The warmth of his touch spread through her. She could not move. She could think of nothing but the feel of his flesh against hers.

'A friend of mine, Lady Beston, is arriving in Monte Carlo within days. She is in need of a companion and I know that you will suit her admirably.'

She fought to think clearly, to take in what he

was saying. His eyes were fiercely intent, unmistakably sincere.

'And until Lady Beston arrives? What will be required of me?' she asked tremulously.

'Not what you fear.' She did not hear the bitterness in his voice. 'There will be no repetition of last night. I shall require your company when I visit the casino. When I visit friends. That is all.'

He did not want her. She had known so all along. Last night had been a mere diversion for him. Her throat felt so tight it made speech almost impossible. 'For me to do so would be to cause speculation,' she said with difficulty. 'It would be believed that I was your . . . that I was your . . .' She could not say the word. 'Lady Beston would not want a young woman with a marred reputation as a companion.'

He said with a crooked smile, 'Have no fears on that score, Charlotte. Your reputation in Monte Carlo is already tarnished. I shall assure Lady Beston that it is so undeservedly. You will find Lady Beston both kind and understanding.'

The table was so small, they were sitting so close to one another, that she could see the tiny flecks of gold near the pupils of his dark eyes. He did not want her for a mistress. He was merely being kind, as he said Lady Beston was kind. She faced him, knowing that she was incapable of walking away from him. That as long as there was the slightest excuse of staying with him, she would stay.

'Thank you, Count Karolyi. I shall stay at Beausoleil under those terms until Lady Beston arrives,' she said stiffly, fighting her pain.

With intense restraint Sandor merely nodded and rang for fresh coffee.

Sunlight flooded the tiny room. French windows led out on to a small, flower-massed terrace. Jasmine wound itself insidiously around the doors so that it was difficult to discern where the room ended and the terrace began.

The maid entered with coffee. It was hot and strong and the coffee cup was of wafer-thin china.

'A croissant?' he asked.

'Thank you.'

He moved the plate in her direction. She reached out a hand and their eyes met. For a heart-stopping moment Charlotte thought she saw desire in the coal-dark depths and then it was chased away and she lowered her eyes, believing herself to be mistaken.

He did not want her for a mistress. He wanted her only to act the part of one. In doing so she would be in his company. She would be able to feast her eyes on him. Talk to him. And she would be spared the lecherous advances of Prince Yakovlev.

She strove to calm her inner tumult. Why had he made such an unusual request? Was it because he did not want another emotional entanglement after the tragic ending of his last love *affaire*? By being seen as his mistress, she would serve to protect him from the attentions of cocottes and ladies of fashion. The ladies of the *demi-monde* would envy her and no one, least of all Count Karolyi, would know of her heartbreak.

His voice broke in on her thoughts, sending her pulses pounding. 'No doubt Jeanne will have already seen to it that a wardrobe has been prepared for you.'

Dark curls tumbled low over his brow. His hand reached out for the butter, strong and olive-toned. She longed to cover it with her own. To feel once again the touch of his flesh beneath hers. She lay down her croissant and clasped her hands lightly in her lap.

'The dresses will be adequate but not entirely suitable. There is a dressmaker in the rue Grimaldi I have heard spoken of very highly. And a milliner. I suggest we pay a visit there this morning. Then perhaps you would accompany me when I pay a call on Mademoiselle

Bernhardt, and I believe I am expected at the Palace for tea. François!'

The secretary entered the room.

'Is it today Prince Charles requires my presence?'

'Yes, sir.'

'Thank you, François. That is all.'

The secretary left the breakfast-room and wondered if perhaps the Karolyi household was about to acquire a new and most unexpected mistress.

Charlotte stared at him. Accompany him on a visit to one of his mistresses? To the palace?

'But will Mademoiselle Bernhardt not object to my presence?'

His brows flew upwards. 'Of course not. Sarah has formed a great affection for you. Drama is her life, both on stage and off. Your action in the Boulevard des Moulins was one that could not fail to enthrall her.'

Her coffee cup was empty. Only crumbs remained on her plate. He rose to his feet and pulled back her chair. 'First of all the dressmaker's and then the milliner's.'

He held out his arm. She felt her cheeks flush. Always before she had seen only the suffering, the impatience in the lines of his mouth. Now she saw the inherent charm. The sensitivity as well as the sensuality.

A Victoria hitched to a pair of perfectly matched grays was waiting on the sun-warmed gravel. Dressed still in her simple gown of lavender, she felt like a princess as Sandor personally assisted her into the carriage. He seated himself where his eyes could rest on her with ease and, aware of his glance, she ostensibly studied the beauty of Beausoleil's garden and the magical view of Monte Carlo below them, its high plateau jutting out into the amethyst blue sea.

She hoped that Lady Beston's arrival in Monte Carlo would be delayed. Old ladies were notoriously unreliable as to their movements. She also hoped that Sandor had not been optimistic in assuming that Lady Beston

would be uncaring of her future companion's reputation. Certainly Princess Natalya would have been uncaring if a man like Sandor had explained the situation and
the truth. But an elderly English lady? She would have
to wait and see and trust in Sandor's judgment.

Sandor studied her face and then, aware of the discomfort he was arousing, lowered his eyes to her hands.
They were folded on her lap, long and narrow with
beautiful almond-shaped nails. A feeling of peace swept
over him. Her presence soothed him, chasing away the
habitual darkness of his thoughts. But only for a little
time. Only until Zara came. Then he would have to
forfeit the sight and presence of Charlotte Grainger and
content himself with the perfumed ladies of the town and
the acquiescent married ladies of society.

'Ah, Monsieur le Comte!' The little French dressmaker hurried towards him welcomingly. 'Of what
service can I be? A day dress for Mademoiselle? An
evening gown?'

'Both, and in profusion,' Sandor said, sitting himself
at ease as the dressmaker's minions hurried to Charlotte's side. 'I shall want gowns ready within days,
Madame.'

'Of course, Monsieur le Comte.' She was beaming,
holding her hand out to Charlotte, leading her away
from Sandor and into a room stacked high with silks and
satins and velvets. Her measurements were taken. Roll
after roll of cloth was unfurled so that her head swam,
and then came the gowns already made.

A pale blue creation, low cut, with a little lace on the
corsage and a posy of flowers at the waist. Charlotte
stared at herself in the long mirror and gasped. Never
before had she worn anything so *décolleté*.

'We will see if it meets with the Comte's approval,' the
little dressmaker said, her eyes sparkling.

Before Charlotte could protest, she was ushered into
the outer room with its expensive oak panelling and

leather chairs where Sandor waited. The curve of Charlotte's breasts glowed, her waist was minuscule. Desire leapt through him and he suppressed it with iron self-control. To allow his feelings to show would be to frighten her away. His look of approval was cool. He nodded.

Charlotte was hurried once more into the rear room with its walls of mirrors. The pale blue creation was removed. A long-sleeved dress of pink Venetian velvet replaced it.

Again Sandor nodded approval.

The Venetian velvet was followed by a white muslin dress that made the breath catch in his throat. The muslin was followed by a pastel linen day dress with full elbow sleeves and a becomingly low neck; then by a dinner gown of cream-coloured chiffon, puffs of tulle framing her shoulders; then a classically severe white velvet dress embroidered with pearls; a green taffeta dress that exactly matched the colour of her eyes.

Suits with narrow fitted bodices, elegantly frogged, and skirts so tight at the ankle it seemed to Charlotte she would never be able to walk in them, were ordered in profusion. And then evening cloaks. Soft white wool, black sable-edged silver fox, an ermine cape that reached to her ankles, chinchilla, swansdown. Her head whirled.

'Mademoiselle Grainger will wear the day dress – the pastel linen. The rest will be sent to Beausoleil.'

'Yes, Monsieur le Comte. It has been a pleasure to do business with you,' the little dressmaker said truthfully.

The discarded lavender gown was about to be disposed of. Impulsively Charlotte stretched out a restraining hand. 'No. I would like to keep that gown, if you please, Madame.'

Madame was too polite to show surprise. She merely smiled graciously and ordered that the simple lavender gown Mademoiselle had entered the salon in, should be wrapped with her own creations and delivered to Beausoleil.

Charlotte turned apologetically to Sandor. 'It was given to me by the Princess. It is all I have left of her gifts to me.'

His pulse throbbed in his throat and he glanced quickly away from her. What other woman would have made such a gesture after being showered with a multitude of new gowns?

Charlotte's heart sank. She had displeased him but she had had no alternative. In silence they journeyed by carriage from Madame Rambert's to the milliner's. Hats laden with flowers were set on her copper curls, approved by Sandor, wrapped in tissue, and placed in lavish hat boxes. Little nonsenses of velvet and feathers followed suit. A small hat fastened by a chenille dotted veil was so exquisite that Charlotte could hardly bear to remove it.

Tentatively she protested at Sandor's extravagance and his brows flew together. Instead of curtailing his expenditure he took her into Monte Carlo's finest jeweller and purchased a rope of pearls, a bracelet of diamonds, a necklace of sapphires, a collar of emeralds.

Seeing her with the emeralds clasped around her throat he paused, his profile grim. The sumptuous stones reflecting the sparkle in her eyes were no match for her beauty. Charlotte had no need of jewels. The simple flowers she habitually wore in her hair were adornment enough. The pearls, the diamond bracelet and the sapphire necklace were purchased; the emeralds returned. The other jewels he had intended lavishing on her were left on their beds of velvet.

As they returned to the carriage he said with a curtness that concealed his true emotions, 'Please try on the pearls with the gown you are wearing.'

With unsteady hands Charlotte looped the single, perfect rope of pearls over her head.

He nodded. The pearls were far more suitable than the emeralds could ever have been.

Charlotte felt a sudden onrush of anxiety. Why had he become so withdrawn from her? Why had he been so curt when she protested at his extravagance? Was it because the gowns, hats and jewels were not for her alone but for those who would take her place?

She blinked back hot tears, and asked in the soft, husky voice that so entranced him,

'Are we going back to Beausoleil now, Count Karolyi?'

'No. We are going to pay a visit to Mademoiselle Bernhardt and you are not to refer to me as "Count Karolyi" but as "Sandor".'

'Yes, Count . . . Yes, Sandor.'

His face was no longer grim. Tentatively she fingered the pearls. 'What will Prince Yakovlev say?'

'And Lady Pethelbridge.' Sandor's mouth curved in a smile. 'And the Countess of Bexhall and Princess Helene?'

Their eyes met and incredibly Charlotte felt laughter well up inside her.

'They will be shocked,' she said, stifling a giggle.

'Outraged.' His eyes danced with devilish amusement.

Suddenly it was too much. Simultaneously they burst into laughter at the thought of the sensation they would create on entering the casino, arm in arm.

The coachman's eyes widened. In ten years in Count Karolyi's service he had never heard the Count laugh so light-heartedly. Whoever the English girl was, she was accomplishing what the royal ladies of Europe had failed to do—chase away the almost palpable burden that lay on Count Karolyi's shoulders.

'Mademoiselle Bernhardt is expecting you, Count

Karolyi,' the hotel manager said, keeping his eyes politely from Charlotte.

They were led by a liveried bellboy along sumptuously carpeted corridors to the wing Sarah had commandeered for her visit. At the bellboy's knock Sarah's voice announced that they might enter with all the seductiveness of a woman about to greet her lover.

Charlotte's unease deepened. What was Sandor doing? As they entered the room and Sarah saw Charlotte, her face lit up with delight.

'My dear Charlotte! What a lovely surprise! How sweet of Sandor to bring you.' Her eyes were mischievous. 'Especially when he was so reluctant for you to enjoy the Comte de Valmy's companionship.'

In that moment Charlotte knew that whatever the relationship was between Sandor and Sarah, it was not that of lover and mistress. Or at least, if it ever had been, it was so no longer. It was only that of two people who liked each other and enjoyed each other's companionship. The lazy seductiveness in Sarah's voice would have been there if she had been merely asking the bellboy for a glass of champagne.

She did not rise to meet them. She lay back on her *chaise longue*, dressed in a long, white, trailing dress, magnificently embroidered and beaded, an enormous wolfhound at her feet.

'My darlings. Do sit down and have some champagne. I've been up all night sculpting a bust of Charlotte and it is absolutely exquisite, but no, Sandor, you *cannot* see it yet. It is not finished.'

The apartment was heavily sprayed with verbena. It was the most crowded, chaotic room that Charlotte had ever been in in her life.

There were easels with dozens of half-finished paintings. There were busts in the rough. There was a covered outline of a head and shoulders that Charlotte could only imagine was the sculpture of herself. There were palettes of paint, clay, all the accoutrements of an artist. In the far corner a skeleton stood as proper and as naturally as a footman. Through an open door beside a chiffon-tented bed, a pink quilted coffin lay open as if ready for instant occupation. There were daintily fashioned chairs, satin couches, vases big as sentry boxes, and towering plants. Manuscripts littered tables, scattered the floor. It was beyond imagination that the room was permanently furnished in such a fashion. Obviously Sarah carried not only clothes and jewels, but also her personal furnishings when she travelled.

Charlotte felt her eyes return again and again to the coffin in the bedroom. Sarah saw the expression in her eyes and laughed throatily.

'A necessity I take everywhere, Charlotte. It is inscribed with my initials and my motto "*Quand même*".'

'And the skeleton?' Charlotte asked, round-eyed.

'My oldest friend. An artist must know about bones and the human body and I am an artist in paint as well as an artist on stage.' Her eyes took on a wide, dreaming expression. 'Monsieur Bertora has asked me to perform in the Casino Theatre. Shall I be Sainte Thérèse in *La Vierge d'Avila* or the Duc in *l'Aiglain*?'

'Whatever you do will be breathtaking,' Sandor said with sincerity.

'But of course.' Sarah's slender shoulders shrugged and she laughed. The wolfhound crossed the room to Sandor to be patted and to lie contentedly at his feet.

Sarah sipped her champagne. 'I have a delightful surprise for you, my little Charlotte. I am expecting another guest very soon. A guest I think you will like to meet very much.'

Charlotte smiled. 'I do not know anyone in Monte Carlo, Mademoiselle Bernhardt.'

'Sarah,' Sarah said, with a wave of her hand. 'Always Sarah, my little Charlotte. However, I think that I must warn you that my guest has a weakness for beautiful women and so, Sandor, you must take great care of Charlotte . . .' Her cat-like eyes teased him '. . . or you may very well lose her.'

Charlotte felt a pang. Even Sarah believed that she was Sandor's mistress.

There was a knock at the door and they all three rose. As they did so Charlotte's skirts brushed against Sandor. He could smell the fragrance of her hair, her skin. Her nearness was a physical pain. Desire washed over him, increasing the heat of his body and pounding in his temples. For an insane moment he was tempted to abandon good sense and do everything in his power to overcome her aversion to him. The moment passed. If he handed the Karolyi estates to Povzverslay's son, he would be nameless and penniless. He could offer her nothing but a future holding perhaps shame and disgrace.

The door opened and a powerfully built, broad-shouldered man with an expansive face and a short, fair beard entered. His bearing was one of supreme ease and the cut of his navy blue serge suit was faultless. A rich silk handkerchief protruded slightly from one pocket of his jacket. He carried a gold-knobbed malacca cane under one arm. The pale grey fedora which he doffed had been worn rakishly a little to the side of his head. The gloves he dispensed with were yellow suede sewn with fine black stitches. Prominent blue-grey eyes under heavy lids surveyed first Sarah and then rested appreciatively on Charlotte.

'Your Royal Highness, may I present Miss Charlotte Grainger,' Sarah said, in her silken voice and, hardly able to believe what was happening to her, Charlotte dropped gracefully into a deep curtsey before her future sovereign.

CHAPTER
SEVEN

'I AM honoured, Miss Grainger,' the Prince said in a deep bass voice. 'I have heard of your bravery and applaud it.'

Charlotte felt hot colour flood her cheeks. Had he also heard of the exhibition that had taken place only hours ago in the Salle Mauresque? Her heart was beating so fast and light she could hardly breathe. He could not have: otherwise he would not have treated her so.

'You are a fortunate man, Karolyi.' The barely disguised amusement in the deep voice shattered her hopes.

The Prince *did* know of the circumstances that had occasioned her to be Count Sandor Karolyi's companion, and was uncaring.

Her chin lifted imperceptibly. No doubt the whole of Monte Carlo was now very well aware that Miss Charlotte Grainger, erstwhile companion to Princess Yakovleva, was now little more than a cocotte, lost like a chattel at a hand of cards.

Sandor, seeing the flash in her eyes and the proud uplifting of her head felt his heart twist with the tenderness and the protectiveness that he could not show. In her innocence she had expected to be shunned by society, not taken up by it. She had still a lot to learn about the ways of the world, and especially about the ways of Monte Carlo.

Aware of his gaze, Charlotte began to tremble and was furiously angry at herself. Because of his behaviour she was being introduced everywhere as if she were his mistress. Even her future king believed her to be a lady of loose virtue. Their eyes met, hers no longer full of laughter but stormy with indignation, his dark with the torment he could no longer hide. Once trapped by his gaze she could not free herself.

Why did he look at her in such a way? Why did he want her company and no more? Why was he so careless of what people thought? The little dressmaker had believed that she was his mistress and he had not enlightened her. And now Sarah did, as did the Prince of Wales. She craved an answer and received none. The Prince was speaking again; Sarah was laughing enchantingly. Sandor was obliged to return his attention to the Prince.

'We should be delighted to join your party this evening, Your Royal Highness.'

'Good, good. Your play at the table should liven up the evening enormously.' He chuckled appreciatively as he seated himself at Sarah's side. 'Devil take it, but I wish I'd been there when you trounced Yakovlev. What did the cur do? Slink out of the casino with his tail between his legs?'

'No!' Sarah sprang exuberantly to her feet. 'He stormed out, so—' She stalked across the room, every line of her body a parody of Prince Yakovlev.

The Prince of Wales slapped his thigh and laughed so uproariously that he had to mop his eyes with his oversize silk handkerchief. Charlotte watched aghast. It had not occurred to her that Sarah had been a witness to her humiliation. Why hadn't she spoken out in protest? Unable to help herself, her eyes slid past Sarah and rested on Sandor.

She had her answer. It would not have occurred to Sarah that any woman would not desire to be won by such a man. Or, having been won, would not be ecstatically happy. But Sarah did not know the other side of Sandor Karolyi. The complex, brooding side of his personality that was so different from the abrasive charm he exercised in public.

Sarah flung her head high, her posture changing, no longer Prince Yakovlev but herself. 'Champagne,' she commanded in her lovely silken voice. 'Champagne to celebrate Sandor's gallantry.'

For a heart-stopping second Charlotte wondered if Sarah knew the truth. That Sandor had won her at cards in order only to offer her his protection. That his action had been prompted by kindness and not desire.

Sarah sat gracefully on the sofa beside the Prince, reclining languidly in a cloud of lace, her features a vision of perfection under a shower of sun-gold hair. Her eyes as they met Charlotte's held a wicked gleam. No, Sarah had not guessed the truth. Her idea of gallantry was that Sandor should have won her publicly as his *cherie amour*.

Gracefully Sarah tugged the bell-pull. Two footmen dressed in royal livery entered. The first carried a bottle of champagne already chilling and two glasses. The second a bottle of Dewar's Black Ball whisky and Appolinaris water. As the champagne was poured into the first glass a faint frown furrowed Charlotte's brow. She did not dislike champagne but neither was she accustomed to it, especially so early in the day. A footman prepared to pour champagne into the second glass.

'Lemonade, if you please,' a rich-timbred voice said easily. The footman nodded, replaced the champagne in the silver bucket of crushed ice and returned speedily with a sparkling glass of chilled lemonade.

Charlotte took the glass and, despite her better intentions, glanced gratefully across at Sandor. He was watching her as she knew he would be. Since they had entered the room his gaze had rarely left her. The unfathomable expression that had been in his eyes and that had so disconcerted her was now absent. He looked merely amused. Incredibly, as she raised the glass to her lips, she felt a smile tug at the corners of her mouth. The answering smile that played about his lips sent her blood racing and she hastily looked away. The Prince of Wales was addressing her, his manner indulgent.

'I understand that you are the talk of Monte Carlo, Miss Grainger.'

It was meant as a compliment, and it had come from the man who would one day be her king. Charlotte held his gaze firmly and said with barely a tremor in her voice,

'No doubt that is true, Your Royal Highness. However, I sincerely wish it were not, and I take no pleasure in the fact.'

There was a hair's breadth of stunned silence and then Edward's eyes began to gleam and a low chuckle started deep in his chest, erupting in jovial laughter. 'God's truth, Miss Grainger. I'm not surprised Yakovlev took your loss so hard.'

'I was not Prince Yakovlev's to lose, Your Royal Highness,' Charlotte said with dignity.

The rumbling laughter ceased. Charlotte's heart hammered as protruding blue-grey eyes held hers intently.

After what seemed an eternity, the Prince nodded his head as if satisfied. 'I believe you, Miss Grainger. You are a young lady of rare quality. However, I hope whatever misunderstanding you have had to endure does not mean you will be abandoning Monte Carlo before we have been able to enjoy your company.'

Relief flooded through Charlotte. 'No, Your Royal Highness, I am remaining in Monte Carlo until Lord and Lady Beston arrive.'

Royal brows moved upwards.

'I anticipate becoming Lady Beston's companion on her journey back to England.'

'Do you, indeed? Then we can only envy the lucky Lady Beston,' Edward said, humour returning to his voice.

A royal footman entered again, this time with a silver

tray bearing a plate of Beluga caviar and plovers' eggs which the Prince proceeded to eat with relish as the conversation turned to people and places Charlotte was unacquainted with.

Mr William C. Vanderbilt and the merits of his new yacht; Mr Frederick Johnstone, in whose villa, it appeared, the king was residing; the Emperor Franz Josef and the pleasures of hunting in Hungarian forests as opposed to the Scottish Highlands.

The Prince was adamant that shooting among heather and bracken was preferable and Sandor remained un-moved in his opinion that it was a poor substitute for the kind of sport available on his own vast estate. The matter was settled amicably with Edward inviting himself to Valeni in the autumn.

Valeni. Was that the name of Sandor Karolyi's home? Curiosity engulfed her. The expression in his voice when he had spoken of it had been one almost of reverence. Charlotte regarded him curiously while his attention was taken by the Prince. He had never mentioned Valeni to her. She had never thought of him as a man with a home and roots. Yet obviously Valeni was where his heart was. How much more was there about him that she did not know? Why, despite his wealth and devastating good looks and the numerous people constantly surrounding him, did he remain so unutterably alone?

Sandor was rising to his feet. Their visit was at an end.

'Until this evening, Miss Grainger,' the Prince said, taking her hand and brushing it with his lips, his gruff voice full of kindness.

'Yes, Your Royal Highness.' Charlotte dropped a curtsey and then, feeling that in the most unlikely of places she had made a true friend, she smiled.

The Prince chuckled, heartily regretted her obvious virtue and, as the door closed behind her, returned his full attention to the delightful Sarah.

*   *   *

'Was the Prince of Wales as you had expected him to be?' Sandor asked as he handed her into the carriage.

Charlotte kept her eyes lowered for a few moments, unnecessarily busy adjusting her skirts. His touch had scorched her skin. When she raised her head and answered, her feelings were once again under tight control.

'No,' she replied truthfully. 'But I liked him exceedingly.'

Sandor laughed and for a moment Charlotte wondered if she had been wrong in judging him to be a man carrying a crushing burden. His thick black hair tumbled low over his brows. His amber eyes were good humoured. He looked for a brief second of time like a man without a care in the world. And then his eyes travelled to her lips and his laughter faded. She turned her head away swiftly, aware that with only one look her whole body responded to him in a way that was shameless.

Silence stretched between them, painful in its intensity. A gentleman, riding as *escort d'honneur* beside the self-driven phaeton of a pretty Parisienne, bent his head in their direction and exchanged a word of greeting with Sandor. As their victoria sped along the palm-fringed boulevard a lady approached them riding a white stallion side-saddle and Charlotte saw that the lady who had so daringly dispensed with her carriage was Louise de Remy. Her jacket was scarlet, lavishly trimmed with gold, her riding skirt was sky blue and a little Louis XV tricorn hat with black ostrich feathers was worn at a jaunty angle on top of her golden curls. The grand duke rode at her side, nodding cursorily as Louise blew a kiss in Charlotte's direction.

'You are acquainted with more people than I was aware of,' Sandor remarked dryly as their carriage bowled past Louise and her companion.

'Mademoiselle de Remy has shown me great kindness.' Charlotte's voice was stiff. She had no intention of apologising for her friendship with Louise.

'Then you are quite right in acknowledging her in public.'

She looked at him uncertainly, but there was no sign of mockery on his lean, handsome face. In the bright sunlight, tilburys and cabriolets rattled past them but she was unaware of them and their occupants.

His nearness overwhelmed her. He was behaving to all outward appearances as if he were her lover. The very thought made her feel weak and light-headed. She remembered the burning glance he had given her on the darkened terrace seconds before he had kissed her, and her hands tightened in her lap. She must not continue to remember it. She must forget it as he had done. He wished for her to act the part of companion. Nothing more.

'We will lunch at Beausoleil before visiting Prince Charles,' Sandor said as the sea was left behind and the carriage headed inland towards Beausoleil.

Charlotte stared at him with incredulity. He could not possibly be proposing that she join him for tea at the Grimaldi Palace. Even Princess Yakovleva had not been afforded that honour.

'Surely it would be improper for me to accompany you?' she protested.

A dark brow quirked queryingly.

'I have not been invited,' she pointed out with charming simplicity.

Sandor waved her objection aside. 'That is of no moment,' he said with easy confidence. 'Prince Charles will be delighted with your company. He is an old man and receives few visitors.'

A deep inner warmth suffused her. His self-assurance was contagious. If Sandor said Prince Charles would be delighted with her company then she believed it.

'Sadly Prince Charles is blind and the scent of flowers

does not agree with him, so wear no posies or perfume on our visit.'

Charlotte was horrified. 'But that is terrible! To be averse to flowers in Monte Carlo, where there are flowers everywhere!'

'He spends very little time in Monte Carlo,' Sandor said, his voice softening at her concern for an elderly man she had not yet met. 'He lives mainly in his mountain retreat. The Grimaldi Palace is generally inhabited only by his son, Prince Albert.'

Charlotte's tender heart ached for the afflicted ruler of Monaco. 'How said to have such a beautiful home and be forced to spend so much time away from it.' She paused, thinking of the home Sandor so obviously loved. Of Valeni, deep in the Hungarian forests. It was a beautiful name. Was it a beautiful house? Was there a lake with swans floating serenely on dark-green water? Did geese fly overhead on their migration south? Were there horses to ride, sleek and sure-footed? And dogs waiting patiently for their master's return?

'Tell me about Valeni,' she said shyly.

Sandor stared at her. He never spoke about Valeni with anyone but Zara but suddenly the temptation to confide in the quietly listening girl before him was almost more than he could bear.

He wanted to tell her of how Valeni meadows were thick with wild flowers in the spring. How wild boar made their home in the forest. He wanted to tell her of the beauty; the solitude; the peace that engulfed him whenever he was on Valeni land. And he wanted to tell her that he was legally entitled to none of it.

The breath caught in his throat. Only to the woman he married would he disclose that terrible truth. Only then would he share his burden. Yet still the urge persisted. He shook his head violently as if to clear it. He was going mad. The idea was preposterous.

Sea-green eyes met his, thick-lashed, honest and

trusting. The loveliness of her face was breathtaking in its purity. Charlotte's love, once given, would not depend on her suitor's wealth or title. It would be unconditional. A constant strength: a haven and a refuge. And it would be given to a man other than himself—a man who had never taken advantage of her. Never shamed her.

His gold-flecked eyes hardened. For a pulsebeat of time he had thought the impossible was possible. Common sense reasserted itself. Monte Carlo was far behind them. They were passing orange and lemon groves. Between the trees Beausoleil's white walls gleamed vividly.

'Valeni is my home.' he said, and shrugged his shoulders dismissively, his voice betraying none of his inner tumult.

Charlotte returned her attention to her clasped hands as the carriage bowled through Beausoleil's magnificent gateway. Had there been a rebuff in his voice? Had she offended him by her question?

The carriage halted. He alighted and held out his hand for her. She took it, acutely aware of the warmth of his grasp, of the sense of power under restraint emanating from his tall, broad-shouldered figure. All too soon his hand released hers and they were walking into Beausoleil. Georges greeted them at the door with a broad smile.

'Lunch is served, sir.'

'Thank you, Georges.'

Through an open doorway Charlotte could see a table laid with white napery, silver and cut glass. Lobster rested on a bed of salad. Champagne was chilling.

A maid relieved her of her gloves and parasol and she was aware that her new dress and long rope of pearls was being much admired by Beausoleil's staff.

She touched the pearls lovingly. They *were* beautiful. The most beautiful things she had ever worn. Her hand fell. She must not become too attached to them. When she left for England with Lady Beston the pearls would have to be left behind, along with the other finery Sandor had purchased for her. To be worn by . . . whom?

Her heart contracted. She must not allow thoughts of the future to spoil the present. Sandor was looking down at her curiously and she forced a smile. She would be happy every minute she was in his company. Desolation and despair could be indulged in later.

'Are you troubled, Charlotte?' He was so near. She longed to rest her head on the snowy-white of his shirt front. To feel the strength of his arms around her. To raise her face for his kiss.

'No,' she lied and prayed fervently that Lady Beston should be long delayed before arriving in Monte Carlo.

The French windows leading on to the terrace and gardens were open and a soft breeze filled the room.

'Lemonade?' Sandor asked, sitting opposite her as he had at breakfast.

'No,' Charlotte replied daringly, 'I would like some champagne please.'

Sandor grinned and as the champagne cork popped and Georges poured the bubbling liquid into their glasses, said,

'And will you also gamble at the tables tonight?'

She was momentarily disconcerted, not knowing whether he was making fun of her or not. The dancing lights in his black eyes were reassuring. He was amused but not in any way at which she could take offence. Laughter suited him. His eyes crinkled pleasingly at the corners. His mouth was no longer a harsh, impatient line but a teasing curve.

'I would *like* to,' she admitted.

White teeth flashed as he laughed delightedly. Outside the room Georges and Jeanne raised their eyebrows.

'But I have no money of my own with which to gamble and it seems so wicked to gamble away that which is not mine.'

Sandor looked at her with unconcealed interest. 'I find you intriguing, Charlotte. I know of no other young lady who would have the slightest qualm at gambling with that which is not hers.'

Charlotte smiled. 'But they perhaps did not have a parson for a father.'

There was a curious edge to his voice. 'You speak in the past tense. Is your father dead?'

Charlotte's eyes clouded. 'Yes. He died two years ago.'

'And your mother?'

'She died shortly before my father. She was ill with a virulent sickness, and Papa nursed her, as he did many others in his parish.'

'And you, in your turn, nursed him?'

'Yes.' Her voice was little more than a whisper.

Sandor reached across the table and it seemed the most natural thing in the world that his strong, olive-toned hands should imprison hers.

'And then?'

She shrugged her slender shoulders. 'I cared for the children of a parson in the neighbouring parish.'

'And you were unhappy?'

Her smile was rueful. 'I discovered that not all homes were as contented as my own had been. I couldn't bear living in a rectory that was cold and cheerless and without laughter. It made my memories all the more painful. So I left, intent on becoming a governess, and found myself companion to Princess Yakovleva.'

'And in Monte Carlo, surrounded by dandies, roués, spendthrifts and the scions of great European families all recklessly gambling away their fortunes?'

'Yes,' she agreed, and her smile once again held warmth.

Sandor regarded her musingly. She was like a flame. Some kind of inner light seemed to illuminate her. The lobster and salad remained untouched. Her hand remained imprisoned in his. She had no need to say how she had delighted in the gaiety and frivolity. He had seen her at Princess Yakovleva's side, watching the glittering throng around her with fascinated eyes; enjoying all that Monte Carlo had to offer and yet remaining totally uncorrupted by it.

'I would like to see you play the tables,' he said, and the curve of his mouth was devilish. 'Beginners bring luck. You might very well make me a fortune this evening, Charlotte.'

'But I might also lose!'

He shrugged. 'No one should gamble who cannot afford to lose.'

'Tell me about gambling,' she said impulsively. 'My father said it brought only ruin but you gamble excessively and you are not a ruined man.'

At her candour Sandor threw back his head and laughed unroariously.

Georges and Jeanne, patiently waiting to enter with the dessert, stared at each other in amazement.

'Your father,' Sandor said at last, still chuckling, 'was a most astute gentleman and perfectly correct. Gambling can become a compulsion and when it does, ruin usually follows.'

'Then it is not a compulsion for you?'

'No. For me gambling is a way of life.'

The familiar darkness touched his eyes fleetingly. A way of life, because there was nothing of greater worth to replace it. No wife to love. No sons to teach to hunt and fish. No daughters to take pride in. Daughters with copper-gold hair and sea-green eyes.

A small frown furrowed her brow as she regarded him, her head tilted slightly to one side. He tightened his hold of her hands and flashed her a devastating smile.

'The first rule is to choose the game you have the most affinity for.'

'Roulette,' Charlotte said unhesitatingly, surprising even herself.

'Why roulette?' He was laughing at her again and this time she was laughing with him.

'I do not know. I just enjoy the excitement of the spinning wheel and the click of the ball, and it does not require the skill of two-pack solitaire or baccarat.'

'And so you will play roulette tonight?'

She was caught up on a tide of recklessness. 'Yes.'

He grinned. 'Then this is what you must do. First of all, seat yourself at the table. Too many people stand in nervous anticipation and then lose money because they become tired. Seat yourself opposite the even chance, red or black, whichever you favour.'

'But how do I know whether to favour the red or the black?' Charlotte asked in perplexity.

Sandor's grin widened. 'That, my dear Charlotte, is a matter of great skill. If your hair is black, favour the black. If it is red . . .' His eyes rested on the halo of her hair. 'Then perhaps it would be best to favour the red.'

Her eyes were full of soft light. He wanted to rise from the table, sweep her up in his arms and carry her to his room. He said,

'Once at the table, make yourself comfortable. Take out a card and pencil the figures one to five down the page. Ignore the other players. You are playing to win and when you have won, you will stop. That is perhaps the greatest secret of all. Your first bet is the sum of the top and bottom numbers on your list. Five plus one. Six gold plaques. If you win you cross out the five and the one on your list and your next bet is the sum of the remaining top and bottom numbers of your column. Four plus two. Your following bets are always the sum of the top and bottom numbers you have *not* crossed out.'

Charlotte stared at him with mystification. 'And will I win if I play as you say?'

His smile was lazy and teasing. 'If you are lucky. If you are *unlucky* you will not lose a great amount because you will stop as soon as all the numbers you have written down have been crossed out. If you win you will not lose your winnings because you will not play again. That is the only way to make a profit out of gambling. Iron self-discipline.'

She nodded her head, intrigued. 'Yes. I see that this way the chances are greater than choosing a number because it happens to be the date of my birth.'

'Then you are wiser than Sarah. She steadfastly refuses to follow any system at all and chooses her numbers at the table by sheer whim.'

Charlotte's smile was mischievous. 'But she often wins. I have seen her.'

'And loses, because she promptly gambles it all back again.'

'That is true,' Charlotte admitted thoughtfully, remembering the times Sarah had called for champagne to celebrate her winnings, and then for more champagne to console herself in her losses.

'Princess Yakovleva did not often play roulette. She preferred baccarat.'

'As I do.' His voice was so tender that it startled her.

He could restrain himself no longer. Her eyes had a captivating slant. Her lips were vulnerably soft. Her presence filled his senses, sending the blood surging through his veins. The desire that laughter had kept at bay showed nakedly in his eyes.

Charlotte tried to hold on to reason and sense, and failed. Her heart seemed to rock within her breast. Slowly he lifted her hand to his lips and kissed the tips of her fingers one by one, his eyes never leaving hers.

If she did not protest now she would be little better

than Louise or Floretta Rozanko. She tried to speak and could not.

Not releasing her hands, he rose from the table and stepped to her side. She could smell his cologne. His tightly trousered legs brushed her skirt.

'No . . .' she whispered, and then he drew her to her feet and she entered his arms like an arrow entering the gold.

The blood pounded in Sandor's ears. She was his. She would always be his.

Her response now was not occasioned by fear. Nor was it a figment of his imagination. He kissed her urgently, hungrily, until she lost her breath in the passion of his mouth. Then, with a groan, he swept her up in his arms and strode from the room like a man demented. He was halted in his tracks by Georges.

'Prince Charles is expecting your arrival at the Grimaldi Palace at three-thirty, Count Karolyi,' Georges said, all too aware of Count Karolyi's intentions.

'The Devil he is!'

Beyond Georges the staircase curved invitingly.

Georges stood his ground determinedly. He had been in Sandor's service for many years and was accustomed to the endless stream of actresses and society beauties that found their way, briefly, into the Count's bed. However, the English girl was different. She was not of loose virtue and she was not protected by a complacent husband. Sandor's brows drew together demonically and Georges quaked in his highly-polished shoes as he said through parched lips,

'Miss Grainger will need to change her attire, and it is already after two o'clock.'

For a long moment Georges and Sandor faced each other and then Sandor reluctantly lowered a bewildered Charlotte to her feet.

'Georges is quite right, sweet love. Your mourning dress will not be suitable for a visit to the Palace.'

From the safety of a far doorway Jeanne hurried forward. 'I have a dress all ready, Mademoiselle. The pink lawn. The cartwheel hat with the satin ribbons will complement it perfectly.'

Charlotte turned to Sandor, her lips bruised and burned by his kisses.

He nodded. 'The pink lawn will be perfect,' he said, his voice thick with the desire he could not suppress.

There was love in his eyes. He would not treat her coolly the next time they met, as he had before. Reassured she ran glowing-faced to her room.

Sandor clenched his hands at his side until the knuckles showed white. He was trembling and there were beads of perspiration on his forehead. Without Georges' intervention he would have made love to her in haste and passion and regretted it to his dying day. He loved her too much to take her in such a manner. In a moment of utter clarity he knew that he wanted her as his wife. He had found what he had long since given up all hope of finding.

'Your diligence, Georges, is to be commended,' he said, wondering when the miracle had happened. When she had ceased to regard him as an enemy.

'Yes, sir. Will you be requiring a brandy, sir?'

Sandor regarded his butler long and darkly. 'Yes, Georges,' he said at last. 'A very large brandy.'

Georges suppressed a smile. 'Yes, sir. At once, sir.'

It seemed perfectly natural to Charlotte that she should be sitting in a crested landau drawn by plumed white stallions, her hand held tightly in Count Sandor Karolyi's, her cheek pressed close against his shoulder, as they approached the Grimaldi Palace. Nothing had been said between them but she knew she would not be returning to England with Lady Beston. Sandor would be as loath for her to leave as she would be.

The crenellated towers of the palace proclaimed that

it had originally been built as a medieval fortress. Charlotte was unimpressed by the interior as they were led up the marble staircase of the Court d'Honneur and along endless passageways towards the State Apartments. The grandeur was drab and without warmth. The palace, Charlotte thought as they were ushered into the presence of the blind Prince Charles, was in need of a woman's touch. It was high time the eligible Prince Albert married and turned the Palace into a home instead of a fortress.

Prince Charles greeted her warmly, complained about the warmth of the weather and asked that his regards be given to Mademoiselle Bernhardt. He declined the suggestion that she visit him on the grounds that she would be enveloped in perfume and that the last time such an invitation had been extended she had arrived not only with her pet wolfhound, but with a monkey as well.

Charlotte's tender heart ached for him. He was blind, helpless and irritable, suffering from prolonged dizzy spells as well as his antipathy to flowers. She found that he had an intense curiosity about England, and though she could not inform him as to Court activities, he was fascinated by her description of Sussex village life and the day-to-day tasks that her father had performed as rector.

'A fortunate man,' he said, time and time again, gazing at her sightlessly. 'Loved, contented, needed. Your father was indeed a very fortunate man, Miss Grainger.'

Charlotte felt her throat tighten. It seemed strange that a prince should envy the lifestyle of her unassuming father, yet she knew that Prince Charles was correct in his judgment. Her father had indeed been fortunate because he had loved and been loved in return.

That evening, as Jeanne dressed her hair, the breath

seemed so tight in her chest that Charlotte could hardly breathe. Within an hour she would appear publicly in the Devil's Palace on Sandor's arm. Every eye in the room would centre on her and everyone would believe that she was Sandor's mistress. She smiled to herself in the mirror as Jeanne adjusted a camellia nestling in the waves of her upswept hair. She was not his mistress yet, but she soon would be. She would be anything he asked of her.

Her gown had been selected by Sandor. It was of classically severe white velvet, daringly décolletée, lavishly embroidered with seed-pearls. Her only adornment was the flower in her hair and a bracelet of diamonds. She looked unbelievably beautiful – like a princess in a fairytale.

Her *toilette* was complete. Sandor was waiting for her downstairs in the marble entrance hall. She took one last glance in the mirror and turned, walking slowly along the corridor and down the curving sweep of the stairs. There was a concerted intake of breath from Georges and Sandor. She seemed to float. Her hair was an aureole of burnished copper. The sparkle in her eyes put the jewels on her wrist to shame. The velvet fell in soft, undulating lines to her feet. Her breasts caught the glow of the candles and her skin glistened in the flickering light.

Sandor's face was inscrutable. Apprehension seized her. Had she disappointed him? Why did he not smile at her? Hesitantly she stood before him and her light perfume enveloped them both. For a long moment he did not touch her, simply claimed her with his eyes, and then he said, his voice thick with emotion,

'Allow me, Georges,' and he took the white satin and sable cloak from Georges' hands and settled it gently around her shoulders.

Georges stepped backwards discreetly. Through a half-open doorway the cook and kitchen maids watched round-eyed. From the balcony above, Jeanne peeped surreptitiously.

Slowly he tilted her face to his, his own brilliant with an expression of such fierce love that it was quite transfigured.

'My love,' he whispered, lowering his mouth to hers. 'My dear, sweet love.'

A sigh, barely audible, sounding as if it had been torn from her heart, was silenced as their lips met.

The maids closed the door. Georges and Jeanne looked away, aware that they had been spectators at the most intimate and momentous moment of Count Sandor Karolyi's life.

CHAPTER
EIGHT

CHARLOTTE'S heart was overflowing with happiness as
the Karolyi coach sped through the night towards the
casino. Her hand was in Sandor's. Her head was resting
against his shoulder. He loved her. Surely he would not
have spoken to her as he had if he did not love her. Like
a small shadow the memory of Irina, Vicomtesse de
Salbris, flitted across her brain. She chased it away.

The Vicomtesse belonged to Sandor's past. She remembered the pain she had first seen in his eyes through
the lenses of Princess Natalya's opera glasses and believed she knew the cause. He was carrying the burden
of the Vicomtesse's tragic death. That was the reason for
his brooding restlessness and palpable unhappiness. In
the darkness her hand tightened on his. There would be
no more unhappiness for Sandor. Tonight would be a
new beginning for them both.

He glanced down at her. 'Are you ready for your
grand entrance, my sweet?'

She smiled, and all the love she felt for him shone in
her eyes. 'Yes, Sandor.'

He gave a low chuckle. 'It's a pity Yakovlev has left
Monte Carlo. Still, it will be a joy to see the expression
on Lady Pethelbridge's face when she has to greet you.'

'But maybe she will not, Sandor.' Apprehension filled
her voice.

Sandor's chuckle deepened. 'She has no choice. The
Prince of Wales has accepted you and we shall be among
his party this evening. The ladies who so churlishly
refused you assistance in leaving Monte Carlo will be
suitably chastened, and serve them right.'

The carriage halted outside the brilliantly lit casino. Charlotte felt a ripple of excitement run down her spine as she stepped into the sweetly perfumed night air.

One of Monsieur Blanc's frock-coated lieutenants hastened to greet them at the doorway. Her sable cloak was lifted deferentially from her shoulders. Sandor slipped her white, elbow-length gloved hand inside the crook of his arm. The soft strain of an orchestra playing in the hall beyond the gaming rooms could be heard distantly.

A lady who had arrived with her escort at the casino for the first time was politely being asked to remove the gardenia she wore in her hair as the flower was unlucky and the sight of it would cause distress to the other patrons.

Chandeliers glittered with a thousand lights. They had yet to enter the Salle Mauresque but already people were looking in their direction.

Camille Blanc was twirling his flowing blond moustache at a pretty actress and wondering whether she could be persuaded to join him for supper. An aide discreetly approached him and informed him of their presence.

'My dear Count. What a pleasure it is to see you again. And . . .' His eyes gleamed wickedly as he took Charlotte's hand, '. . . your delightful companion.'

Charlotte, well aware that Monsieur Blanc knew very well how she had been acquired as Sandor's companion, merely smiled with the utmost composure and felt almost regal as she continued her procession towards the gaming rooms on Sandor's arm.

At the entrance to the crowded Salle Mauresque Sandor halted. Princess Helene, about to place her plaques on red number nine, paused, her eyes disbelieving. Lord Pethelbridge, engrossed in pursuing the Martingale system and doubling up to the limit, choked on his cigar and wondered what the devil the world was coming to. The Countess of Bexhall ceased her search for Justin and raised her eyebrows.

Conversation ceased. Tables were stilled. For a long, sensational moment no ivory balls twirled around the roulette wheels.

Monsieur Blanc's eyes were admiring. Twice in the same number of days the English girl had done the impossible and silenced his glittering gaming room.

Lady Pethelbridge turned slowly in her seat and flicked her ostrich feather fan shut with a snap. The girl was shameless. Flaunting herself as if she were a lady when everyone knew she was little more than a lady's maid. Her aristocratic features set in a tight line. Her breasts heaved indignantly over their formidable corsetry. This time Count Karolyi had gone too far. She rose majestically to her feet, stared full-face at Charlotte and then very slowly and deliberately turned her back. English nobility eyed each other uneasily. Lady Pethelbridge clearly expected her example to be followed. Yet there had been rumours . . .

The source of the rumours strode curiously into the room from the concert hall, intent on discovering what had stilled the usual clamour. Cigar smoke wreathed his royal head. There was a flower in the lapel of his dinner jacket. The bottom button of his lavishly embroidered waistcoat was characteristically left undone. Sarah glided gracefully at his side, exotic and flamboyant, alight with jewels.

Edward surveyed the scene with relish. He liked to be entertained and here was entertainment in plenty. With all the skill of a professional actor, he milked the moment for all it was worth, puffing contentedly on his cigar as Lady Pethelbridge remained standing, her back set squarely against Charlotte. The tension mounted. Charlotte remained at Sandor's side, her back straight, her head high. The Prince of Wales grinned and stepped towards her.

'I commend you, Mademoiselle Grainger. Your beauty has stilled even the gaming tables.'

An ugly red flush stained Lady Pethelbridge's face and neck. All around her, her social equals deserted her, milling forward, eager to become acquainted with the breathtaking English girl who had been won at a hand of cards and who was being fêted by the Prince of Wales. Lord Pethelbridge, knowing his hours of gambling were at an end, sighed regretfully and crossed to his wife's side.

'You've done it this time, old girl,' he said unsympathetically, and led her, frozen-faced, from the room.

'My darling Charlotte. You look absolutely ravishing,' Sarah said, kissing her affectionately on the cheek. 'The Hotel de Paris has insisted that I remove my cheetah from their premises and Bertie is being very English about it and very unhelpful.' She tapped the Prince of Wales on his chest reprovingly with her forefinger and Charlotte assumed quite rightly that Bertie was Sarah's name for the Prince.

'Now I wonder if Sandor would be more understanding.' Her feline eyes gleamed speculatively.

'No,' Sandor said emphatically. 'I am not giving a home to your cheetah, Sarah.'

'But it would only be for a *little* while, Sandor. And he is really very well behaved.'

'No.' Sandor was adamant.

Sarah looked up at him from beneath her shower of gold-red hair. '*Please*, Sandor darling.'

'No. Beausoleil is not a zoo.'

Sarah pouted provocatively. 'You are being very ungallant. Where will my poor little cheetah go?'

'You could send the damned creature to my nephew,' the Prince of Wales suggested darkly as a slightly-built gentleman with a withered arm and heavy dark moustaches entered the room, followed by a retinue of aides.

Uncle and nephew glared at each other with dislike

and then greeted each other with outward signs of
cordiality. Charlotte dropped into a curtsey before the
future Emperor of Germany, and was aware that not
even Sarah's gaiety could lighten the gloom that suddenly seemed to have descended.

'I was not aware that you were in Monte Carlo,'
Crown Prince Wilhelm said stiffly to his British uncle.

'It is a short visit,' Edward said, with none of his usual
bonhomie.

The stilted conversation continued for a few moments
while royal equerries waited patiently and Sarah raised
her long cats' eyes to heaven expressively.

Etiquette satisfied, the Crown Prince took his leave of
them and made his way to the Salon Privé.

Edward tugged bad-temperedly at his short, fair
beard as Sarah said undeflected, 'If the Hotel de Paris
orders my cheetah to leave, *I* will leave also!'

Edward sighed, humour returning once more to his
heavy-lidded blue-grey eyes. 'Then I think, my dear,
that Count Karolyi has no alternative.'

Sandor was just about to say that he had every alternative, when Charlotte pressed his arm lightly with her
fingers.

'Please, Sandor. It will be exciting to have a cheetah
at Beausoleil.'

He looked down at her, a smile tugging at the corners
of his mouth.

'The cheetah,' he conceded, 'but no wolfhounds, and
definitely no monkeys.'

Sarah threw her arms around his neck. 'Darling Sandor. You are too, too kind. And now I must play the
tables and win a fortune in gold.'

'Not at baccarat,' the Prince of Wales said firmly. 'Not
until my nephew has taken his leave of the Salon Privé.'

Sarah sighed. 'Roulette then. Look, there is Princess
Helene playing two wheels at the same time!'

The Rubenesque elderly Princess was attracting a

great deal of attention. In between sips of champagne, she was placing bets on the same numbers on two tables simultaneously. Her losses were astronomical.

Louise de Remy's protector stepped forward and offered her a word of caution but the princess ignored him and with a hiccup and a flamboyant flourish, halved her remaining gold plaques and placed half on thirty-two on one table and the other half on thirty-two on an adjacent table. Impassive-faced, the croupiers spun the wheels. Princess Helene covered her eyes with her hands. The balls slowed and the crowds at the tables held their breaths.

'Oh *please*,' Charlotte found herself whispering and Sandor shot her an amused glance. She had already forgotten Princess Helene's unkindness to her.

A ball clattered snugly into thirty-two on one table and into thirty-two a fraction of a second later on the other. The room erupted in applause and the triumphant Princess waited patiently while the croupiers took ten minutes to count out her winnings.

'*That* is how I want to win,' Sarah declared, but her royal escort was unimpressed.

'It wouldn't happen again in a hundred years,' he said good-temperedly, making no attempt to part with any of his wealth.

'You are the most *careful* prince in Christendom, Bertie,' Sarah remonstrated gaily, and enveloped in perfume, trailing yards of chinchilla in her wake, she clung to the arm of her chuckling escort.

Sandor's grip tightened on Charlotte's arm as they seated themselves beside Edward and Sarah at a roulette table that had magically cleared in deference to the Prince.

'You are going to play?' Sandor asked, his rich dark voice holding an undertone that made her nerves throb.

'In the company of the Prince?' she asked, round-eyed.

He laughed softly. 'This evening you are the Prince of Wales' guest, Charlotte. I think it would be most discourteous if you did not enjoy yourself to the utmost.'

Edward was beaming jovially at her, gratified at being flanked by the two most beautiful women in the room.

'How do you play, Miss Grainger? Do you resort to your birthday or astronomy, or the hymn number currently on display in the local church?'

Charlotte smiled. 'No, Your Royal Highness. I play to a system.'

Royal brows rose upwards. 'Do you indeed? Then please proceed. If you win I shall ask for your secret.

What to Charlotte seemed an incredible number of gold plaques was placed in front of her by Sandor.

'Remember, my sweet,' he said softly, 'all you require is luck, courage and coolness.'

Sarah had already begun to play with uncharacteristic caution. Time and again she lost to the table.

'Bertie, *cherie*, being careful is no fun. I shall call on the gods for inspiration.' And she closed her eyes, her fingers resting lightly on the table, rapt in concentration. Suddenly her eyes flew open and with the confidence of a mystic, she put a fortune on red nine.

Edward leaned back in his seat, indolently at ease, a huge cigar clamped between his teeth. Sarah's scream as the gods decreed that black should win reverberated throughout the room. Edward guffawed with laughter. It had not been his money that had been lost.

'I shall die!' Sarah exclaimed dramatically, clutching at her chest. 'I shall jump from the cliff and end it all!'

'Nonsense, my dear Sarah. We are having supper at the Café de Paris,' Edward said, with good-humoured practicality.

Sarah groaned and demanded that pink champagne be brought to the table in order that she might be revitalised.

Meanwhile Charlotte had withdrawn a small piece of

paper and a pencil from her jewelled evening bag and was following Sandor's instructions carefully. She won once, twice.

'Sweet Mary,' Sarah exclaimed devoutly. 'The child is playing like a professional.'

Charlotte giggled as more gold was shovelled across the table in her direction. Then, when it seemed as if her winning streak would never come to an end, she calmly ceased to play.

'But you can't stop now,' Sarah shrieked, aghast.

Charlotte's green eyes danced, 'I wish to keep my winnings, Sarah. Not lose them to Monsieur Blanc.'

Edward's deep laughter rumbled explosively. Sarah flung her head back, eyes closed, as if momentarily overcome by unconsciousness at such a display of English coolness.

'Congratulations, Miss Grainger,' the Prince of Wales said as champagne was poured into her glass. 'I hope your skill at baccarat does not exceed your luck at roulette.'

'I have never played baccarat, Your Royal Highness,' Charlotte murmured, her eyes sparkling.

'Then I am relieved.' He turned to the equerry standing at a discreet distance behind them. 'Has the Crown Prince left the Salon Privé yet?'

'I will ascertain, Your Royal Highness.'

Sarah, revived, demanded that she be told Charlotte's secret but on being shown Charlotte's card and neatly written figures, declared that numbers were a mystery to her and proceeded to gamble once more, this time using the hour of her birth for inspiration.

Charlotte gazed around the room, the recipient of eager smiles and nods as society ladies and ladies of the *demi-monde* sought to catch her glance and claim acquaintance.

Louise de Remy's grand duke was desolately alone. Charlotte's eyes searched the room but could see no sign of the effervescent Louise. In deep dudgeon the grand duke lit his cigar with a mille note and with slumped shoulders made his way out on to the terrace.

An ageing member of the royal house of Austria adjusted her lorgnette and studied Charlotte unnervingly, Charlotte smiled. For the first time in years withered lips attempted the semblance of a smile in return.

A gentleman, his chest covered in medals for gallantry on the field, stood with his back to the table he was playing, unable to stand the pain of watching while the roulette wheel spun and his stakes were raked away.

The Countess of Bexhall was playing trente-et-quarante listlessly, her eyes repeatedly leaving the table and scanning the throng. Her husband seemed unaware of her inattention, genially greeting familiar faces.

'Put down your glass of champagne,' Sandor's deep-timbred voice ordered.

Charlotte looked up at him, startled.

'I am going to take you out on the terrace and kiss you as I have wanted to all evening.'

The expression in his eyes sent her pulse throbbing in her temples.

'You cannot,' she protested, feeling the strength leave her legs. 'We are in the Prince's company.'

'The Prince,' Sandor said, his fingers caressing the nape of her neck, 'will be perfectly understanding.'

'It would cause comment,' she protested weakly.

'It would cause even more comment if I began to make love to you at the table,' Sandor replied purposefully.

She began to giggle. 'You wouldn't.'

'I would,' and to prove it he tilted her face to his and kissed her with lingering expertise.

Heat surged into Charlotte's cheeks. Not even the escorts of the grande cocottes behaved in such a cavalier manner. To add to her confusion, the Prince of Wales merely surveyed them with approval and insisted that they join him at the baccarat table and that Charlotte, as a beginner, should test the legend of beginner's luck.

'Now we cannot go on to the terrace,' she whispered to Sandor, her eyes mischievous.

'In that case . . .' He leant towards her again and was only halted on seeing the expression in her eyes change to one of incredulity as she looked beyond his shoulder to the couple who had just entered the room.

Louise was drenched in jewels. A cluster of diamonds secured the ostrich plume in her hair; a collar of diamonds hugged her throat and cascaded in glittering droplets on her half-naked breasts. Armlets of sapphires circled her upper arms, bracelets of pearls her wrists. The topaz silk of her gown clung sensuously, sweeping aside in Grecian folds at a point far above her ankles into a demi-train, revealing an indecent amount of shapely leg.

Her arm was proprietorily through that of Justin, Comte de Valmy.

Sarah's attention, too, was riveted on Louise and her escort.

'I thought de Valmy was an officer in the *Chasseurs à Cheval*, not possessor of the Russian crown jewels,' she whispered incredulously.

Now that de Valmy was no longer a contender for Charlotte's favours, Sandor surveyed him with equanimity.

'The lady's jewels will not have come from that source. They will be her *cache* from the grand duke – and his predecessors.'

Unerringly Louise made her way to the table where her friend Charlotte sat in company with the future King of England.

'Charlotte, *ma cherie*! How ravishing you look.'

Charlotte took a deep breath. How was she to introduce one of France's grande cocottes to the Prince of Wales? She need not have worried.

Edward was in his element, well aware of Louise's

reputation and, within the walls of the casino, uncaring of it.

'I have long wanted the pleasure of meeting Your Royal Highness,' Louise purred as she curtsied charmingly, clinging silk scarcely skimming her breasts.

'The pleasure, mademoiselle, is mine,' Edward replied, determined it would be before he departed Monte Carlo.

Justin's gaze remained steadfastly on Charlotte. She avoided his eyes, she had not seen him since the day of the Princess's funeral. He had behaved with kindness to her then but she could not forget the embarrassment of their carriage ride together. Or the damage that she had caused his hand when she had slammed the carriage door so violently behind her.

'Your hand, was it badly hurt?' she asked with concern.

'It was and deservedly so.'

'I am sorry. I . . .'

'The apologies are mine, Charlotte. I behaved disgracefully that afternoon and I beg your forgiveness.'

The warmth of her smile put Louise's jewels to shame. 'You have it, Justin. It was my fault for being so innocent as to have accepted your invitation without realising that . . .' She broke off, blushing prettily.

'Your innocence is worth more than gold, Charlotte. And it is a quality I think you will carry to your grave.' His glance flicked across to Sandor who had forsaken equanimity and was glaring at him with barely controlled rage. Good sense precluded the conversation from continuing.

'The terrace,' Sandor said grimly to her, taking her arm and steering her away from the Prince and Sarah and Louise and Justin.

'Sandor! Surely we need the Prince of Wales' permission to leave his presence?'

Sandor was uncaring, striding purposefully through

the crowded room, his hand firmly gripping her elbow, forcing her to half-run in the effort to keep up with him.

Gasping for breath Charlotte could see the Countess of Bexhall glaring malevolently across at Louise; could see the Turkish pasha dismiss his adoring companion bad-temperedly as his eye caught sight of a pretty new face, could see Floretta Rozanko, Louise's rival, making a flamboyant entrance, half a dozen attentive gentlemen in her wake.

'Sandor, please. You are hurting my arm.'

The brilliant chandeliers and spinning roulette wheels were left behind. They were out on the terrace, sheltered by a semi-circle of flowering shrubs.

'Damn your arm,' Sandor growled, spinning her round to face him. 'What do you mean by flirting with de Valmy?'

'I was not,' she protested indignantly, her hand against his chest as his arms encircled her. 'I was merely apologising for the injury I did his hand.'

Sandor's frown deepened. 'And do you mind telling me under what circumstances you managed to accomplish that admirable deed?'

'No.' She sighed rapturously. He was jealous. Beneath her fingers she could feel the fierce thudding of his heart.

'You deserve spanking,' he said, and instead kissed her with fierce passion.

Her arms slid up and around his neck. Fireflies danced in the darkness around them as his hands moved caressingly over her body and she trembled in his arms.

His hands cupped the softness of her breasts. He was burning with a desire he had never previously known: never believed to be possible.

'Charlotte,' he murmured hoarsely, against her hair, 'My sweet, beautiful Charlotte.'

She pressed herself closer and closer against him. It

was as if he had a right to her body; as if she were already his wife.

'My dear, no one knows who she is,' an autocratic female voice said, unaware that the object of her conversation was only yards away, half hidden by oleanders. 'Some say she came to Monte Carlo with a Russian Princess. Others that she arrived with a rich, young lover and instantly discarded him for Karolyi.'

'She's certainly different from the usual run of adventuresses,' her lady companion said with less condemnation in her voice. 'Her manner is both charming and modest.'

'Really Henrietta! How can the girl be modest? She was *won* by Karolyi at a game of cards!'

'So I have heard, but do you not think it romantic, Sophronia?'

The ladies were rapidly approaching the bower of oleanders. Regretfully Sandor lifted his mouth from Charlotte's.

'And to risk her life for a child!' Henrietta said admiringly.

'Sheer melodrama.'

In the darkness Sandor grinned down at her. 'There will be more melodrama unless we return to the gaming rooms, my love.'

She giggled and slid her hand comfortably into his. As they stepped forward from the concealing bushes, Henrietta and Sophronia gasped in alarm.

'Good evening,' Sandor said genially to the two elderly ladies. 'I am happy to see you are enjoying the night air and a little gossip,' and swept past them, Charlotte on his arm, leaving Sophronia gasping for breath and Henrietta more admiring than ever.

'That was most unfair of you,' Charlotte chided. 'You could have at least pretended not to have heard what they were saying.'

'Why? Perhaps in future that gorgon, Sophronia, may

be a little more careful before she speaks of someone she has no personal knowledge of.'

The laughter and chatter of the Salle Mauresque enveloped them. Charlotte's eyes widened. 'Good heavens, Sandor. What *is* Floretta Rozanko about to do?'

The gipsy-dark Floretta, eyes flashing, smile dazzling, was swaying voluptuously towards the Prince of Wales' table, determined not to be bested by Louise.

Her progress was watched with bated breath. At last, with no escort, no one to introduce her, Floretta stood before the Prince of Wales and with the cheek of the Paris gutter from which she had sprung, said in fractured English,

''Allo, Wales.'

Before the royal equerries could hurry her away, she blew him a kiss and sprang on to a table, launching into an exuberant can-can. From beyond the gaming room the orchestra hesitated, and then, French to every last man, proceeded to play merrily for her.

Floretta's gartered legs kicked provocatively before the Prince of Wales. Lavishly laced petticoats whirled.

The Prince of Wales grinned broadly. This was just the kind of entertainment that he loved.

As the music reached a crescendo Floretta leapt from the table, executed a perfect cartwheel, and fell into the splits at the Prince's feet, her head thrown back triumphantly, her arms held high above her head.

The stunned silence was broken as Edward applauded gustily. Soon the sound of clapping and cheering filled the room. Louise smiled sweetly at her rival, concealing her rage with exquisite self-control.

Sarah's feline eyes held a dangerous gleam. She had no desire to lose the Prince's company while she remained in Monte Carlo.

Sandor's arm tightened around Charlotte's waist as he

said with a grin, 'It would seem Mademoiselle Rozanko has stolen the evening.'

Charlotte gazed at the breathless Floretta dazedly and could only nod in agreement.

A royal equerry stepped forward and said deferentially, 'Crown Prince Wilhelm has now left the Salon Privé, Your Highness.'

'Good.' Edward rose to his feet. 'I would appreciate another display of your art later on this evening at the Café de Paris, Mademoiselle.'

Floretta flashed a brilliant smile and then, uncaring of the watching bystanders, winked quite openly at the Prince.

Edward chortled and led the way to the Salon Privé. Sarah took his arm, glaring ferally in the direction of the unrepentant Floretta.

Louise refused to allow Floretta the pleasure of knowing the extent of her fury and twined her arm through Justin's, making quite sure that Floretta knew he was her new conquest.

Justin was unaware of her, his eyes on Charlotte's retreating back. He had been a fool. He had acted crassly and without finesse and he had lost Charlotte to Karolyi. The knowledge brought with it a surge of desolation he had never before experienced.

Charlotte was no Louise, to be enjoyed and discarded without thought. Justin's eyes were reflective. Karolyi had never been known to indulge in long standing *affaires*. He was a notorious breaker of hearts. He would remain in Monte Carlo and if Charlotte should be in need of consolation, he would give it. Honourably. He thought of the marriage arranged for him in September and shrugged. Extricating himself from such an obligation would be unpleasant, but would be a small price to pay for a lifetime spent with Charlotte.

Charlotte's slender figure disappeared from sight. With reluctance he returned his attention to Louise.

*   *   *

'I am damned if I want to spend tonight playing baccarat,' Sandor said bad-temperedly, acutely aware of the soft rise and fall of Charlotte's breasts as she made her way up the stairs.

'Shush, the Prince will hear you.' Charlotte was alight with happiness. Sandor had offered her shelter out of kindness and had grown to love her. Any doubts she had previously entertained had fled. She was now quite sure that his reputation was undeserved; that he had suffered acutely over the death of the Vicomtesse and that his suffering had caused him to be grim and forbidding. He was so no longer. His narrow black eyes lit with pleasure whenever they fell on her. Which was constantly. The harsh, impatient lines of his mouth had given way to dazzling smiles and to laughter.

Male eyes gleamed appreciatively as she entered the salon on Sandor's arm. Sandor drew back her chair and she sat down at the baccarat table in the room reserved for only the most distinguished patrons.

The croupier sat at one end of the oblong table, Sandor the other. That meant that Sandor was going to be the banker. Charlotte had watched enough games of baccarat to understand that the banker was the individual who put up the money for the others to play against. And the amounts were always high. There were not many people, even among the Russian royals, who could afford to play for the stupendously high stakes that Sandor set.

Edward seated himself comfortably, lit another of his cigars, and lovingly fingered counters engraved with the Prince of Wales feathers.

Sarah sat opposite Charlotte, her willowy body betraying none of the tension and excitement she felt at the prospect of such dangerous play.

Edward's other guests were introduced and seated. An English lord and his wife; a French duke and his Russian mistress. The gentlemen placed their stakes and cigarette cases around the edge of the table, the ladies their lucky mascots.

Sandor, aware that it could be early morning before he would once again have Charlotte to himself, breathed a sigh of irritation and began to deal.

The novelty of the game was such that the hours at the table were not so tedious to Charlotte as they were for Sandor. She had watched Princess Yakovleva play baccarat and her quick wits accomplished the rest. Occasionally Edward would raise a royal brow in her direction as she played unfalteringly and she knew that he was amused by the knowledge that it was the first time she had played.

Sandor dealt another three cards, one to himself, one each to the player on his left and right and imprisoned her with his eyes. She read the impatience there, the desire. Demurely she lowered her eyes, aware of the heightened colour in her cheeks.

Sandor reluctantly turned his attention to his cards. He held a natural, a six and a three, and was obliged to declare it. No one could match it and so, once again, he won.

When, several hours later, play ended and the Prince of Wales invited his guests to join him at the Café de Paris, Sandor politely declined.

Edward, aware of Sandor's eagerness to have Charlotte to himself, accepted his refusal with good grace. He didn't blame his friend. Miss Charlotte Grainger was a young lady of exceptional charm and beauty.

'Thank goodness for that,' Sandor said as he hurried her down the gilded staircase. 'I thought we were going to be at the card table until morning.'

'We nearly were,' Charlotte said as they stepped out of the casino and into the waiting Karolyi carriage. 'Can you see how the sky is pearling to dawn beyond the horizon?'

'Damn the dawn,' Sandor said, and as the coachman

cracked the whip and the carriage rattled off in the direction of Beausoleil, he pulled her towards him hungrily, kissing her with barely suppressed violence.

To Charlotte, the return to Beausoleil was like returning to a dearly loved and familiar home. The white walls of the villa shimmered, dreamlike, in the early morning light. The spiky green leaves of exotic shrubs gleamed with the first drops of dew. Roses, magnolias and lilies hung their closed heads, waiting for the sun.

As she stepped from the carriage she paused and looked up at him, her eyes shining with love.

'Thank you for a wonderful evening, Sandor. I shall never forget it.' Standing on tiptoe she kissed him lovingly.

From the doorway of the villa came a discreet cough. Without releasing her, Sandor raised his head. 'Lady Beston has arrived, sir,' Georges said apologetically. 'She is distressed and is resting in the main salon.'

She could feel his body tense, see the expression in his eyes change.

'Thank you, Georges. Tell Lady Beston I shall be with her immediately.'

Swiftly he strode towards the open doorway. Charlotte ran after him, her satin pumps uncomfortable on the harshness of the gravel.

In the entrance hall the pendants of glass in the magnificent chandelier tinkled as Georges closed the door after her. Sandor began to walk swiftly towards the main salon, and then stopped, swinging round on his heel to face Charlotte

'I shall be some time with Lady Beston, Charlotte,' he said. 'It would be best if you retired.'

'Yes.' Her voice was barely audible, her disappointment acute.

Lady Beston's arrival had altered Sandor's whole demeanour. He had asked her to retire as politely and indifferently as he might have asked any guest. The magic of the last few hours seemed suddenly to have disappeared. His eyes when they had looked at her had been the eyes of a stranger.

Unhappily she began to climb the stairs to where Jeanne waited to help her undress. From the main salon came the distant throb of voices. Sandor's and that of a female voice, thick with emotion.

Charlotte paused, one hand on the balustrade, cold fear gripping her heart. Surely Sandor could not intend that she still return to England with Lady Beston? Her breathing steadied. She was being ridiculous. Of course he would not. He would be faced with the unpleasant task of informing his elderly friend that she must look elsewhere for a companion. She climbed another two stairs and halted again. Princess Yakovleva had been eccentric and irascible, but even she would not have descended on a gentleman friend in the hours before dawn, waiting like an outraged matriarch for his arrival.

She turned her head. The door to the main salon was ajar. Curiosity engulfed her. It was quite probable she would never have another opportunity of seeing the lady who had so nearly become her employer.

Quietly she retraced her steps and from the foot of the stairs took a quick peep into the salon. At what she saw her heart ceased to beat and her blood froze in her veins.

This was no patchouli-scented *grande dame* greeting Sandor, but a woman at the height of her beauty; a woman with an olive-toned skin and shining black hair piled high in an intricate *coiffure*. A woman with violet dark eyes glistening with tears of joy. A woman clasped close in Sandor's arms. She heard the break in his voice as he said hoarsely, 'Zara, it's been so long, my love. So long,' and then she was stumbling up the stairs, her fist pressed tightly against her mouth to stifle the cry of pain, her world in ashes, the truth all too cruelly clear.

CHAPTER
NINE

BROTHER and sister clung together in the candlelit salon, Sandor's eyes overly bright, Zara's wet with unshed tears.

'Sandor! How good it is to see you again! I can't tell you how ghastly things are!'

The tears spilled down her cheeks and he rocked her fiercely against his chest. 'Don't cry, my love.'

'But I can't help it, Sandor. Beston is unbearable. He tells me that I am stupid and useless and nothing that I do pleases him. He seems to take a delight in distressing me and . . .' her voice was barely a whisper. 'He . . . he accuses me of having improper relations with gentlemen I scarcely know.'

'Where is he now?' Sandor's voice was low and tight and terrifying.

'I don't know. I heard him tell his valet he would not be back until morning. He often stays away all night.' She raised her face piteously to his. 'He doesn't love me. I don't believe he ever has. He married me because he thought I would bring him wealth. When he discovered that the Katzinskys had little but their title he accused me of deceiving him.' She began to sob again, this time hysterically. 'I dare not think what he would do if he ever discovered that I was not of true Katzinsky blood.'

His fingers tightened on her shoulders and his eyes darkened, filled with shadows. So much suffering from one heedless afternoon of sin. He wondered if his mother had truly loved the flashing-eyed gypsy who had seduced her. If she had thought the world well lost for love. Had she ever imagined the anguish that her children would suffer when they learned the truth of their parentage? His jaw tightened. She was dead and he could feel no bitterness towards her. Her impulsive, passionate blood flowed in his veins as it did in Zara's. Hadn't he, too, allowed his heart to rule his head?

Zara rested against his chest with a little moan. 'If only I had never married him. If only we could meet openly as brother and sister.'

Sandor held her close. If . . . If only Count Istvan Karolyi had reared Zara as his child as well as himself. If only the Count had legally adopted him. If only he had written a will leaving him the wealth and lands that he intended him to have. But he had done none of those things.

Zara had been given to the childless Katzinskys. No legal adoption had ever taken place, for Count Istvan had believed that such action would make his wife the object of rumour and gossip. No will had been left because the old man had not deemed it necessary. The world regarded Sandor as his son. Therefore he would inherit Valeni. To Count Istvan the matter had been simple. It would not be so if Lord Beston ever discovered the truth. Gently Sandor lowered his sister on to a sofa.

'There must be a way of freeing you from him,' he said, pouring a brandy.

Zara shook her lovely head. 'We are doomed, Sandor. Both of us are doomed because our lives are a lie.'

He wanted to tell her about Charlotte but now was not the time. Her eyes were dull with fatigue and misery.

'You must get back to the Hotel de Paris,' he said tenderly, helping her to her feet. 'If Beston should arrive and find you absent, the situation would only be made worse.'

'Yes.' She picked up her cape of black fox and trailed it on the floor after her as she walked to the door. 'If I were absent whose bed would he accuse me of sleeping in? Lord Romberry's? The Duke of Steene? The Earl of Lale? According to Beston each and every one is my lover. As are a score more.'

Thin white lines etched the corner of his mouth. 'You will not suffer such calumnies for much longer, Zara. Trust me.'

She smiled up at him sadly. 'He is my husband, Sandor. He can abuse me as he pleases.'

Sandor's jaw tightened and his eyes were scarcely recognisable. 'You are my sister, Zara, and he cannot.'

He walked outside with her and handed her into the carriage. She was tall and willow-slim with hair as black as his own and eyes the colour of velvet-dark pansies. Her skin tone was the same as his, a honey gold that lent an exotic quality to her dark beauty. It never ceased to amaze him that the likeness between them was never commented on.

'Darling Sandor,' Zara said softly, oblivious of the bedroom window open above their heads. 'If I could not see you, even for a little while, I think I should die.'

'You will see me tomorrow,' Sandor said, kissing her cheek. 'I shall make it my business to call on Beston.'

'Yes.' Such visits were always made. Outward civility between Sandor and her husband was the only thing that made it possible for her to enjoy Sandor's presence in public.

'Goodnight, dearest Sandor.'

'Goodbye, dear love.'

The carriage rattled away in the early morning light and Sandor remained immobile, watching it until well after it had disappeared, a tic throbbing at the corner of his jaw, his eyes mere slits as he considered Lord Beston, pillar of English society and destroyer of his sister's happiness.

Charlotte stared sightlessly at the ceiling, exhausted from her tears, drowned in grief. The emotionally charged conversation that had taken place beneath her window left no room for doubt. If Sandor had spurned Irina, Vicomtesse de Salbris, it had been because of Zara, Lady Beston. If he carried a burden of grief and love, it was for Zara, Lady Beston, wife of one of England's peers.

The depth of feeling in his voice had not been that of a man for a casual mistress. It had been that of a man who loved, and who loved deeply.

She had discovered his secret at last and it was as if a dagger had been driven into her heart. She had been correct in her first assumption, that he had taken her in at Beausoleil so that she might be of use to him. Not, as she had so fondly supposed, that she might protect him from amorous females whilst he recovered from the death of the Vicomtesse, but so that with Monte Carlo society believing her to be his mistress, he could more openly associate with the married woman who held his heart.

The woman he had had the effrontery to suggest she accompany back to England. She rose from the bed and stood at the window, watching in desolation as the first flush of dawn tinged the sky and pearled the distant sea.

She would do as he desired. She had very little option. Once in England she would rebuild her life, as she had rebuilt it on the death of her parents. It would be unbearably hard, crucifyingly lonely, but no other future lay open to her.

She remained at the window staring sightlessly as the grey of the sky deepened to blue; as the sea warmed and shone; amethyst and jade, aquamarine and sapphire.

When Jeanne entered with her morning tray of hot chocolate and croissants, she was barely aware of her. Or of the maid's stunned shock at seeing her still gowned in white velvet and seed-pearls.

With firm gentleness Jeanne removed the gown, ordered that a bath be drawn and ushered an unprotesting Charlotte into the rose-scented water. Using her own discretion, Jeanne selected a pretty day dress patterned in pastel roses and after brushing Charlotte's hair once more into a *coiffure* of upsweeping deep waves and curls, helped her to dress, looping the long, single rope of flawless pearls over her head.

'Mademoiselle looks very beautiful,' she said sincerely, hoping for some response in the unutterably sad eyes.

'Thank you, Jeanne.' Charlotte's voice was soft and gentle – and heartbreakingly sad.

'Count Karolyi is already breakfasting,' Jeanne ventured.

Charlotte rose from her dressing table stool. He would have to be faced. She could not hide in her room for ever. The charade must continue.

With reluctant feet she walked slowly along the opulent corridor and down the vast, sweeping staircase.

Georges greeted her with a smile, but he was concerned at the lacklustre of her usual sparkling eyes. Had the Count and the English girl quarrelled? Were Beausoleil and Valeni to be bereft of the mistress their staff so desired?

Sandor's night had been as sleepless as Charlotte's. Nevertheless, at the sight of her his heart warmed.

'I didn't expect you to rise until much later,' he said, rising from the table, drawing a chair out for her, dismissing the footman so that he might pour her coffee himself, breakfast with her in delicious privacy.

'I was not tired.' It was a blatant lie. She was exhausted.

He frowned. 'Is everything as it should be, Charlotte?'

She did not trust herself to meet his eyes. How could he ask such a question? Hadn't he only hours ago abandoned her to be reunited with the woman he loved? Hadn't Lady Beston told him passionately that she would die if she could not see him, even for a little while?

And hadn't Sandor promised that they would meet again that very morning?

'Yes, thank you.' Her voice was cool and remote.

His frown deepened. 'As you know, Lady Beston has arrived in Monte Carlo. I plan to call on her this morning.'

There was silence from the other side of the table. He leaned forward, covering her hands lovingly with his. 'You will be able to see what an ideal employer she would have made.' Beneath the heat of his hand her blood seemed to freeze. He no longer wished her to accompany Lady Beston to England. Perhaps he was afraid that she would be indiscreet. That Lady Beston would discover that he was not against engaging in flirtations when she was absent. She kept her eyes firmly averted from his.

'I am sure Lady Beston would still make a most admirable employer,' she said stiffly.

He stared at her. 'What do you mean, Charlotte? You cannot imagine that after what has happened I still intend that you should accompany Lady Beston to England?'

She raised her head and braved his eyes. 'But of course,' she said, as if it were the most natural thing in the world. 'How else am I to reach there?'

His incredulity was total. 'You cannot mean it, Charlotte!'

Her coffee remained untasted, her croissant untouched. 'I am afraid that I do. I enjoyed yesterday exceedingly, Count Karolyi, but now I must think of my future.' She was talking to him as if she were at an afternoon tea party with a stranger.

Sandor felt himself held in the grip of a nightmare. This conversation could not possibly be taking place. Either she was mad or he was. His brows flew together, his eyes blazed.

'Your future is here! With me!'

She felt faint, as if she were poised on the edge of a precipice and about to plunge headlong into a void from which there was no return. If she wanted, she could remain outwardly his mistress. It was what Sandor desired. In Budapest and Vienna, in Paris and Monte Carlo, he could meet Zara and the world would be no wiser. For an insane moment she was tempted to capitulate. To live with him on any terms he offered. And then she remembered the sight of Lady Beston in his arms and knew that such recurring pain was beyond endurance.

'I am afraid not, Count Karolyi,' she lied politely. 'There is a gentleman to whom I am betrothed waiting for me in London. He has little finances but he is honourable . . .'

'*God's teeth!*' Sandor rose to his feet in a fury, coffee cups spilling, plates scattering to the floor. 'You have the *audacity*, the *effrontery* to tell me that you are returning to England to marry!'

Charlotte placed her napkin on the table with a trembling hand and rose to her feet.

'Yes, I am sorry that I did not tell you earlier. It did not seem important.'

With a savage oath he crossed the space between them and seized her. For a terrifying moment she thought he was going to strike her and then he said savagely,

'So your betrothed is honourable, is he? It's more than I can say of you! Louise de Remy and Floretta Rozanko could learn a lot from your wiles, Mademoiselle Grainger!' and, crushing her to him, he kissed her with cruel viciousness.

She could not free herself from his bruising mouth. Her hands pushed in vain against his chest, but he was too strong for her. She could smell his skin, hear his heart beating, feel her body responding to his even as she struggled.

As he raised his head from hers, blood seared her lips.

'We will leave in fifteen minutes! I expect you to be ready and waiting.' He spun on his heel and stormed from the room.

She steadied herself on a chair and wiped the blood from her mouth. She had disrupted his plans and incurred his wrath. The devil incarnate Princess Yakovleva had called him. Now she understood why.

She steadied her breathing. She had played her part well. Even Sarah could not have played it better. Her pride had been salvaged. Sandor Karolyi was disabused of any belief he might have had that he had won her heart. And now she must tend her lip, resume her play-acting, and meet the woman whose reputation Sandor had gone to such lengths to protect. Zara, Lady Beston.

On the carriage ride to the hotel, Sandor felt as if his world had fallen apart. She sat opposite him, eyes lowered, hands lightly clasped in her lap. He had seen the bruises on her lips and had felt remorse mixed with murderous rage. Dear God in heaven, had she taken him for a fool right from the beginning? What had happened that he, Sandor Karolyi, a man whose reputation was notorious, should have fallen for the charms of a nineteen-year-old English girl? He cursed inwardly. At thirty-two he had thought himself immune from such foolishness. Now he was so deeply embroiled that even knowing how little she cared for him, his feelings remained unchanged. He loved her. She was in his blood and in his bones. He would love her to the day he died.

The perfume that emanated from her hair filled his senses. He had to clench his hands into fists to prevent himself from seizing hold of her and crushing her once more against him. Her skirt brushed against his leg as they entered the hotel and he felt as if every nerve ending in his body were raw.

The Bestons' suite was in the opposite wing of the hotel to Sarah's and bore no trace of its occupants' personalities as Sarah's so lavishly did.

Lord Beston was clearly not pleased at receiving visitors. He was tall and narrow-shouldered, his moustaches immaculate and flecked with grey. His hand barely touched Charlotte's as Sandor introduced them. Looking up into his colourless, almost opaque eyes, Charlotte felt an unpleasant chill touch her spine. Lord Beston was a man it would be wise not to cross. Or to be alone with.

'Lady Beston,' Charlotte was aware of the underlying throb in Sandor's voice. 'Miss Charlotte Grainger.'

Charlotte took a deep breath and looked directly into the eyes of the woman Sandor loved.

Shock reverberated through her. The face was vaguely familiar, but from where? When? Blue-black hair was upswept in deep, undulating waves. Instead of the creamy white skin so treasured by professional and society beauties, Lady Beston's skin seemed sun-kissed, as if she had dispensed with protective parasols and broad-brimmed hats. Her face was oval, her cheekbones high, and her eyes held a tantalisingly familiar slant. Her smile was warm and gracious, but the limpid pools of her thickly-lashed eyes held such suffering that all hostility drained from Charlotte's tender heart.

'I'm very pleased to meet you, Miss Grainger.'

Charlotte stared at her helplessly. The dislike she had expected to feel was absent. She saw only a woman who was bitterly unhappy. A woman who lived only for the brief moments when she was in Sandor's company. As she herself did. A woman who was graciousness itself.

'I understand you have lately been in Vienna,' Sandor was saying to Lady Beston. 'Did you enjoy the opera?'

'My wife would not know a good opera from a bad one,' Lord Beston said unkindly.

Charlotte saw two high spots of colour appear in Lady Beston's cheeks.

'I am sure you are mistaken, Lord Beston,' Sandor said smoothly. 'I have heard it said that your wife is a keen patron of the arts.'

'She is a keen patron of dressmakers and jewellers, but an understanding of the arts is unfortunately not within her grasp.'

Charlotte stared at him. Did he know how much his carelessly spoken words were wounding his wife? She saw the expression in his eyes and shivered. He knew, and he did not care.

Sandor was speaking civilly to him about the Prince of Wales's presence in Monte Carlo and Charlotte saw that Lady Beston's eyes were fixed almost beseechingly on Sandor, as if willing him to keep her out of the conversation and away from the attention of her husband.

As the minute hand on the clock moved up to the hour, Charlotte ached to escape from the claustrophobic confines of the room. Lady Beston's unhappiness was palpable. Sandor's eyes rarely rested on her, but Charlotte knew that he was acutely aware of her and that he entertained nothing but contempt for the man to whom he was speaking. It was with overwhelming relief that she saw Sandor was rising, that they were about to take their leave. Lord Beston turned away to summon service imperiously. In that brief moment Lady Beston's and Sandor's eyes met, the love each felt for the other nakedly exposed.

Charlotte felt the knife in her heart plunge deeper, inflicting even more pain, and then they were saying goodbye and she was dimly aware that Lady Beston was risking her husband's wrath by sweetly asking that she call on her for tea the next day. The door of the Beston suite closed behind them. The stilted and joyless meeting was at an end.

Her heart was racing as if she had run a great distance.

She felt sick and dizzy. Sandor had not mentioned to Lady Beston that Charlotte was to be her companion back to England. He had introduced her to the Bestons as his guest. Surely Lady Beston would not expect to employ a young lady she had met socially, as a companion?

Her head throbbed. If Sandor had thought that his behaviour would make such an appointment impossible, he had underestimated her. She had been invited to tea the following day by Lady Beston, and she had accepted. It would be the ideal opportunity to ask Lady Beston if she might accompany her in an official capacity back to England.

She began to put on her gloves and realised she had dropped one in her distress. They were nearing the lobby. The glove was nowhere to be seen.

Hastily she retraced her steps. The white net glove was on the floor outside the door of the Beston suite. As she bent to retrieve it she could hear the sound of heart-rending tears. Feeling like an eavesdropper, Charlotte snatched up the glove and hastened to where Sandor waited impatiently in the hotel lobby.

'I am sorry. I dropped my glove.'

Taut-faced he escorted her into the brilliant sunshine. Yesterday had been the happiest day of his life. Today he was faced with the difficulty of extricating Zara from a marriage that was untenable and of pondering on the identity of an unknown Englishman of no financial resources who had succeeded in winning from him the only woman he would ever love.

Charlotte's emotions were in turmoil as Sandor handed her into the landau. She had gone to the Hotel de Paris fully expecting to feel bitter jealousy for Lady Beston. She had left feeling only compassion for her. Lady Beston was not of the same ilk as Lady Pethelbridge and the Countess of Bexhall. Her sad mouth had held sweetness, her tragic eyes kindness. Help from that quarter would never have been refused.

Sandor struggled for self-control. He wanted to seize Charlotte's slender shoulders and shake her until she promised that she would not leave Beausoleil. Instead he said caustically,

'May I be permitted to ask the identity of your future husband, Miss Grainger?'

Charlotte's imagination failed her. 'I do not think such details can be of any interest to you, Count Karolyi,' she said tightly.

The sun blazed down from a cloudless sky. Ladies in passing carriages bent their parasol-shaded heads in acknowledgment on seeing the unmistakable Karolyi stallions.

'But it is of the greatest interest,' he said relentlessly, fixing her with a steely gaze. 'After all, if it had not been for my intervention, you would not have been in a position to return to the gentleman concerned.'

She felt hot colour stain her cheeks. 'I have no wish to discuss my future husband,' she said, avoiding his eyes. If Lady Beston were not returning to England for some while, she would ask if she would lend her the necessary money, so that she herself could return to England immediately. Her pride, where Lady Beston was concerned, would not be at stake, and she would return the money as soon as she had found herself a position. Nor would the request be refused. She knew that intuitively. Never in her wildest dreams had she imagined that she would be reduced to such lengths, but there was no way she could remain in Sandor's company. His anger cut through her like a knife. She was no longer 'Charlotte' to him, she was 'Miss Grainger', and she could no longer call him 'Sandor'.

'As you choose,' Sandor said, his jaw tightening, and his eyes blazing.

Her heart began to throb painfully. Why was he so angry? Surely he could acquire another lady to provide a foil for his public meetings with Zara? The sun blinded her eyes. Is that how he had used the Vicomtesse de Salbris? And had the Vicomtesse, like herself, fallen in love with him?

The landau entered Beausoleil's sub-tropical gardens, the palms giving fleeting and cooling shade.

'If you will excuse me, Count Karolyi, I must rest. I have a headache.'

With a leap of concern he saw the paleness of her face, the blue shadows beneath her eyes. 'Of course.' His voice was stiff. He dared not trust himself to express his true concern.

Once in her room she closed the shutters, plunging the room into blessed shade. When Jeanne knocked and asked if she could be of assistance Charlotte merely allowed her to help her out of her dress and then said that she would like to rest and not be disturbed.

Jeanne retreated respectfully and Charlotte lay motionless on her bed. Roulette *coups*. *Grande cocottes* dancing can-cans in front of the Prince of Wales. Dazzling sun. Exotic flowers. Sarah's witchery. Louise's pertness. How would she accustom herself to life without them? And without Sandor?

She passed her hand across her eyes. How was it possible to love a man so much that she should suffer with him in his despair at not being able to make the woman he loved his wife? Her heart ached. For herself For Sandor. For Zara. It seemed that none of them was destined for happiness.

Lord Beston left his hotel suite shortly after Sandor and Charlotte had departed—his destination the villa of his English mistress.

Zara remained on the sofa where she had fallen in a flood of tears. Why had she married him? Vaguely she remembered the austere charm he had taken pains to exercise when courting her. Her longing for a fresh start in life. Her escape from her adopted home and its perpetual reminders of her bastardy. Through the long afternoon she remained on the sofa. If only she could live openly as Sandor's sister then she would be happy, but to do so would mean telling Beston the truth about her birth, and so would mean Sandor's ruin. Beston would not keep silent. He would tell Povzervslay that he had a claim to Valeni and then Count Istvan Karolyi's last wishes would be denied. Valeni tenants would not live happily under Sandor, but would be ruled in terror by Jozsef Povzervslay. It was a prospect too hideous to contemplate.

Her despair was total. She was thirty-two. Her husband did not love her; did not even care for her. She could see no happiness in her future, no peace or serenity.

She rose and poured herself a glass of mineral water, seeing with vague surprise that the shadows in the garden of the hotel were lengthening. Dusk was approaching. How much longer would Beston be gone? Dare she risk hurrying to see Sandor for a few snatched moments at Beausoleil?

She moved swiftly, setting a hat of flowers and veiling upon her blue-black hair, picking up silk gloves, a lace-fringed parasol, her hands trembling.

Rigid in his carriage, Lord Beston's pale grey eyes were like slivers of ice. It had been three months since he had last seen his mistress, the wife of a fellow peer, and he had expected his welcome to be a warm one. Instead he had been received with languid indifference. The lady in question had grown bored by his absence and had sought diversions elsewhere. The interlude was over. Lord Beston had not endangered his pride by asking that the lady reconsider. He had feigned dignified relief at the news and untruthfully stated that he, too, had embarked on a new *affaire* of the heart. With barely concealed hostility he had taken his leave of his former mistress and, reluctant to return to the hotel immediately, ordered his coachman to drive up into the hills.

Damn it to hell, but he would have to have a new lady on his arm to flaunt or it would be obvious that he had been lying. Calculatingly he reflected on the ladies in residence in Monte Carlo. None of them stirred his appetite. He had a sudden mental picture of Count Karolyi's companion and at the thought of Charlotte's red-gold hair and luminous green eyes the blood leapt along his veins. She was a beauty. Outstandingly so. And Karolyi would not be squiring her so publicly unless her pedigree was above reproach.

A thin smile curved his lips. Karolyi was not in love with her. He was in love with Zara. They thought he was a fool and unseeing, but he had known so for years. He had known also that his infuriatingly pure wife had not yet graced the Count's bed and it was for that reason he had remained silent. When she did so he would use the knowledge to break her spirit completely. God, how he hated her! So irreproachable. So long-suffering. He had married her believing he was aligning himself to a family of wealth. A family who had only one daughter to leave that wealth to. A daughter who was a princess. He remembered preening himself on his conquest the day the announcement of their betrothal had appeared in *The Times*. And he remembered his stunned incredulity after the wedding when he realised there was no wealth. That the Katzinskys had only an ancient family name littering the pages of the Almanac de Gotha like confetti.

An ugly red stain mottled his cheeks. His own greed had been his downfall and he had blamed his folly on his beautiful young wife. Never a day passed without he belittled or ridiculed her, wishing her dead so that he could marry advantageously elsewhere.

His eyes narrowed speculatively. What spirit she had

he had nearly broken. She spent her days weeping,
eating only enough to keep a bird alive. If Karolyi should
succeed in coercing her into his bed and he, Beston, then
faced her with the truth, she would be a broken reed and
might even lose the will to live. Zara was not like the
majority of her contemporaries, entering lightly upon
liaisons and *affaires*. Her purity was almost nun-like.
The shame of breaking her wedding vows would be
monumental.

He smiled grimly to himself as his carriage returned to
the hotel. She had barely taken her eyes off Karolyi
when he had visited that morning, and Karolyi, too, had
not been as circumspect as usual. The tension in the air
had been almost palpable.

He opened the door of his suite and froze Zara in the
act of leaving. Slowly he closed the door behind him.
'And just where do you think you are going?' he asked
softly. 'Who are you intending to see?'

'I . . . no one.' Trembling convulsively Zara removed
her hat and lay down her gloves. Beston eyed her
curiously.

'I'm not a fool, Zara,' he said, and the very silken
quality of his voice intensified her fear.

'I . . . I have just come in.' She forced a smile. 'I would
like to retire now. I feel most unwell.' Nervously she
reached a hand out to ring for her maid, but her husband's hand closed around hers, restrainingly.

'I think perhaps you have something to tell me, Zara.'

'No. It is just that I feel most unwell.' His touch on her
flesh made her shrink with revulsion. Sweat broke out on
her forehead and the palms of her hands.

'I am reliably informed that guilt often has that effect,'
Beston said smoothly, noting with satisfaction that the
blood had drained from her face and that her heart was
palpitating wildly.

'Guilt?' Her eyes widened and Beston felt a *frisson* of
pleasure. She was hiding something. Had she received a

communication from Karolyi? Had she been on the point of capitulation? Had she, incredible thought, already capitulated? Was she already Karolyi's mistress? Was now the time to strike?

'Perhaps you would like to tell me his name, my dear, and relieve your conscience of its burden?'

'There is no one. I swear . . .'

Beston laughed softly. 'I doubt if an onlooker to this morning's little reunion would find that believable.'

Zara's throat contracted with fear. Her mouth opened and she tried to speak but no sound would come. Her husband released her hands and seated himself comfortably on the nearest sofa, pinning her with his eyes as if she were a butterfly on a mount.

'I think the moment for truth has finally arrived, Zara.'

Zara's fingers splayed helplessly in an effort to find something upon which to lean for support. 'I . . . I don't know what you mean. I was just going for a carriage ride. . . .'

Her distress held a quality he had never seen before. His suspicions became certainty.

'You told me a moment ago, my dear, that you had just returned from a carriage ride.'

'I . . . I am confused.'

Beston rose to his feet and poured himself a brandy. 'Your talent for lying is as negligible as your other talents. And it is completely pointless. You see, my dear, I know the truth about you and Sandor Karolyi.'

Zara's nails dug deep into the back of a chair. 'No . . . It isn't possible.'

Her husband sighed with satisfaction. 'So . . . I *was* right in my assumption. It *is* true.'

'Yes . . . No . . .' Zara began to weep unrestrainedly.

Something near to heat warmed Lord Beston's glacial gaze as Zara fell half senseless across the chair.

'Do you realise the shame you have brought on my

name?' he said relentlessly. 'The ignominy.' His voice was like a whiplash. He rose to his feet, his shadow falling threateningly across her.

Zara clutched at his hand, falling to her knees. 'No one need know! Oh please! Promise me you will not speak of it again. It will break Sandor's heart to relinquish Valeni!'

Lord Beston began to speak and then halted. Valeni. Why the devil should Karolyi be obliged to relinquish the family estates? The sixth sense that never failed him prompted him to silence.

'It was my father's dying wish . . .' Zara was incoherent. Her head hurt. She could no longer think clearly. She had to protect Sandor. Had to make Beston see how important it was for him to keep silent. Tears strangled her throat.

'I know you have no love for me, but I beg of you to keep it silent. To do otherwise would be to kill me.'

Lord Beston's eyes glinted. 'Then let us have some truth, Zara. I think you have deceived me long enough.'

'But there was no other course open for me.' Her eyes were wide, distraught. What she had lived in fear of all her life had occurred. Beston knew her secret. Knew Sandor's secret.

'Who told you,' she sobbed, wrapping her arms around her body, as if to hold herself against an inner disintegration.

'It is of no moment.'

'But it is! Oh! What if he should tell Povzervslay? What will become of Valeni?'

Lord Beston was aware of a rising excitement that took all his self-discipline to control. 'You must tell me everything yourself, Zara. Right from the beginning.'

Zara moaned and for a moment Beston was afraid that she was going to lose consciousness.

'Count Karolyi loved Sandor as if he was his own son. He always meant Valeni to be Sandor's.'

Lord Beston felt the blood throb in his temple. Dear God, what was she telling him? That the arrogant Hungarian was one of the old Count's by-blows?

'If only he had adopted Sandor, then Povzervslay would have no claim to it . . .' She was crying again and her husband could scarcely prevent himself from shaking her shoulders.

'Yes?' he prompted, leaning forward, his eyes gleaming with anticipation.

'But he wouldn't. He loved our mother too much. He thought that if he adopted Sandor, news of his action would leak into society and then there would be speculation and gossip.

'*Our* mother?' Beston repeated softly, hardly daring to breathe.

Zara closed her eyes. She had feared this moment all her life, now there was a strange relief in saying:

'There was no question of Count Karolyi adopting me. He gave me to Prince and Princess Katzinsky when I was only days old . . .'

Beston's breath hissed. 'Your mother was Count Istvan's wife?'

'But of course!' Her eyes flew open. Her husband was smiling. 'But you knew that! You told me you knew!'

'I know all I need to know,' he said with exultant satisfaction. 'I know that you're not a Katzinsky but an illegitimate nobody. I know that you married me under false pretences and that I can now be freed of this marriage without any damage to my own reputation.' His teeth showed wolfishly as his smile widened. 'I know that your bastard brother has no right to the title he holds.'

Zara felt as if she was falling into a bottomless pit. A pit of her own making. 'No!' she gasped, falling on to her knees before him. 'Oh, promise me you will say nothing. Povzervslay is a man of blood and violence. His tenants live in mortal fear of him. He must not be allowed to wreak his wrath on Valeni tenants.'

Lord Beston picked up his silk hat and gloves. 'Povzervslay's actions are immaterial to me. However, honour demands that I inform him that he has been usurped.'

Zara flung her arms around his knees dementedly. 'It was Count Istvan's dying wish that Sandor inherit!'

'Then he should have taken the precaution of legally adopting, and legally willing Valeni to your brother. As it is . . .' Beston shrugged his shoulders expressively and turned for the door, sending Zara sprawling.

'No! Oh, no!' Imploringly she stretched out her hands towards him.

Her husband laughed. 'I imagine Povzervslay will be exceedingly grateful to me, but before I have the pleasure of telling him the truth, I shall indulge myself in telling Monte Carlo.'

'You . . . are . . . a . . . devil,' she whispered, and fell unconscious at his feet.

Lord Beston laughed, adjusted his hat and closed the door on his stricken wife.

A first Charlotte wondered what sound had awoken her with such a start. She stared perplexedly at the darkened shutters. No light filtered through the slats. Had dusk already fallen? If so, she had been asleep for several hours, overcome with an emotional exhaustion. The sound that had woken her came again, this time umistakable. A female cry of anguish.

Hastily Charlotte sprang from the bed and stepped into her dress, fastening the tiny buttons with hurrying fingers as desperate sobs reverberated through the villa. She ran along the corridor to the top of the staircase and at the sight that met her eyes, halted, her hands flying to her throat.

Zara was sobbing, her words strangled, barely coherent. Sandor was holding her in his arms, rocking her against his chest with unutterable tenderness.

'He knows everything, Sandor! He's going to the casino now to make the news public! He's going to ruin you, my love.'

'There is nothing to fear, Zara. I will speak with Beston.'

'It is no use, he is evil.' She began to shiver uncontrollably. 'He will not rest at vilifying you and myself. He will have Mama's name disparaged in every salon, at every card table.'

Gently Sandor extricated himself from her grasp. 'That he will never do, Zara,' he said, and at the tone of his voice Charlotte's blood chilled. 'Georges, attend to Lady Beston for me. I am going to the casino.'

Charlotte felt her heart begin to beat in slow thick strokes. The dark menace that surrounded him like an aura had finally been unleashed. Charlotte had no doubt that on behalf of the woman he loved, Sandor was capable of murder. He strode to the door, ignoring the jacket that Georges held out for him. His white shirt was slashed open at the throat, every muscle in his body taut and tense like that of an animal about to spring on its prey.

Charlotte felt the strength leave her legs. If he confronted Lord Beston in such a demonic fury then only tragedy could result. She clung to the banisters for support as Georges called after him agitatedly,

'No, sir, I beg of you to consider!'

The door slammed and rocked on its hinges and Zara threw herself prostrate on the chaise longue and began to sob as if her heart would break.

CHAPTER
TEN

CHARLOTTE forced herself to move, to run down the crimson carpeted stairs.

Jeanne was leading the semi-conscious Lady Beston into the main salon. The door of Beausoleil was flung open. The dusk had deepened. The moon was rising as Charlotte ran out into the night. The carriage was still there but in the distance she could hear the galloping of hoofs. Georges was at her side, white-faced and shaking. She grasped his arm urgently. 'The carriage, Georges. I must take the carriage.'

Georges did not demur. As she stepped inside she heard him order the coachman to drive at full speed for the casino after Count Karolyi.

The whips cracked. The carriage lurched into motion. She found that she was praying aloud. He could not kill Lord Beston. The consequences would be too terrible to contemplate. The road she had taken so often now seemed endless. Pine trees soared starkly against the moonlit sky. Orange and lemon groves loomed grotesquely.

'Faster,' she urged beneath her breath. 'Oh please, *faster*!'

Revellers turned in alarm as the Karolyi coach hurtled to the entrance of the casino. Charlotte flung open the carriage door herself and ran heedlessly past the startled gentlemen at the casino's entrance.

He was not in the Salle Mauresque. Jewelled heads turned in her direction. Eyebrows rose in surprise. Her gown was not suitable for such a venue. Louise smiled in her direction and was perplexed as Charlotte stared at and through her sightlessly.

Where was he? In the Salon Privé? In the theatre? The answer came unerringly. He would not face Beston in such a throng. He would confront him on the darkened terraces.

Fluttering fans, smiling faces, pressed in on her on every side. She pushed through them. She must reach the terrace and Sandor's side before it was too late.

Lord Beston paused in his conversation with his companions in a side doorway and gazed after her thoughtfully. The girl was distressed and alone. He crushed out his cigar in an onyx ashtray, excused himself and followed her at a discreet distance.

Charlotte hurried out of the casino and on to the darkened terrace. Couples, hands closely entwined, strolled languidly, laughing flirtatiously. The night air was soft and warm, heavy with fragrance. Charlotte picked up her skirts and began to run along the flower-bordered terrace, down the steps where oleanders and dark-green shrubs lent privacy and seclusion. It was here that Sandor had first kissed her. From here that she had run from him, burning with shame at the response that had consumed her.

What would be his reaction when she caught up with him? Fury? Indifference? Certainly he would not take kindly to her interference, but she could not stand idly by whilst his murderous rage led to actions he would surely regret. His meeting with Lord Beston would end in violence, there could be no other outcome. And Lord Beston was not a lackey who could be thrashed and forgotten. He was a man of high public standing—a peer of the realm. A man whose capacity to hate far exceeded his capacity for love.

Her heart hurt in her chest. He was not there. The lower terraces were empty. Despairingly she turned, intent on once more searching the glittering rooms of the casino.

'You appear to be searching for someone, Miss Grainger. Would it be Count Karolyi?'

Charlotte's hand flew to her throat as Lord Beston stepped from the shadows. Her first reaction was one of overwhelming relief that Sandor had not, as yet, confronted him. Her second, one of apprehension as he moved towards her, barring her way.

'No,' she said, gathering her scattered wits, forcing herself to smile and be civil. 'I was simply taking some air. The gaming rooms are intolerably hot this evening.'

'And you, Miss Grainger, are incredibly beautiful.' In the darkness his tall, narrow frame seemed far more substantial that it had by daylight. The moon sailed from a bank of cloud and she could see the expression in his curiously colourless eyes clearly. They held the same hungry gleam that Prince Victor's had held. Charlotte's apprehension deepened into fear. She struggled to keep her voice light, praying that he would not detain her.

'Thank you for the compliment, Lord Beston, but I must now be returning to the tables. My presence will be missed.'

'I think not,' Lord Beston said easily. 'You did not, after all, enter the casino with any companions. Nor speak to anyone on your whirlwind tour of the rooms.'

'I was simply observing who was present this evening, and now, Lord Beston, if you will excuse me . . .' Determinedly she moved forward but to her alarm Lord Beston did not step aside.

'I think, Miss Grainger, it is time we had a little *tête à tête*.' Unhurriedly he removed a cigar from his inside pocket, lit it and blew a wreath of blue smoke upwards.

Charlotte did not move. She sensed that to do so would be to precipitate action on Lord Beston's part. Then he might detain her by force. At last he said,

'You seem inordinately fond of Karolyi, and, knowing

that gentleman as I do, I feel obliged to acquaint you with some unsavoury aspects of his character.'

At the prospect of hearing of Sandor's love for Lady Beston from Lord Beston himself, Charlotte felt panic well up in her. 'I am not a close friend of Count Karolyi and I have no desire to learn any more about him than I already know,' she said through parched lips.

Lord Beston puffed contentedly on his cigar, certain of victory. She was lying of course. She was Karolyi's mistress but she would not be so after tonight. Not after he had embellished his story with unpleasant innuendos about the depth of affection between brother and sister. She would be devastated and distraught, and he would console her. The prospect was an immensely pleasing one.

'Count Sandor Karolyi is a man about to face ruin.'

'Then I am sorry, but it is none of my affair.' Dear God, she had to escape. She could not endure to hear of Sandor's love for Zara from Beston's lips.

Purposefully she tried to step past him but he laid his hand on her arm restrainingly.

'The man is an impostor. A usurper.'

Charlotte halted, rigid with shock. This was not the revelation she had expected. Lord Beston's eyes were triumphant.

'He has duped Baron Povzervslay out of his rightful estate, and he has aided and abetted my wife into deceiving me.'

Charlotte stared at him in bewilderment. 'I am afraid I do not understand you.'

'You will,' Lord Beston said with an unpleasant laugh. 'And so will everyone else when I disclose the truth.' He glanced down to where his hand grasped Charlotte's slender wrist. Desire licked through him. 'So you see, Miss Grainger,' he said, drawing her protesting hand to his lips and kissing it passionately, 'he is not a man it is wise to be seen with.'

'And you, sir,' Charlotte retorted, aware of a note of rising hysteria in her voice, 'are not a man it is wise to be alone with!' She tried to wrench her hand away from his hold and failed.

Lord Beston laughed and caught hold of her waist, pressing her body so close to his that Charlotte could feel the buttons of his jacket pressing painfully against her breasts.

'I like you exceedingly Miss Grainger. . . . Charlotte. Let us be friends, eh?' His lips sought her averted face, his moustache brushing her skin unpleasantly.

'No!' Charlotte gasped. 'Your behaviour is infamous. I demand that you release me instantly.'

'Not until I have told you the truth about the man you feel such misplaced loyalty for,' Lord Beston said, his voice hardening. 'He has no feelings of affection for you. None for any woman except his sister; my wife.' He began to laugh again and in his laughter was the sound of madness.

Charlotte felt revulsion flood her body. His words made no sense to her but it was obvious that his hatred of Sandor was sufficient to endanger Sandor's life if they should meet.

Lord Beston's mouth sought hers with desperate urgency. 'So no more Count Karolyi,' he panted as she struggled against him. 'No more Zara. Let them comfort each other in penury while we . . .' His mouth fastened on hers. She could feel his teeth biting her lips, smell the sickly sweetness of his breath.

Lord Beston was not a man who normally let passion rule his senses, but the enormity of his wife's revelations had temporarily deranged him. His power over the unsufferably self-assured and arrogant Count Karolyi was absolute. And as if to prove it, he had every intention of possessing Karolyi's mistress, with her consent or without it.

Sheer terror lent Charlotte strength. She clawed and

kicked but the harder she fought the more she inflamed Lord Beston's senses. His hand grasped the silk of her bodice and pulled with terrifying ferocity.

'No! Oh please God! No!'

Twisting and struggling, they had moved from the spot where he had detained her. She felt her back slammed into the hard trunk of a tree and then he was upon her, grasping and kneading her tender flesh.

She could taste blood in her mouth, feel her strength ebbing. His knee pressed between hers and then she felt the touch of his hand beneath her skirts, and she screamed Sandor's name.

Lord Beston had not been in the Salle Mauresque when Sandor entered. Sandor had wasted little time in his search of the downstairs rooms. If Beston was at the casino he would no doubt be playing in exclusive company upstairs. His search there was fruitless. As Lord Beston entered the main gaming room and watched Charlotte's hurried entrance, Sandor was in conversation with Monsieur Blanc, asking if Lord Beston had entered the casino that evening. On being told that his lordship was indeed present, Sandor had demanded to know which private supper room Lord Beston was entertaining in. Monsieur Blanc had assured Sandor that his lordship was in none of them.

Grim-faced, Sandor strode through the jostling throng, ignoring smiles and calls of greeting. Where the devil was Beston?

Louise de Remy excused herself prettily from her escort's side and hurried across to Sandor in a rustle of silk and a cloud of feathers.

'Excuse me, Count Karolyi, if you are looking for Charlotte she stepped out on to the terrace some ten minutes ago and has not returned.'

'Charlotte?' Sandor paused, his dark brows flying together.

'She seemed a little . . . agitated,' Louise ventured, her heavy lashed eyes concerned. 'Lord Beston followed her. I think perhaps he, too, realised she was not her usual self.'

In that moment Louise de Remy knew full well how Sandor Karolyi had earned his devil-dark reputation. She heard the hiss of his indrawn breath, saw the glitter of his eyes and was suddenly aware of the primitive and feral nature of his masculinity.

'Which way did they go?' he rasped, his voice slicing across her nerve-ends like a whip.

'I do not know,' Louise faltered, regretting her boldness and trying to tear her eyes away from his before the angry blaze in them consumed her.

Sandor cursed and spun on his heel, shouldering his way towards the terrace with little heed for those in his path. His anxiety grew as he saw that Charlotte and Beston were not among the couples enjoying the evening air within earshot of the gaming rooms. Fear was an emotion that he was not familiar with, but it gripped him now as he ran down the shrub-bordered steps to the lower terrace. A couple enjoying a close embrace in the shadows sprang apart guiltily at his approach. Sandor ignored them. Swiftly he strode along the darkened terrace and then Charlotte's scream shattered the stillness, abruptly curtailed as Beston's hand smothered her mouth.

Sandor hurried down the seldom used steps to the wilderness of Madame Blanc's tropical garden. For a terrifying moment, although he could hear the sound of a violent struggle, he could see only the silhouettes of palms and eucalyptus and then, against the darkness of the trees, he saw the flash of silk.

With the speed and agility of a wild animal, Sandor covered the distance between himself and Beston in a couple of seconds. He had sought him that evening to talk with him, reason with him—now he desired only to kill him.

Charlotte's gown was ripped from her shoulders, her breasts exposed, and in the moonlight Sandor could see the cruel imprint of Beston's fingers on her soft flesh. Her skirts were disarranged, pushed high towards her waist. She was sobbing, still struggling as Sandor's hand closed like a vice on the collar of Beston's jacket and he hauled him off her protesting body.

'What the . . . ?' Lord Beston began, and was immediately silenced as Sandor's fist made violent contact with his jaw.

'*That!*' Sandor snarled, 'is for making my sister's life a misery. *This!*' Another blow sent Lord Beston to his knees, bloody-faced, 'is for having the temerity to lay hands on the woman I love.'

Lord Beston struggled to his feet and lashed out in vain. The blow skimmed Sandor's face and Sandor's clenched fist drove deep into Lord Beston's stomach, doubling him up with pain.

'*That*, is for all the other women you have no doubt taken advantage of and who have had no one to defend them. And *this!*' He dragged Lord Beston upright, steadying him with one hand and slamming his fist into his jaw with the other, 'is to ensure that you never lay a finger on Charlotte again!'

Lord Beston fell and Sandor turned to Charlotte, his breath coming in harsh gasps.

'Are you all right, my love?'

'Yes . . .' She began to shake as he helped her gently to her feet, holding her against his pounding heart as if he would never let her go. Why was he treating her so? Did he think she was Zara? She clung to him, heedless of his reasons, grateful only for his strength and his tenderness, wanting to stay for ever in the safety of his arms.

'You will pay for this, Karolyi,' Beston panted, his

voice slurred as he stumbled to his feet. 'I'll tell the whole world of your bastardy.'

Blood blinded his eyes, he began to weave backwards, away from Sandor and Charlotte, and towards the low wall that protected nocturnal strollers from the cliff face.

'Be careful, Beston,' Sandor warned. 'The cliff is only yards behind you.'

'You will be ruined! Ostracised in every capital of Europe!'

'You are going to fall, Beston.' Sandor's voice held true alarm.

Beston laughed. 'Incest. That's what I'll accuse you of. I'll destroy you! Force you to your knees!'

Like a man overcome by drink, Lord Beston continued to stagger backwards.

'For God's sake man, move no further!' Sandor shouted.

'Povzervslay can slaughter every one of your tenants in cold blood for all I care,' Beston crowed, and then his heel struck stone and he tottered, losing his balance.

For a hideous second Charlotte saw the gleeful expression on his face change to one of concern and then terrified comprehension. His hands clutched vainly in Sandor's direction as Sandor leapt to save him. His fingers caught hold of Beston's jacket and Charlotte heard the sickening tear of the material and then Lord Beston's crazed scream as his own weight wrenched him from Sandor's grasp and he toppled, arms flailing wildly, over the low wall and down the rock-strewn cliff.

Feeling as if she were in the grip of a nightmare, Charlotte forced herself to walk to Sandor's side, staring horrified at the dark abyss into which Lord Beston had fallen. No sound came. No cry for help. No moan of pain.

'Is he dead?' she asked fearfully.

'Dead or mortally wounded,' Sandor said grimly and then the first of those to be alarmed by Lord Beston's screams came running down the steps towards them.

'Good God, Karolyi, what's happened?'

In seconds they were surrounded and Charlotte clutched the remnants of her gown to her breasts as Sandor's arm circled her shoulders.

'Lord Beston,' Sandor said briefly. 'There has been an accident and he has fallen.'

Sharp eyes flew from the smears of blood on the white linen of Sandor's shirt to Charlotte's state of disarray and Charlotte could hear the whispers fly.

'A fight?'

'I always said Karolyi was born to be hung.'

'Was it murder?'

Monsieur Blanc forced his way through the gathering crowd. 'What happened?' he asked Sandor urgently.

'Lord Beston,' Sandor said briefly, pointing down the cliff face. 'You will need to get men down there immediately. He may still be alive.'

Agitatedly Monsieur Blanc issued orders to his staff for lanterns to be lit and a search to be made. Then he turned once more to Sandor. 'I must call the *gendarmes*,' he said in distress. 'I have no alternative.'

Charlotte stared at the faces around her, at Monsieur Blanc's bowed shoulders, at the skin stretched like parchment across Sandor's cheekbones. It had been an accident but in that moment she knew that if the truth were told it would not be believed. Sandor would be accused of murder.

Suddenly she began to sob, tearing herself from Sandor's grasp and throwing herself into Monsieur Blanc's arms.

'Oh, Monsieur Blanc. What will happen? Will I be accused of murder? I did not mean it. Truly I did not. Lord Beston was so pressing in his attentions and when I refused him he grew angry.'

She no longer attempted to disguise the rent in her gown. All those present could see that it was ripped from the neck to the waist. A lace camisole gleamed provocatively. Bared breasts rose and fell as she wept in Monsieur Blanc's arms.

'I begged him to desist, and when he did not I pushed him and he fell against that little wall, and . . .' She shuddered expressively. 'Count Karolyi heard my cries for help and he came just as Lord Beston fell. He tried to reach Lord Beston and I believe he has injured himself.'

Eyes swivelled to the blood on Sandor's shirt. Sandor tried to interrupt her and gain Camille Blanc's attention, but failed. The Frenchman's concentration was given entirely to comforting the delightfully distressed English girl.

The members of his staff who had stumbled into the darkness with lanterns to locate Lord Beston's body returned without haste.

'The gentleman is dead, Monsieur Blanc.'

Charlotte gave a little scream and Monsieur Blanc tightened his hold on her shoulders as he ushered her through the crowd, away from the scene of the tragedy and towards his private suite. Again Sandor attempted to speak to him, but Monsieur Blanc merely said,

'It was an unfortunate occurrence, Count Karolyi. And one that the *gendarmes* will handle discreetly. The young lady was protecting her honour. The fall was an accident,' he shrugged expressively.

Justin de Valmy took hold of Sandor's arm. 'A brandy, I think, Karolyi.'

'No. I must speak to the *gendarmes*.'

'The *gendarmes* will handle the situation far more discreetly without your presence,' Justin said drily.

'But you don't understand, de Valmy, it was not as Charlotte says.'

'Then I advise you to keep silent about that fact. The *gendarmes* will let Charlotte off lightly. She is a woman, she is beautiful, and she is distressed. What Frenchman could resist such a combination?'

'But I cannot allow her to take the blame for Beston's death when the fool caused it himself,' Sandor hissed.

'For the love of God, keep your voice down,' Justin chided, keeping a firm hold of his arm as they climbed the steps to the casino. 'The matter as it stands is simple. Charlotte accidentally pushed Beston over the wall, while defending her honour. Don't complicate the simple affair unnecessarily.'

Charlotte was ahead of them, crying softly, Monsieur Blanc's arm protectively around her shoulders. All around them they could hear the buzz of sympathetic gossip.

'The poor child is half out of her mind.'

'My dear, the man must have been an animal. Did you see the state of her gown?'

'Such a sweet girl too.'

'Princess Natalya was devoted to her.'

They were at the door of the de Valmy carriage. 'Get in,' Justin said to him. 'The sooner we leave the better.'

'No. I cannot leave now,' Sandor retorted. 'I must go to Charlotte.'

Justin sighed with exasperation. 'Charlotte can manage quite well on her own, Karolyi. You are forgetting that if it is as you say, it is her quick wit that has saved you from arrest. That *she* pushed Beston and he fell is acceptable and will not be regarded as murder. That *you* should admit to doing such a thing . . .'

'Damn it to hell, man! No one pushed Beston over that parapet! He fell to his death unaided.'

Justin laughed grimly. 'Considering Charlotte's dishevellment, I doubt if you will find anyone to believe that. Follow my advice. Leave Charlotte to exonerate you both and join me for a brandy.'

'No. My place is with Charlotte,' and with that Sandor wrenched his arm from Justin's hold and marched through the crowd of fevered spectators after Monsieur Blanc and Charlotte.

No one detained him as he entered Monsieur Blanc's lavishly appointed office. Charlotte was still crying quietly and being comforted by Monsieur Blanc. As Sandor entered the room her eyes flew to his, pleading for him to remain silent. He had known he had loved her for a long time, but not until that moment did he realise the enormity of his love. In that moment he knew that if it were necessary Charlotte would lay down her life for him. As he would for her.

Within minutes the *gendarmes* arrived, headed by the inspector of Monte Carlo's small police force. Monsieur Blanc greeted him warmly. He was an old and trusted friend. Cognac was poured.

'Mademoiselle Grainger is a young lady of irreproachable morals,' he told the inspector. 'You will remember the incident in the Boulevard des Moulins? It was Mademoiselle Grainger who risked her life in saving the child from the bolting horse. She was companion to Princess Yakovleva and the Princess was devoted to her.'

Above Charlotte's head Monsieur Blanc's eyes met those of the inspector. The inspector nodded. So—the young lady was not a cocotte. Not an adventuress. Blanc, one of the most respected citizens in Monte Carlo, was prepared to vouch for her character.

'What happened, mademoiselle,' he asked gently.

Charlotte clutched the torn bodice of her gown to her breasts. 'It was hot in the casino and I was taking some air on the terraces. I had wandered further than usual for I enjoy solitude and there were many other strollers on the upper terrace.' She paused and shivered convulsively. 'I was about to return when Lord Beston barred my way. He . . . he tried to detain me in conversation but I told him I wished to return to the gaming room and then he . . .'

She gazed up at Monsieur Blanc as if for support. 'He told me that I was beautiful and seized my hand, kissing it most passionately.'

The inspector's subordinate nodded. The Englishman had been overcome by the girl's beauty, had tried to take advantage of her and had behaved clumsily and failed. No Frenchman would have made such an error.

'And then . . .' the inspector prompted kindly.

'I tried to free my hand from his grasp, but he pulled me against him and tried to kiss me against my will.'

Sandor's face was demonic. A pulse beat furiously at his jawline and his hands were clenched so tightly that the knuckles showed white.

'I begged of him to desist, but he would not. I think . . . I think he was not quite sane. He tore off my bodice and then he forced me to the ground . . .' Tears convulsed her.

Monsieur Blanc leant gallantly towards the inspector and saved her from continuing.

'Attempted rape,' he whispered in the inspector's ear.

The inspector coughed appreciatively.

'I screamed, and that must have been when Count Karolyi heard my cry and began to run to my assistance. As I did so Lord Beston tried to silence me and that was when I managed to free myself of him. He caught hold of me again and I pushed him and he fell against the parapet. Count Karolyi ran on to the terrace and tried to seize him, but Lord Beston was too heavy for him.' She covered her face with her hands and her torn gown fell to reveal her breasts to the pleasure of every onlooker but Sandor.

'You have my deepest sympathy, Mademoiselle,' the inspector said, envying Blanc his task of comforting such a delectable creature.

Charlotte managed a tremulous smile and Sandor could contain himself no longer. Savagely he brushed Monsieur Blanc aside and draped his evening jacket over Charlotte's naked shoulders. There was a knock at the door and Dr Deslys entered.

'You have seen the body?' the inspector asked, regretting the Hungarian's chivalrous action.

Dr Deslys's sharp eyes moved from Charlotte's dishevelled gown to Sandor's grim face, and back once again to Charlotte's pleading eyes.

'I have. A full autopsy will have to be carried out at a later date, but I think I can assure you that death was occasioned by the fall.'

'Were there any blows inflicted on the body? Any signs of violence?'

There had been four quite definite blows and Dr Deslys could well imagine how they had been caused. His eyes held Charlotte's. 'No. There were several contusions of course, and a great deal of bleeding, but then that was to be expected. There was nothing of a suspicious nature,' he lied smoothly.

Charlotte fought the urge to fling her arms around the good doctor's neck and forced herself to remain sitting.

'Then there is nothing more for me to say to you, mademoiselle,' said the inspector, 'except to offer you my deepest sympathy for the ordeal you have undergone.'

With a sweeping bow he took his leave of her, taking Dr Deslys and his entourage with him.

Monsieur Blanc wiped his brow with relief as he closed the door after them. Another scandal had been avoided. Lady Beston would no doubt be distressed at the manner of her husband's demise, but all in all the outcome had been satisfactory. When he turned to say as much to Count Karolyi, he found the Count otherwise engaged.

The second the inspector had left the room, Sandor had swept Charlotte into his arms, kissing her like a man demented.

Charlotte clung to him, ecstasy and despair inextricably mixed. He was grateful to her. That was the reason for his wild kisses. Zara was now a widow. There was nothing to prevent their marriage.

Monsieur Blanc gave a discreet cough. Sandor raised his head from Charlotte, his arm still circling her body.

'There is a side entrance and I think it would be most wise of you to avail yourself of it, Count Karolyi. Gossip is still rife in the gaming rooms and will only be intensified if Mademoiselle Grainger appears in her present condition.'

'Thank you. I am deeply indebted to you for your handling of the affair,' Sandor said, as Monsieur Blanc led them down his private stairway and out into the moonlight where the Karolyi carriage in which Charlotte had arrived in such distress, still waited.

The men shook hands, Monsieur Blanc kissed Charlotte gallantly on each cheek and then Charlotte was entering the dark intimacy of the carriage with Sandor at her side. Apprehension flooded over her. He had thanked Monsieur Blanc. Would he now thank her? If he did so, she would be unable to bear it. It was not his gratitude that she desired, it was his love.

'Charlotte! Oh my God, Charlotte!' His arms were around her, his lips were on hers, hot and sweet. At last, as his lips moved to her eyelids, her temples, she could bear it no longer.

'Will you now marry Lady Beston?' she asked in a voice little more than a whisper.

Every muscle in his body was struck with such rigidity that she pulled away from him in alarm, certain that he had been taken ill. The carriage rattled at high speed towards Beausoleil and in the moonlight that streamed through the windows she could see the stunned incredulity in his eyes, the thick tumble of his hair, the lean, high planes of his cheekbones.

'What did you say?' His voice was frightening in its intensity. His hands seemed to crush the bones in her wrists, so tight was his grasp.

'Lady Beston,' she faltered. 'I know that you love her and now that Lord Beston is dead . . .'

He groaned, pulling her against him. She could feel his heart beating strongly against hers. Feel the strength and safety she always felt when in his arms.

'Oh Charlotte! My sweet, foolish, beautiful Charlotte.' Tenderly he raised her face to his. 'It is you I wish to marry, Charlotte. You that I love.'

She gazed up at him in wonderment, all the love she felt for him shining in her eyes.

His fingers wound caressingly in her hair. 'If you are to be my wife, Charlotte, you must know things about me no other person knows save for my sister.'

'Your sister?' She remembered Lord Beston's incomprehensible words and her eyes widened.

He took her hands, holding them in his.

'Lady Beston is my sister. Beston only discovered the truth tonight and he was determined to use the knowledge to ruin me.'

'But how? I do not understand.'

He lifted her hand to his lips, searing her upturned palm with the heat of his kiss. She trembled, overcome by love for him.

'My mother was the wife of Count Istvan Karolyi, but Count Karolyi was not my father.' His eyes burned with anguish. 'Zara is my twin. When we were born Count Istvan, out of love for my mother, reared me as his own son and gave Zara to Prince and Princess Katzinsky who were childless.'

She pressed close to him, wanting to ease his suffering, wanting to tell him that none of it mattered any more. The thing that mattered was that *they* loved each other. That they would have children who would live life without any dark secrets, any burdens.

'I loved the Count as my father and he grew to love me as if I were indeed his son. He wanted me to inherit his title and his lands when he died but he made no legal will.' He ran a hand through his tumbled hair, his eyes tortured.

'When Zara married Beston, I feared his wishes would not be fulfilled. Beston had no love for Zara. He married her believing the Katzinskys were wealthy and that as their only child, Zara would inherit. When he discovered differently he treated her with coldness and callousness. It was obvious that if he ever discovered the truth of Zara's birth, he would not keep it secret. And I would lose Valeni.'

Tears glistened on Charlotte's cheeks. 'Oh, my love! Is that the pain you have carried within you all these years? That Count Istvan's wishes would not be fulfilled? That you would lose all you hold dear?'

Wonderingly, he lifted her face to his, tenderly kissing away the teardrops, his voice hoarse with love.

'In these last few days, Charlotte, I have discovered that all I hold dear is you. I love you Charlotte, and I will love you till the day I die. You are my fortress and my peace. I want you to be my wife. To bear my children. To be at my side every waking moment of every day. To lie in my arms every night. If I lost Valeni and I still had you, I would still be the richest man on earth.'

She smiled up at him, her voice unsteady. 'You will have me and you will have Valeni, Sandor. Just as Count Istvan wished. Lord Beston is dead now. He is a threat no longer.'

Sandor's voice was tight. 'I did not wish him to die but God knows, I cannot grieve for him.'

'And nor will Zara,' Charlotte said with sound practicality.

'And your English fiancé?' His hands tightened on hers so that she gasped. 'You will write to him immediately? You will tell him that you are marrying elsewhere?' Every nerve in his body was tensed, his eyes blazing with heat as he waited for her answer.

'Oh Sandor! There never *was* a fiancé in England. It was only silly pride which made me say there was. I loved you so much and I thought you did not care for me.'

'God's teeth!' Sandor blasphemed as the carriage rocked to a halt outside Beausoleil. 'Have I tortured myself in vain over a man who does not exist?'

Charlotte's eyes sparkled at the thought of Sandor suffering jealous rage on her account. Her gurgle of delighted laughter was her answer and Sandor swooped his dark head to hers, silencing her with fiery kisses that rendered her breathless. She was his without reserve. His, as she had been since the moment she had first set eyes on him.

'From now on you will remain in no doubt of the depths of my love for you,' Sandor said grimly, when at last he raised his head from her flushed and radiant face. 'I've been patient long enough. I can be patient no longer.'

With consummate ease he swept her into his arms and carried her from the coach.

'I've been teased and tormented till I'm nearly insane and I'm damned if I'll stand for it another moment!'

Charlotte sighed and clasped her hands even tighter around his neck; his black curls brushed her skin, sending her senses tingling.

'But it could be weeks before we are able to be married,' she murmured provocatively.

'It will be days!' Sandor growled as he strode purposefully with her towards the villa. 'Hours if I can arrange it, and I shall move heaven and earth to do so!'

'Good evening, sir. Good evening, mademoiselle,' Georges said, disguising the anxiety he had suffered during the last few hours, and gallantly averting his gaze from Charlotte's entrancingly near-naked breasts.

'Lady Beston is sleeping. Shall I wake her and inform her of your return, sir?'

'No, Georges. I have a matter of extreme urgency to deal with first,' Sandor said, not halting in his progress across the vast hall. 'I do not wish to be disturbed, Georges,' he continued, mounting the stairs, Charlotte's arms still tightly entwined round his neck, 'Not for anything, is that understood?'

'Yes, sir,' Georges said with a dazed expression on his face as Count Sandor Karolyi strode with his willing captive towards the master bedroom and, on entering, kicked the door firmly shut behind him with a booted foot.